DANIEL RE staff, he is on leave to visit his family in Virginia, only to find himself pressed into service to guard a shipment of gold vital to the funding of the revolution.

ROXANNE DARRAGH STODDARD—Bound to America by her love for freedom and for Daniel Reed, she is expecting their first child, but not the deadly enemy who is sailing across the sea to kill her and her baby.

ELLIOT MARKHAM—The son of a prominent Tory, he finds himself torn between his loyalty to friends and family and his ardent belief in the patriot cause.

CYRIL ELDRIDGE—A high official in England's Ministry of War, he is also the Crown's number one spy, but he has a far darker, more personal reason for coming to America than either espionage or assassination.

CASEY—A beautiful young prostitute, she plies the infamous "Holy Ground" district of New York City but also traffics in secrets that can be helpful to the patriot cause . . . or destroy it.

JETHRO TYLER—A ruthless cutthroat from the Virginia hills, he leads his gang of murderers and thieves from Monticello to Philadelphia on the trail of a fortune in patriot gold.

PATRIOTS—Volume VI

STARS AND STRIPES

Adam Rutledge

BCI Producers of **The First Americans,**
The Holts and **The Frontier Trilogy.**

Book Creations Inc., Canaan, NY • *Lyle Kenyon Engel, Founder*

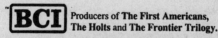
BANTAM BOOKS
NEW YORK • TORONTO • LONDON • SYDNEY • AUCKLAND

STARS AND STRIPES

*A Bantam Domain Book / published by arrangement with
Book Creations Inc.*

Bantam edition / October 1994

*Produced by Book Creations Inc.
Lyle Kenyon Engel, Founder*

*DOMAIN and the portrayal of a boxed "d" are trademarks of
Bantam Books, a division of
Bantam Doubleday Dell Publishing Group, Inc.*

ISBN 0-553-56316-5

Published simultaneously in the United States and Canada

*Bantam Books are published by Bantam Books, a division of Bantam
Doubleday Dell Publishing Group, Inc. Its trademark, consisting of the
words "Bantam Books" and the portrayal of a rooster, is Registered in
U.S. Patent and Trademark Office and in other countries. Marca Regis-
trada. Bantam Books, 1540 Broadway, New York, New York 10036.*

PRINTED IN THE UNITED STATES OF AMERICA

OPM   0 9 8 7 6 5 4 3 2 1

To patriots everywhere

Chapter One

Daniel Reed clutched the railing of the storm-tossed ship and tried not to let the sickness in his belly overcome him. Wind and rain lashed against his face, washing away the beads of sweat on his forehead. This was not his first sea voyage—he had sailed across the Atlantic from America to England only a few weeks earlier—but the vessel that carried him on that trip had not run into weather as bad as this. Dark, wind-torn clouds that looked like fangs scudded across the sky, bringing a torrent of rain and gusts that sent the French ship *Bonaventure* into a welter of waves higher than the vessel's topsails. After the *Bonaventure* crested each wave, it plunged into the next trough, and as it did, Daniel's stomach rebelled.

"Good Lord," he muttered as he hung on to the

1

railing. If he was this sick from the storm, what must it be doing to Roxanne in the cabin below? After all, she was with child and near the time of her delivery.

Daniel dragged a deep breath into his body, coughing a little as he inhaled some spray from the wild waves. He straightened his body and wiped away the moisture on his face, a futile gesture, but it made him feel a little better. Roxanne needed him, and he had no business being anywhere but at her side, he told himself sternly. He waited until the ship had crested another wave, then in the brief lull turned away from the railing and headed for the door to the forward companionway.

The corridor at the bottom of the short flight of stairs was lit by candles set in wall sconces, and the reddish, flickering light seemed to Daniel like the illumination that might be found in the bowels of Hades. It was only his terrible seasickness that made it appear that way, he decided, that and his concern for Roxanne and the child she carried—*Daniel's* child.

One of the cabin doors opened, and a solidly built young man a little shorter than Daniel emerged, reeling slightly because of the motion of the deck under his feet. Hamish MacQuarrie clutched Daniel's arm and said, "There ye be! I was about t' come looking for ye!"

Daniel felt a surge of alarm and would have bolted past Hamish into the cabin had it not been for the Scotsman's grip on his arm.

"Is it Roxanne?" Daniel asked anxiously.

"Aye. She's been calling for ye."

"Damn!" Daniel knew that he shouldn't have left the cabin, not with this storm going on, but Roxanne had seemed to be asleep, and he had thought it would be safe to go on deck for a breath of fresh air. He had intended to be back before she woke up.

Hamish released his arm, and Daniel hurried into

the cabin. The room was small, barely big enough for the bunk that took up most of the space. The *Bonaventure* was a cargo ship with little room for passengers. Its hold was filled with medical supplies bound for America, supplies sent by the French government to help the burgeoning rebellion in the colonies. Daniel had negotiated the arrangement with the French on behalf of General George Washington, on whose staff he served. The diplomatic mission, while important, had not been Daniel's real reason for the trip, however. From France he had been smuggled into England to rescue the woman he loved from her British captors.

He had saved Roxanne, who had been convinced that Daniel was dead, but there had been surprises in store for Daniel, as well. Roxanne was pregnant with the child they had conceived in Massachusetts just before her capture by a party of redcoat raiders. And she was no longer Roxanne Darragh; she was Roxanne Darragh *Stoddard,* wife of the British aristocrat Bramwell Stoddard, Lord Oakley. But now Bramwell Stoddard was dead, and Roxanne was a widow.

In the weeks since Roxanne and Daniel had fled Stoddard's estate, Ilford Grange, along with Stoddard's servants, Hamish and Moira MacQuarrie, Daniel had learned the whole incredible story. It only reinforced the truth Daniel had held dear since the day nearly three years earlier when he had come to Boston from Virginia to visit relatives and enroll at Harvard College in nearby Cambridge.

That truth was a simple one: The world could turn upside down with little or no warning, and when it did, all a person could do was hang on for dear life.

Moira MacQuarrie, Hamish's wife, looked up from where she knelt beside the bunk. With her freckled face and red hair, Moira was an attractive young woman, but at the moment her features were etched with worry lines.

"So there ye be, Mr. Reed," she said tartly, echoing Hamish's greeting. "We heard th' lady callin' out for ye, but ye seemed t' be nowhere around."

Daniel repressed a surge of anger; he was in no mood to be scolded.

"I'm here now. How's Roxanne?"

The woman lying on the bunk opened her green eyes and looked up at him. "I'm fine," she said in a voice that she tried to make firm and steady, but she could not control the tremor in it. Roxanne's complexion had always been fair, but now it was ashen, and perspiration plastered some of her thick red hair to her forehead.

Daniel leaned over her and gently brushed some strands away from her eyes. "I'm sorry I wasn't here when you woke up," he said softly.

"The . . . the storm's still going on, isn't it?"

The squall had been blowing for nearly twenty-four hours now, although it seemed longer than that since the *Bonaventure* had first encountered it. The French captain had attempted to steer around it, but to no avail.

"I'm sure it'll be over soon," Daniel told Roxanne. "I've spoken to the captain, and he says it's rare for one of these spring storms to last more than a day."

"A day . . ." Roxanne repeated. "It's been at least a week already, hasn't it?"

Daniel smiled faintly. He understood the feeling all too well, and *he* wasn't pregnant.

The smile left his face. What if all the commotion caused Roxanne to go into labor and deliver the child early, right here on the ship? The French doctor who had examined her before the *Bonaventure* left Le Havre had told Daniel not to expect the baby to be born for several weeks, but doctors had been known to be wrong.

Besides, these were unusual circumstances, to say the least.

The *Bonaventure* was bound for Norfolk, Virginia, and from there Daniel and Roxanne planned to travel to the plantation of Daniel's parents, Geoffrey and Pamela Reed, in the Piedmont region some miles inland.

Daniel felt another cold chill at the thought of the baby being born on the ship. There was no doctor on board, but at least Moira had served as a midwife on several occasions. If the baby started to come, they would just have to handle it as best they could.

Roxanne must have seen the anxiety in his eyes, because she reached up and touched his cheek with soft fingertips. "I'll be all right, Daniel," she said, "and so will the baby. You worry too much."

"Who could *not* worry at a time like this?" he asked. "It's impossible to be certain of anything anymore."

Roxanne shook her head. "No. You can be certain of one thing, Daniel Reed. I love you."

He felt a surge of shame. He needed to be the one who was strong for Roxanne, and here she was comforting him. He caught her hand and squeezed it gently but firmly.

"You're right," he said, his voice strong. "We'll be in America soon, and everything will be fine."

"Yes," Roxanne murmured, "on land that will one day be free."

A faint smile crossed Daniel's face as her eyes closed and she slipped into a restless sleep. Even under such dire circumstances as these, her devotion to the patriot cause shone through like a beacon.

"I'll keep an eye on her if ye'd like, Daniel. And 'tis sorry I be tha' I was sharp with ye earlier," Moira said quietly.

"We're all on edge," he told her. A fresh wave of nausea hit him as the ship rolled through another trough in the storm-tossed ocean. "It's this infernal storm. We'll all feel better when it's over."

"Aye," Hamish agreed, looking slightly green himself. "I'm a lad made for dry land."

"Another two or three days ought to see us in Norfolk," Daniel said, putting a hand on his friend's shoulder. "Until then, I suppose we'll just have to suffer."

As promised by the French captain, however, the storm blew itself out by nightfall, and by the time the moon and the stars were shining brightly in an ebony sky, a strong breeze out of the east filled the sails and the vessel was skimming over a calmer sea.

Daniel stood at the railing again, watching the waves go past, grateful that his stomach had settled down. Roxanne was feeling better, too, and had been able to take some broth for supper. She was sleeping now, and Daniel would soon be ready to turn in himself.

The captain saw him at the rail and strolled over. Jean-Claude LeMonde was a veteran seaman, lean and weathered by years of sun and ocean winds. He nodded to Daniel and said in excellent English, "Good evening, Lieutenant Reed. I trust the lady is feeling better now that we have left the storm behind."

"Much better, thanks," Daniel replied. "Do you know whether or not that squall blew us very far off course, Captain?"

"My navigator has been taking sightings all evening with his instruments. We should know soon."

Daniel looked up at the sky. He was no expert on steering by the stars, but he hoped the encounter with the storm wouldn't delay their arrival in Virginia.

It was important to Roxanne that their child be born on American soil. That meant something to Daniel, too, although he was more concerned with the safety of both mother and baby.

He chatted for a few moments with Captain LeMonde. Then the Frenchman suddenly stiffened and tightly grasped the railing as he peered out across the waves lit by silver moonlight. After a moment he said sharply, "There!" He lifted a hand and pointed. "Do you see them, Lieutenant Reed?"

Daniel, frowning in concern at the captain's abrupt change of behavior, looked where LeMonde was pointing and saw nothing but moonlight dancing on the water. Then a pair of darker shapes slid across the surface, and Daniel felt a surge of alarm.

"Whose ships are those?" he asked.

Quickly LeMonde took a spyglass from inside his jacket and stretched out the arrangement of tubes and lenses to its full length. As he lifted the glass and peered through the eyepiece, a cry of alarm sounded from the crow's nest high above the deck. Daniel spoke enough French to know that the sailor on watch had spotted two ships off the starboard bow.

LeMonde lowered the spyglass and closed it with a curt motion. "It might have been better had the storm remained," he said. "This moonlight is both blessing and curse. We can see the enemy, but he can also see us."

"Those are British ships?" Daniel asked tensely.

"They fly the Union Jack," LeMonde replied.

Daniel frowned. "They won't attack us, will they? England and France aren't at war with each other."

"Not at the moment," LeMonde said. "But there is no shortage of ill feeling between the English and my country, let me assure you, Lieutenant. Besides, the British Ministry of War is well aware that France would like to see your colonies succeed in their rebellion. The English suspect us of furnishing aid and assistance to the Americans—as of course we are doing. It is possible that the English captains, recognizing the *Bonaventure* as a French vessel, might decide to attack."

"What are you going to do?" Daniel asked.

"There is nothing we can do that we are not already doing," LeMonde replied with a Gallic shrug. "We are running before the wind, and we will continue to do so. If the British pursue us, *c'est la vie*."

"Perhaps they won't," Daniel said grimly.

LeMonde strode briskly to the bridge, saying over his shoulder, "You had better go below, Lieutenant Reed, and warn the others that there could be hostilities."

Daniel felt a worm of fear gnaw at his gut as he hurried belowdecks. He had faced danger many times in the past year—at Concord Bridge, on Bunker Hill, in the rugged Berkshire Mountains—and he knew that only a fool risked his life without fear. But this was different. This time Roxanne was in danger, too, not to mention Hamish and Moira MacQuarrie.

When he reached the door of Roxanne's cabin, Daniel opened it quietly and peered inside. She was sleeping peacefully, and Moira dozed on a small chair beside the bunk. Daniel hesitated, then decided not to wake either of the women. Let them rest while they could, he told himself.

He went down the corridor to the cabin Hamish shared with Moira and knocked lightly on the panel. After a moment Hamish opened the door. He looked sleepy, and his hair was tousled.

"What is it, Daniel?" he asked.

"There are British ships nearby, and Captain LeMonde thinks they might attack."

Hamish's air of drowsiness vanished instantly. "Is there aught we can do t' help?"

"Not unless it's to say a prayer," Daniel answered. "I'm going back up on deck. Do you want to come with me?"

"Aye," Hamish answered without hesitation, reaching behind him to pick up his jacket. He shrugged into it as he came out into the corridor. "I want t' see what's goin' on. I dinna like bein' cooped up down here." As they passed the door of Roxanne's cabin, Hamish inclined his head toward it and asked, "Wha' about th' lasses?"

"They were both asleep when I looked in there a few minutes ago. I think we should leave them alone for now."

"Aye."

Roxanne might be angry with him later for keeping the news of their danger from her, and rightly so, Daniel reflected. They had always been honest with each other. But at the moment, Roxanne and Moira were as helpless as Daniel and Hamish were, so he saw no point in disturbing them.

The two men climbed the steps of the companionway and ran to the starboard railing, the wind plucking at their jackets as they did.

Responding to the commands called out by Captain LeMonde from the bridge, sailors were scurrying about on the deck. The helmsman spun the wheel, and the *Bonaventure* veered slightly so that the sails could catch the wind at a more favorable angle. Daniel looked up at the white canvas shining brightly in the moonlight and knew that it would be clearly visible, just as he could now spot the sails of the oncoming vessels.

"I see 'em," Hamish said as he leaned on the railing next to Daniel. "Is the cap'n sure they're British?"

"According to the flags they're flying, they are. I'm not sure what they're doing this far south, though."

Daniel's uncle, Benjamin Markham, was a partner in a shipping line that had been highly profitable before the war, and Daniel had spent quite a bit of time in the Markham household, visiting his cousin Elliot. He knew something about shipping, and most trans-Atlantic trade had followed a more northerly route. The British effort to suppress the growing rebellion was concentrated in the northeast, so it made sense that warships would travel more often in those latitudes.

During his brief stay in England, Daniel had heard rumors that a large British fleet was about to sail for the colonies, carrying munitions, supplies, and reinforcements for the king's forces there. Perhaps two of those ships had run into the storm, as the *Bonaventure* had, and been blown off course.

Daniel shook his head. The how and the why did not matter. The only important thing was that the British warships were out there, still a good distance off to starboard but angling ever closer. As he watched them for several minutes in the moonlight, all doubt vanished from his mind. The two ships were trying their best to intercept the French vessel.

Where was a nice, thick bank of clouds when you needed one, Daniel wondered as he looked up at the clear sky. If the moon and the stars were obscured, the *Bonaventure* could probably slip away in the darkness. But there were no clouds in sight, nothing to offer a chance of escape.

"Great God in Heaven!" Hamish suddenly exclaimed as orange fire blossomed from one of the ships. "What was that?"

Daniel listened, heard the faint, faraway boom and then a high keening whistle before water shot up a hundred yards to starboard. His hands tightened on the railing. "They're trying to get the range," he said. "That was a cannon shot."

"Damned English bastards!" Hamish cursed fervently. "Do they mean to sink us?"

Judging from what they had just seen, Daniel thought, the answer was yes.

As a cargo vessel the *Bonaventure* was not heavily armed, but the ship did have several small cannon on board for self-defense. Captain LeMonde shouted the order that sent gun crews leaping to their stations. One of the cannon emplacements was located only a few feet from where Daniel and Hamish stood. The gun was a three-pounder, similar to some of the artillery Daniel had helped Henry Knox transport across the mountains of New York and Massachusetts from Fort Ticonderoga to be used in the siege of Boston. If need be, Daniel thought, he could pitch in and help load and fire the cannon.

He was not going to have that opportunity, however. LeMonde spotted him and Hamish and bellowed, "Get belowdecks *now,* Lieutenant Reed!"

Daniel did not want to go and for an instant considered defying the captain's order. But the Frenchman had more than enough problems facing him at this moment. Daniel nodded curtly and said to Hamish, "Come on. We'd better do as he says."

As they reached the companionway, they heard LeMonde give the order to fire, and the two cannon on the starboard side of the ship erupted in smoke and flame and thunderous noise. Daniel paused and craned his neck to see where the cannonballs landed. He thought he saw twin spurts of water, well short of the British ships. LeMonde did not have the range any more than did the enemy, but despite being outnumbered and outgunned, he had announced his defiance.

Reluctantly Daniel and Hamish went belowdecks. There was no more cannon fire from the *Bonaventure,* but Daniel thought he heard several more blasts from the British ships. Evidently none of the shots came close, however.

The volley ordered by LeMonde had been enough to jolt both Roxanne and Moira out of their sleep, and Moira was waiting anxiously in the open doorway of Roxanne's cabin when Daniel and Hamish reached the corridor.

"What is it?" Moira asked. "What's goin' on up there?"

"Just a skirmish with a couple of British ships," Daniel told her.

Roxanne called out to him, "Daniel! Is that you?"

Moira stepped back and let him into the cabin. Roxanne was sitting up in the bunk, the thin pillow propped behind her back and head. Daniel knelt beside her and took her hands in his.

"What's happening?" she asked.

"We're being pursued by a pair of British warships. They've opened fire on us."

"Are they going to catch us?"

Daniel's jaw tightened, and he replied honestly, "I don't know."

"Is there anything we can do?" Roxanne asked, her hands clasping his firmly.

He shook his head. "Captain LeMonde is doing everything he can."

"I'll be loadin' those pistols," Hamish said from the doorway. "Come along and give me a hand, Moira."

Daniel glanced around at his friend and nodded. There were several pistols stored in the bags the travelers had brought aboard, and they might be needed if Daniel and Hamish were called upon to help repel boarders from the British ships. Preparing them would also give Hamish and Moira a few minutes alone with each other.

Roxanne moved aside on the bunk, sliding over as much as she could. "Sit with me, Daniel," she said quietly.

Perching a hip on the side of the narrow bunk, he slid an arm around her and drew her against him. They had been through a great deal together; each had been certain that the other was dead, but fate had brought them back together more than once. Daniel refused to believe that they would be torn apart now.

"What will happen if we're caught?" Roxanne asked in a voice that was little more than a whisper.

"If the ship isn't sunk, we'll be returned to England. Both of us are wanted on espionage charges."

He was not telling her anything she did not already know. In the past, as members of the patriots' intelligence network, they had contributed to several important setbacks for the British. The Crown considered them mortal enemies, and they could expect no mercy if they were captured.

In the distance, the English cannon continued to boom, but the *Bonaventure*'s guns did not reply. Daniel supposed the French sailors were devoting their energies to the attempt to outrun the British warships, and there was a chance the effort would be successful. The English vessels, heavily loaded as they would be with cannon and munitions, were not made for speed. With skillful sailing, the *Bonaventure* might elude them.

But for the time being, all Daniel and Roxanne could do was wait, and Daniel tightened his embrace around the woman he loved as a fresh shudder went through her every time the cannon roared.

Daniel had thought that the storm lasted an eternity, but the grim chase that followed it seemed even longer. For the rest of that night and most of the next day, the British warships pursued the *Bonaventure*, firing occasionally at it.

Their attempt to strike at an angle and intercept the *Bonaventure* was a failure, however, as Captain LeMonde took advantage of every puff of wind to outdistance the enemy to the crucial point where he slipped in front of them and forced them to fall in directly behind him. Then the engagement became a chase, pure and simple, and gradually the *Bonaventure* took the measure of the British ships following it. The gap between pursuers and quarry slowly widened.

The British commanders were stubborn, though, and stayed on the heels of the French ship, struggling mightily to close to within cannon range but just falling short. Some of His Majesty's seamen lined the forward rails of the nearest warship and blazed away with muskets, but that fire was even more futile than the cannon shots. The *Bonaventure* was out of reach and stayed that way all through the day.

The morning had dawned as clear as the night before, and it would have been a beautiful day under other circumstances, but Daniel, Roxanne, Hamish, and Moira were in no mood to appreciate the weather. Their nerves were frayed, and no one on board was more relieved than they were, late that afternoon, when the lookout in the crow's nest sang out that the British ships were turning aside from the pursuit.

The cry spread across the ship, and Captain LeMonde sent a crewman to the cabins to let the passengers know that the danger appeared to have passed. Daniel and Hamish hurried up on deck to see for themselves.

"Yonder they go!" Hamish exulted when the two young men reached the railing at the stern. He pointed excitedly at the British ships, dwindling now in the distance to the north.

"Why did they give up?" Daniel called to Captain LeMonde on the bridge.

"There is no way of knowing, Lieutenant Reed. Perhaps they decided we were getting too close to the American coastline. Or perhaps they had followed us as far as their orders would allow. Whatever the reason, we should have clear sailing the rest of the way to Norfolk."

Clear sailing, Daniel thought. He liked the sound of those words.

For the rest of that day and all of the next, LeMonde's prophecy proved to be correct. With the storm behind them, Daniel's seasickness subsided, and with the British no longer pursuing them, taut nerves finally relaxed. On the evening of the day after the English warships abandoned the chase, Roxanne felt well enough to ask Daniel to take her up on deck.

Holding her arm to make sure she did not trip on the companionway steps, Daniel led her to the deck and over to the starboard railing. Hamish and Moira came along, too, and the four young people leaned on the rail and enjoyed the breeze as twilight settled over the ocean. The moon had not yet risen, but the stars were beginning to wink into life in the huge sky arching overhead.

" 'Tis a lovely evening," Hamish declared. "Nothing prettier than th' stars comin' out in th' gloaming."

Daniel agreed and gently led Roxanne forward along the railing until they had put some distance be-

tween themselves and the MacQuarries. When he
stopped, Roxanne laid a hand softly on his arm.

"What is it, Daniel? I can tell when you have something on your mind."

He had searched his soul for the words, but he still
found it difficult to begin.

"I've been thinking, Roxanne. We've been through
so much together, and now with the child coming . . ."

His voice trailed off, and she smiled as she folded
her hands on her swollen belly. "Are you worried about
being a father, Daniel?" she asked, a roguish smile on
her lips. "If so, then you shouldn't have been quite so
forward that day in Lemuel Parsons's barn."

"It's not that," Daniel said quickly. "I'm excited
about the baby, you know that. And I agree with you
that the child needs to be born on American soil. But I
see no reason why the two of us should not be married
before that takes place." He saw her stiffen and hurried
on, "It's the customary thing, you know, for a child's
parents to be married."

"You've no need to tell me that, Daniel," Roxanne
said sharply. "I've heard as much gossip as you about
women with babes but no husbands. But that's not the
case with us. I'm a widow, remember?"

"I remember. And I'm not saying anything against
Bramwell Stoddard, or against you for marrying him.
You believed I was dead, and Bramwell was a fine man
. . . for an English aristocrat."

"He was a fine man no matter what he was," Roxanne whispered. "He only wanted what was best for me
. . . and for the child. That's why he bribed the officials
to falsify the records and make it appear he and I were
married before the baby was conceived."

"I know all that," Daniel said, keeping a tight rein
on his temper. "I know that in the eyes of the English

law, the child is Bramwell's and is the heir to his estate. But that doesn't change the facts. This baby is mine, and you and I should be married."

Roxanne's chin lifted slightly, a sure sign that stubborn anger was building up inside her, too.

"I agree," she said. "But I can't do anything now to cast a shadow on the legitimacy of the child. After more time has passed—after the war is over—then you and I can be married, and you can adopt the child. You'll be the only father he or she ever knows."

Daniel turned away sharply, his hands gripping the rail tightly.

"I don't understand," he said. "You never cared about money. Why is it so important to you now not to take any chances with that inheritance? Surely you're not worried about the title! Or is that it? If our child is a son, do you want him to be Lord Oakley so badly that you refuse to marry me?"

For a moment Daniel thought he had made her angry enough to strike him, but finally she said, "You just don't understand. The money and the title mean nothing to me. But Bramwell Stoddard saved my life, Daniel. He saved the life of our child, too, and this is what he wanted. I . . . I'm honoring the man's final request, that's all." She drew herself up slightly. "Besides, if the inheritance doesn't pass to the baby, Eldridge will claim it."

Daniel's grip on the rail tightened even more. Cyril Eldridge, Bramwell Stoddard's cousin and one of the top spymasters for the Crown, had been the man responsible for Roxanne's captivity at Ilford Grange, the Stoddard estate. Eldridge and Major Alistair Kane, the king's leading intelligence agent in America, had worked together to get as many details as they could concerning the patriot espionage network from her, only to consistently fail in their efforts. Eldridge had done his best to kill both Daniel and Roxanne before their escape from Ilford Grange, and Daniel could understand why Roxanne despised the man and wanted to frustrate his ambitions.

Daniel sighed and rubbed his lean jaw. What Roxanne said made sense—of a sort—and after all, she only wanted to postpone their union for a time. He supposed he could live with that.

"All right," he said finally. "But I'm not going to pretend to my family that the child isn't mine. My parents will be a bit scandalized, perhaps, but I will *not* renounce my own flesh and blood in my own home."

"Nor would I ask you to," Roxanne said. She slipped her arm through his and leaned her head against his shoulder. "All in good time, my darling Daniel. All in good time."

"Lieutenant Reed!"

The urgency in the voice made Daniel look up. Captain LeMonde was leaning on the rail around the bridge nearby, pointing to the west. "We have sighted land, Lieutenant."

Excited, knowing that the closest land in that direction had to be the Virginia coastline, Daniel and Roxanne peered into the starlit gloom, hoping to make out the dark, low-lying shape that marked their destination.

They saw more than they expected, however, as did the others on the ship as word of the sighting spread. Hamish and Moira came forward to join Daniel and Roxanne, and several members of the crew crowded to the rail as well. Daniel's eyes widened when he saw the flickering red and yellow lights in the distance, lights that were much more visible than they should have been from several miles at sea.

"What is it?" Roxanne asked in a whisper.

"A fire," Daniel said softly. He turned to look up at LeMonde. "Captain, is that about where Norfolk should be?"

"*Oui*," the Frenchman answered grimly. "I am sorry, Lieutenant, but it appears that the city is in flames."

Chapter Two

"If there be a prettier land than this, I have no' yet seen it in all my wanderings," Murdoch Buchanan said as he paused at the top of a ridge to lean on the butt of his long-barreled flintlock rifle.

"That's the Piedmont," Quincy Reed said as he stood next to Murdoch. "The land where I grew up. The frontier was exciting, but it's good to be home again. Almost home, I should say. We've still got a ways to go."

Quincy had begun to look older than his years—which numbered eighteen—in recent months. He had the same tall, lean build as his brother, Daniel, who was five years his senior, and a similar shock of tousled hair that was a light chestnut color, in contrast to Daniel's dark brown locks. The dangers Quincy had endured since leaving Boston after the outbreak of hostilities be-

tween the British and the colonists had aged the young
man, and the fact that he was now married and about to
become a father had matured him as well. The carefree
daredevil he had been only two years earlier was gone.
But at times like this, some of the old devilish light
sparkled in Quincy's eyes once again, and he felt like a
boy—a boy who was going home.

Murdoch Buchanan was also excited by the prospect of a visit to the Virginia plantation owned by Geoffrey and Pamela Reed, the parents of his friends Quincy
and Daniel. A tall, brawny, redheaded Scotsman in
buckskins and coonskin cap, Murdoch was a wanderer
and had been since coming to the colonies as a young
man, almost two decades earlier. A long hunter, an ex-
plorer, a frontiersman, Murdoch had been up and down
the Ohio River and to the fringes of civilization. In all
his roaming he had never crossed the Blue Ridge Mountains that were now behind the party of travelers, nor
had he been to the Piedmont, the plateau of rolling,
wooded plains that made up the central section of Virginia.

Quincy turned and walked back to the wagon he
had parked just below the crest of the ridge. His wife,
the former Mariel Jarrott, sat on the wagon seat with her
brother, three-year-old Dietrich. The youngster had the
same pale-blond hair as his sixteen-year-old sister. Dietrich was jabbering away, but Mariel was not paying
much attention to him. She was watching Quincy instead, and when her husband returned to the wagon, she
asked, "Are we almost there?"

Quincy grinned. "It's all downhill from here, as they
say. There won't be any more mountains to cross, although we may have to ford a few creeks and rivers. Lots
of streams run through the Piedmont. But we ought to
get to my parents' place in another day or two."

"I will be very glad to get there." Mariel smiled tiredly. "This has not been an easy journey, my husband."

She wasn't telling Quincy anything he didn't already know. They had left their small settlement on the Ohio frontier weeks earlier, saying farewell to their friends Ulysses and Cordelia Gilworth and Cordelia's father, Gresham Howard. Cordelia and Howard had shared quite a few adventures with Quincy and Murdoch as they made their way to the frontier from New York. It was during that time that Mariel and Dietrich had become part of their group, following the massacre of the rest of the Jarrott family by hostile Mohawk Indians working for the redcoats. Quincy and Mariel had gone from comrades-in-arms to friends and then lovers, and they were going to be parents soon as well. After all his wife's harrowing experiences on the frontier, Quincy couldn't blame her for wanting to give birth in a safe environment. That was why Mariel and he, along with Murdoch and Dietrich, had set out across the Appalachians, bound for Virginia.

Quincy just hoped they made it to the Reed plantation before Mariel gave birth. The baby was not due for a while yet—at least according to what Cordelia had figured out before Quincy and Mariel left Ohio—but such calculations were hardly an exact science, Quincy knew. In fact, the whole business was so arcane and mysterious to him that he had no real idea *when* to expect the baby. All he knew was that Mariel had gotten a lot bigger than he had expected, and he would have been less frightened by facing half of old German George's army than he was by the prospect of delivering a baby out on the trail.

He swung lithely onto the seat beside Mariel and took up the reins. Standing on the ridge, Murdoch waved them forward. Quincy flapped the reins and shouted at the oxen pulling the wagon, and the massive beasts lumbered into motion. The wagon topped the rise and started down the gentle slope on the other side.

Quincy had never been this far west in the Piedmont. During his boyhood he had ranged all over the area around his parents' home on the Rivanna River, and he had been up and down the Tidewater plain along the Atlantic. But until this journey from the west, he had never seen the Great Valley between the Appalachians and the Blue Ridge, had never seen the Shenandoah or the rugged foothills at the base of the Blue Ridge. Before the day was over, they would leave those foothills behind and travel across the Piedmont plateau itself. It was beautiful country, as Murdoch had said, with rich farmland, dense forests, and the hazy blue line of mountains always in the distance. Despite his weariness from the long weeks on the trail and his increasing nervousness about Mariel's condition, Quincy enjoyed himself as he steered the wagon across fields and alongside streams.

They made camp that night beside a tree-lined creek and set off again early the next morning. Before midday they passed some farms, and Mariel smiled when she saw the houses and barns, knowing them to be signs of civilization.

Quincy patted her knee. "We'll be there soon."

"I know. I hope your mother and father aren't too upset when they find out that you are married."

"How in the world could they be upset?" Quincy asked with a grin. "I know they'll fall in love with you right away, just like I did."

She leaned her head against his shoulder, and Quincy felt a glow of happiness spread through him. After everything that had happened—after the battles and desperate flights and hairbreadth escapes from danger—it was going to be mighty good to spend some time at home and enjoy the peace and quiet. The war could not be forgotten, of course; it loomed much too large for that. But for a while he certainly intended to ignore it. From the Boston Tea Party to Fort Ticonderoga, Quincy had done his part, and now it was time to worry about his own family for a change.

Another day and a half went by, and the travelers made steady progress, Murdoch tirelessly striding along in front of the wagon and Quincy handling the team of oxen with the skill born of long weeks of practice. They were following a road now instead of blazing a trail of their own, and Quincy was beginning to spot some familiar landmarks. He recognized a particular hill, a stretch of woods, the way a stream made a sharp bend around a sandy spit of land. Late in the afternoon they reached a larger stream, and Quincy said excitedly, "This is it! This is the Rivanna. Daniel and I used to hunt along here when we were boys."

That made it sound like a time so far in the past, Quincy thought, when actually it had been only a few years.

"Do ye recollect where yer folks' place is from here?" Murdoch asked.

"Four miles that way," Quincy said, pointing down the river.

Murdoch nodded, his brow furrowing in thought. "Too far t' make it 'fore we lose the sun. Might as well make camp here tonight."

"Make camp?" Quincy echoed, sounding surprised. "We should push on! I know this ground, Murdoch. We won't have any trouble."

Murdoch tugged at an earlobe and then scraped an iron-hard thumbnail across the reddish stubble along his jawline. "I dinna ken, lad. Traveling at night can be a tricky proposition."

"We can make it, Murdoch, I know we can." Quincy turned to his wife. "What do you think, Mariel? Shouldn't we push on, since we're this close? I know there are no Indians around here. We'll be safe enough."

"What about British patrols?" Mariel asked.

"Th' lass is right," Murdoch said. "We've no' been told what th' situation is 'round here with th' war. There could be redcoats all over these hills."

"We've seen no signs of British activity, and people have been working in the fields on the farms we've passed. The countryside wouldn't look so peaceful if the war had reached here already."

"What ye say makes sense, lad. I dinna reckon 'twould hurt t' push on for a while longer."

With a grin of anticipation, Quincy got the oxen moving. He could feel home pulling at him.

Night settled down, but there was enough light from the stars and the rising moon for Quincy to make out the road. Murdoch strode along in front of the wagon, and Quincy kept the oxen moving in their slow, plodding gait. From time to time they passed a farmhouse with the warm yellow glow of lamplight visible through the windows, and the tightness in Quincy's chest grew strong as he remembered other warm spring evenings like this one. He had not realized he was so homesick until now.

Even in the darkness Quincy knew when they were approaching his parents' plantation. He saw the split-rail fence alongside the road, then the peach orchard and the large fields of tobacco, cotton, and peanuts. Spotting a scattering of lights off the main road, Quincy knew they came from the main house and the outbuildings. He wished he could goad the oxen into a faster pace, but the massive beasts moved only as fast as they wanted to.

"This is it, Murdoch," Quincy called out to the big frontiersman. "There'll be a lane turning off to the left about fifty yards farther on. It'll take us right to the house."

"Aye," Murdoch replied. "I'll be watching for it."

A few moments later, Quincy spotted the two towering pine trees that flanked the entrance to the lane, marking it like a gateway. As he swung the wagon toward the trees, there was a sudden flicker of movement, and someone stepped out from behind one of the thick trunks.

"Stand fast," a man's voice called. "You're covered."

The threat in the stranger's tone was unmistakable, and as Quincy brought the wagon to a stop, he heard the distinct sound of a flintlock's cock being pulled into firing position. Murdoch had stopped in his tracks at the challenge, and the Scotsman was holding his own rifle tightly, ready to lift it and fire in a split second.

"Hold on!" Quincy cried hurriedly to the sentry. "We're friends. This is the Reed place, isn't it?"

"That it is," the shadowy stranger replied without lowering his weapon. "But who might you be?"

"I'm Quincy Reed." Something about the man's voice now struck him as familiar. "Is that you, Cornelius?"

"Master Quincy?" the man exclaimed in surprise. "Is it really you?"

Quincy was certain now that the man standing beside the tree was Cornelius Johnson, the plantation's overseer.

"If you'll let me climb down from the wagon and come closer without taking a potshot at me, you can see for yourself."

"Come ahead," Cornelius growled. "But tell that big backwoodsman not to get any ideas. I don't like the way he's holding that rifle."

"Ye'll like it less happen I decide t' use this old leadspitter, mister," Murdoch rasped. "I dinna fancy folks pointing guns at me."

"Nor do I," Cornelius snapped back.

Quincy climbed down quickly from the wagon seat after patting Mariel on the knee and assuring her that everything would be all right. He strode forward, his tricorn shoved to the back of his head so that Cornelius could get a good look at his face in the moonlight.

"No doubt I've changed some in the past couple of years," he said, "but surely you remember me, Cornelius."

The man lowered his rifle and broke into a grin. "Aye. It *is* you, Master Quincy! Welcome home!" He stepped forward and threw an arm around Quincy's shoulders in a rough hug.

The tension left the air, and to make sure things stayed relaxed, Quincy said, "This is my friend Murdoch Buchanan. Murdoch, meet Cornelius Johnson, my father's overseer."

The two men shook hands. Both were brawny specimens, Cornelius several inches shorter than Murdoch but sporting even broader shoulders. With the introduction complete, Quincy gestured at the wagon and went on, "And this is my wife, Mariel."

"Wife?" Cornelius repeated, clearly shocked by the news. "But you're just a boy!"

"Boys turn into men quickly these days," Quincy

said, just a shade of grimness in his voice to hint at the things he had seen and done.

"Indeed, that's all too true." Cornelius tugged his hat off and bowed to Mariel. "Pleased to meet you, ma'am."

"Hello, Mr. Johnson," Mariel said. "My brother Dietrich is asleep in the back of the wagon. I'm sure you'll meet him later."

"Yes, ma'am."

"What's going on here, Cornelius?" Quincy asked. "Why are you standing watch out here? Father never put guards on the road before."

"We've never been at war with the blasted redcoats before, either."

"Has there been fighting 'round here?" Murdoch asked.

"Not close. The British attacked Norfolk some time ago, and there was word that the city was in flames and all but destroyed. Rumor has it that the bloody British are going to invade Virginia and try to sweep right across the Tidewater. If they do, they'll not find the going so easy when they reach the Piedmont, I can promise you *that*!"

Quincy heard the fierceness in the overseer's voice and recognized it as the sound of a man ready, willing, and able to fight to defend his home. That was something the British, in their arrogance, had not counted on, and it was what would one day bring liberty to this land, Quincy mused.

"Your father thought it would be a good idea to keep an eye on the road at night," Cornelius went on. "It was my turn for the duty tonight."

"And it's probably a good idea," Quincy said.

"What are you doing here, Master Quincy?" Cornelius asked, unable to contain his curiosity any longer.

"The last I heard, you were up in Massachusetts somewhere."

"It's a long story," Quincy told him. "I'll explain all of it to you and the boys later, but right now I'd like to get to the house so Mariel can rest. We've had quite a journey."

"Of course." Cornelius lifted a carved-out horn, much like a powder horn but open at both ends. He blew on it, producing a strident note that carried through the night. "That way the lads at the house will know there's someone coming in," he explained.

Quincy and Murdoch exchanged a look in the moonlight. Even though the war had not yet spread to this part of Virginia, there was no escaping its influence.

Quincy hopped up onto the wagon seat and got the oxen moving. It took only a few minutes to travel up the lane to the house, an impressive, whitewashed, three-story frame structure surrounded by a stand of pine and spruce. A high, colonnaded veranda ran along the front of the house, and the double doors stood open as Quincy pulled the wagon to a stop in front of them. Light spilled from the house and silhouetted the man who hurried outside.

"Who's that?" the man demanded. "Who are you, sirs?"

"Father!" Quincy cried, unable to restrain himself. He leapt from the seat and flung himself into the arms of his startled parent. "It's Quincy, Father! I've come home."

"Quincy?" Geoffrey Reed whispered, disbelief in his voice. He put his hands on his son's shoulders and stared at him. Quincy had grown, and he was taller now than the stocky Geoffrey. "My God, is it actually you?"

"It's me, Father, and I want you to meet someone very special. Father, this is my wife, Mariel."

Geoffrey looked every bit as shocked as Cornelius Johnson had been. He sputtered, at a loss for words, and Quincy hurried on, "Mariel, this is my father, Geoffrey Reed."

"I'm so pleased to meet you, Mr. Reed," Mariel said. "Quincy has told me all about you and his mother."

Geoffrey finally regained his composure. "Well, don't just stand there, boy! Help the lady down from that wagon. I'm sure the seat can't be *that* comfortable."

Grinning, Quincy gave Mariel a hand as she climbed down gingerly. He glanced at his father and saw that Mariel's condition had not been lost on Geoffrey. He led her over to the older man, who took her hand and shook it, then laughed and embraced her.

"This comes as quite a surprise, Mariel," Geoffrey said, "but welcome to the family!"

Murdoch reached inside the wagon and picked up the sleeping Dietrich, leaving the long rifle on the seat. With the toddler cradled in his brawny left arm, he strode up to Geoffrey and said, "Since Quincy has no' got 'round t' introducing me, I'll do it meself. I'm Murdoch Buchanan, friend t' both o' yer sons, and this wee bairn be Dietrich Jarrott."

"My brother," Mariel supplied.

Geoffrey shook hands with Murdoch and said, "I'm very pleased to meet you, Mr. Buchanan."

"Murdoch," the big frontiersman said firmly. "Where I hail from, we dinna stand on ceremony."

Geoffrey grinned. "Nor do we around here. Welcome to my home, Murdoch." He turned back to Quincy, who had slipped an arm around Mariel. "Let's get all of you inside. I'm sure your mother is very curious as to who our visitors are. We don't get very many these days."

"I imagine with all the war talk, people are staying pretty close to home," Quincy commented as the group crossed the veranda to the front doors.

"That they do," Geoffrey agreed. "There haven't been any hostilities here yet, but I'm afraid it's only a matter of time."

That grim discussion came to a quick halt when they entered the house and Geoffrey called out, "Pamela! Come see who we have here!"

A moment later Pamela Reed appeared at the head of the broad staircase that swept up from the foyer. An attractive woman whose thick blond hair and unlined face belied her middle years, she put her hands to her mouth and cried out in joy at the sight of her son standing at the bottom of the stairs.

"Hello, Mama," Quincy said quietly, tears springing to his eyes.

Pamela hurried down the steps and threw her arms around Quincy, hugging him tightly for a long moment as if she could not really believe he was here. Then she stepped back, clasped his hands, and looked up at him.

"You've grown so much," she said. "We . . . we were afraid we would never see you again."

No point in telling her how many times that fear had come close to being realized, Quincy decided. He smiled and proudly introduced Mariel instead. His mother exhibited the same surprise and excitement and joy that his father had.

"Come into the parlor and sit down," Pamela said as she linked arms with Mariel and led her out of the foyer. "I'm sure you must be tired, and you all must have so much to tell us!"

That is an understatement, Quincy thought. For now, he would just touch on the highlights of the past couple of years.

Dietrich had slept through all the greetings, and now Murdoch placed him gently on a divan with his head on a throw pillow. The boy snuggled down and settled into deep slumber. The adults sat down as well, Quincy and Mariel on one sofa, Geoffrey and Pamela on a facing one, and Murdoch in a heavy armchair. The Scotsman stretched his long, buckskin-clad legs out in front of him. Furnished comfortably but not sumptuously, the parlor of the Reed house was a warm, inviting room. But Quincy knew that Murdoch would be somewhat ill at ease in such surroundings. He was much more at home in the woods or on the trail.

For half an hour, Quincy, Mariel, and Murdoch answered Geoffrey's and Pamela's eager questions and told of some of the adventures they had been through. Then Quincy asked, "Have you heard anything from Daniel?"

Geoffrey's features grew solemn. "We were hoping you'd have some recent news of him. We received a message from him several months ago. It was brought here by an army courier, and it said only that your brother was all right. Nothing about what he was doing or where he was."

Quincy sighed. It was clear to him that Daniel had continued his involvement with espionage and intelligence efforts on behalf of the patriots, or he would not have been so reticent in the message to their parents. Quincy was unsure how much to explain to Geoffrey and Pamela, so he said, "Daniel is often involved in things that have to be kept quiet, but I wouldn't worry too much. He can take care of himself quite well, you know. He helped capture a wagon train full of British munitions while Murdoch and I were at Fort Ticonderoga with Colonel Ethan Allen and the Green Mountain Boys."

Geoffrey shook his head slowly. "It's incredible. Here we thought you lads were going to Boston for an education, and you wind up involved in practically every dramatic event of this war so far."

"It's just happenstance," Quincy said with a shrug of his shoulders. "And there's so much going on everywhere now, it's difficult to avoid getting mixed up in the war."

"I wish that wasn't so," Pamela said quietly. "I never thought being a colony was so terrible. I'm not sure why we have to fight with the British."

"They refuse to give us our rights," Quincy responded. "All we ever wanted was fair treatment, and we went to war only when it became obvious the British were never going to relent."

"Let's not argue politics," Geoffrey said quickly. "Not on the night that you've come home, my son. I can assure you that your mother and I support the efforts of the patriots, even if we wish things had never come to this."

"Well, I wish the same." Quincy realized that was true. He had been a firebrand once, eager for hostilities to break out, but those days were in the past, before he had seen some of the results of war firsthand.

Geoffrey leaned forward on the sofa and rubbed his hands together. "I think we should give a party," he said. "The occasion of our youngest son's safe return, along with the news of his marriage, is enough to warrant a celebration, don't you think, dear?"

Pamela frowned slightly. "A party? No one around here has been giving parties lately, Geoffrey."

"I'm well aware of that, and perhaps that's one reason such gloom has settled over the countryside." Geoffrey stood up and paced back and forth, clearly excited by the notion he had advanced. "I think a ball is an excellent idea. Something to celebrate life."

"I don't know," Quincy said hesitantly. He looked over at his wife. "What do you think, Mariel?"

"I think it would be fine," she replied. "Remember the way the people danced in the settlement where we stopped on the way west? The music and the dancing drew them together, Quincy. It made them feel better."

"Aye, there's nothing like some fiddle playing and high stepping t' make folks feel like there be a reason t' go on," Murdoch added.

"That's the spirit!" Geoffrey said. "A party to mark the homecoming of Quincy and his new wife, and a celebration to get everyone's mind off the war for a bit. Under the circumstances, we'll invite only the people around here, instead of the whole colony, as we would have at one time, but that'll be enough." He looked at his wife. "You'll see, Pamela. Everyone will enjoy themselves, I warrant."

She returned his smile. "I never could argue very successfully with you, Geoffrey. And you're probably right. It would be so nice to have our friends here again, for the house to be full of music and laughter."

"We'll issue the invitations right away. I'll have Cornelius send some of the lads around with them tomorrow."

Quincy leaned back and tightened his arm around Mariel's shoulders, a warm feeling inside him. It was good to be home, and it would be nice to see his old friends and acquaintances.

But he had nearly everything he needed right here beside him and in this room, he realized. His parents, his good friend Murdoch, little Dietrich . . . and most of all, Mariel and the child growing within her.

The only one missing was Daniel, and Quincy found himself wondering just where his brother was and what he was doing. There was no way of knowing.

But one day—one day soon, Quincy dared to hope —the Reed brothers would once again be together.

Chapter Three

Elliot Markham turned up the collar of his light-weight coat and shivered a little as a chill wind blew from the East River over the island of Manhattan and the settlement at its southern end known as New York City. Despite the fact that it was May and spring should have been in full force, the evening breezes off the harbor were cold. Elliot pulled his tricorn down tight on his head and wondered what the weather was like in Boston.

It had been two and a half months since the patriot siege of Boston had forced the British troops to withdraw from the city in March of 1776. When the redcoats evacuated, the Tories left in Boston had had no choice but to flee as well. The loyalists who supported King George and the Crown knew they could expect little sympathy from the rebellious colonists. In fact, it would

have been quite dangerous for the Tories to remain in
Boston, a fact Elliot knew all too well, so he had urged
his parents to leave when loyalist ships began sailing
from Boston Harbor bound for safer ports to the south.
Elliot was glad that his father Benjamin had agreed. In
the past, Benjamin had been stiff-necked and stubborn
—and proud of it.

That was before the violence of the war had
touched the Markham family personally. Benjamin had
never been the same since the vicious beating he received at the hands of the Liberty Legion, a gang of
criminals who took advantage of anti-Tory sentiment in
the city to extort money from loyalists.

With the help of his cousin Daniel Reed, Elliot had
put an end to the activities of the Liberty Legion, but
there was nothing he could do to restore his father to the
man he had once been.

The situation in New York had not helped matters.
The patriots controlled the city, despite the fact that
Mayor David Matthews was a staunch loyalist. Patriots
outnumbered the Tories by a considerable margin, and
the loyalists who had fled to New York from Boston
were a hated and despised minority. But New York *was*
safer for the Tories. True, they were segregated in a
certain part of the city and risked harassment if they
ventured beyond its bounds, but there had been no
hangings, floggings, or burning down of houses, as there
had been in Boston when Tories foolish enough to remain without the protection of British troops were discovered. News of these frightening events had reached
New York, and the loyalists there lived in fear.

Food and fuel were in short supply, too, just as they
had been in Boston, where some people had starved to
death during the siege. Many once-fine houses had been
gutted, the furniture used for firewood during the cruel

winter. Again, the situation was not yet that bad in New York, but the day could come when it would be, Elliot knew.

Shivering from the chilly wind, he reached his destination, a tavern known as Jessup's. Elliot went inside, relishing the warmth and the distinctive blend of odors: pipe smoke, sawdust, and ale. In earlier days—not that long ago—he had been a frequent patron of Boston's taverns, from the finest inns to the most squalid grogshops. The surroundings had never mattered much to Elliot, as long as there were drinks, gambling, and lusty serving wenches to be had. He had been a proper wastrel of a young man, spending his father's money with vigor and style and having a high old time.

That, like everything else about him, had changed with the coming of the war and his grudging involvement with the patriot espionage network set up by Benjamin Tallmadge and Robert Townsend, two of his cousin Daniel's friends from Yale. Almost against his will, and despite his family's solid Tory background, Elliot had found himself working for the colonial spymasters as a secret agent, sometimes designated as Operative Five. And all the while, he lived a double life, continuing to play the role of a dedicated loyalist.

It was somewhat akin to trying to balance on the blade of a razor, Elliot had thought more than once. A slip either way would be fatal.

Jessup's was only half full this evening, and Elliot wished there were more customers in the place so that he would be less conspicuous. He told himself he was worrying needlessly; no one in the tavern seemed to be taking the slightest interest in him except the bartender, who gave him a bored glance as he approached the bar.

"What can I do for you, mate?" asked the bartender, a gangling man with a protruding Adam's apple.

"I'll have a mug of ale," Elliot replied, taking a coin from his pocket and dropping it on the bar. "And I'm looking for someone, too. A man named Carruthers." He kept his voice pitched low, but the bartender didn't seem surprised by the question.

The man drew a mug of ale from a keg and placed it in front of Elliot, then nodded toward a rear booth and said quietly, "Back there."

Elliot slid the coin across the bar and picked up the ale without waiting for change. That was the price of the information, he knew. He sipped the strong, bitter brew and then carried it with him as he ambled toward the booth the bartender had indicated.

The man sitting there alone and drinking wine was well dressed, something of a fop, in fact, with tight cream-colored breeches, a silk shirt ruffled in the French style, and a cinched, dark blue jacket. His black tricorn sported a small feather in its band, and the silver buckles on his shoes gleamed in the lantern light. His dark hair had silver in it, just enough to make him look distinguished. As Elliot approached, the man looked up and smiled.

"Jermyn Carruthers?" Elliot asked.

"Indeed I am," the man replied. "And you are? . . ."

"My name is Elliot Markham. May I sit down?"

"By all means." With a languid hand motion, Carruthers indicated the seat opposite him.

Elliot instinctively disliked Carruthers, but if the man could help him get what he needed, Elliot didn't care how he felt personally.

"I'm told that you have contacts within the shipping industry," Elliot said.

"That is correct. Who mentioned my name to you?"

"That's not important," he answered without hesitation. It had taken him several weeks of asking discreet questions to finally come up with Carruthers's name. Elliot didn't want to jeopardize any of the contacts he had made.

"I'd like to know if it would be possible to buy some food from you," Elliot stated.

Carruthers smiled, the expression more a sneer than anything else. "I'm not a greengrocer, lad."

"I know that. I'm talking about the next cargo of food that comes in on one of your ships from the southern ports."

"Ah, then you're a patriot, are you?"

Elliot hesitated, then shook his head. "No. My family and my friends are all Tories."

That was only a small lie, Elliot thought. His parents and the acquaintances he had here in New York were definitely Tories, but as for the others—his cousins Daniel and Quincy, the frontiersman Murdoch Buchanan, his former partner in espionage, Roxanne Darragh—they all supported the cause of liberty with their hearts, souls, and lives . . . as did Elliot. But he could not sit by and watch innocent people starve to death, no matter what their political stance.

Carruthers was frowning slightly at him across the table. "I sell only to those who support the patriot cause," he said. "To do otherwise would be imprudent and not good business at all, I'm afraid."

"That's not what I've heard," Elliot said boldly. "I've heard that for a price, you can deliver goods to patriots and Tories alike."

Carruthers drew himself up and gave Elliot a withering stare. "Are you accusing me of smuggling in supplies for the Tories, young man?" he demanded.

"I'm saying that you're a good businessman," Elliot replied smoothly. "And as such, you know that the highest price can be gotten from the ones who need your services the most."

"Well, that's true enough, I suppose." Carruthers leaned forward. "Just how much money are we talking about?"

Elliot felt a surge of relief, but he tried to mask the emotion. He knew that he had come to the right man.

"A hundred pounds," Elliot said.

Carruthers burst out laughing. As Elliot's jaw tightened in anger, Carruthers picked up the glass on the table in front of him and drained the last of the rich red wine.

"A hundred pounds for a shipload of food?" he asked as he placed the empty glass on the table. "You're either joking or insane, Mr. Markham."

"It's all we have," Elliot said. He wasn't negotiating; he was telling the truth. The hundred pounds was all he and his family and their acquaintances had been able to scrape together. With it they had hoped to buy enough food on the illegal market to last them at least a month.

"You might as well go back where you came from," Carruthers said coldly. "I'm a legitimate businessman with strong connections to the patriots. I cannot afford to jeopardize those connections for less than five hundred pounds."

"But that's a fortune!" Elliot exclaimed. "You can't be serious!"

"I am indeed, and I'll thank you to keep your voice down. If a hundred pounds is the best you can do, you should leave now, before you annoy me even more."

Elliot bit back a blazing retort. As angry as he was, he was still rational enough to know that challenging Carruthers would accomplish absolutely nothing. The man was right. He had the goods and could name his own price, and there was not a thing Elliot could do about it.

Tossing back the rest of the ale, Elliot thumped his mug down on the table and glared at Carruthers. "I'm leaving," he said. "But it would be only fitting for a scoundrel like you if I revealed the business you've been doing with the Tories!"

"No one would believe you," Carruthers said. "Unlike you pitiful loyalists, I've some influence in this town."

For a few seconds longer Elliot glowered across the table, then stood up and stalked out of Jessup's tavern. This foray had been unsuccessful, and the failure was made worse by the knowledge that Carruthers was smiling mockingly at him as he left.

Elliot was so angry that he did not feel the dank chill in the air as he walked toward the small house where he and his parents were living. The building was a fraction of the size of the Beacon Street mansion in Boston in which Elliot had grown up. The exiled Tories all lived in cramped quarters, including Benjamin Markham's business partner, Theophilus Cummings. The Markham & Cummings line had once been one of the most prosperous shipping concerns in the colonies. Its vessels had plied the trade lanes between England and North America with full cargoes both ways, making the two men rich. Now the once-proud Markham & Cummings line had been reduced to three ships sitting idle in New York Harbor. The only reason the ships had not been destroyed already was that the patriots might one day decide to confiscate them and place them into service against the British. When that day came, it would be the final blow for his father, Elliot feared.

Theophilus Cummings and his wife were staying in the modest house next to the one occupied by the Markham family. Their married daughter, Sarah Wallingford, lived there, too, along with her husband, Avery. That arrangement had proven difficult for Elliot to endure, since for several years he had been engaged to the lovely, blond Sarah Cummings, only to have her break the engagement and marry Avery Wallingford, whom Elliot despised. Elliot no longer loved Sarah, he was sure of that, but he was still fond of her and hated to see her saddled with an ineffectual, selfish, self-centered individual such as Avery.

If only Carruthers had been reasonable and agreed to sell them some much-needed supplies! Elliot thought. Approaching the man had been Elliot's idea, and now he had to return to the others and admit failure, but perhaps he could find someone else who could bring in some food—

He stopped in his tracks, blinking hard at the thought that had just occurred to him. Carruthers brought in food from the agricultural colonies along the Atlantic seaboard: Virginia, Carolina, and Georgia. What would prevent someone from going the other direction—to Canada—and returning with a ship filled with supplies? The settlers in Canada were still firmly entrenched as supporters of the king, and they would surely be willing to provide provisions for the beleaguered Tories in New York for a reasonable price.

And there were the Markham & Cummings ships sitting in the harbor, just waiting to sail. . . .

There was a new lightness in Elliot's step when he moved on. He felt excitement growing within him as he turned over the idea in his mind. It could be done, he told himself, and it would solve many of the Tories' problems. The shortage of food and fuel was their most pressing concern at the moment.

His parents were not alone, Elliot saw when he entered the front room of the rented house a few minutes later. In addition to Benjamin and Polly Markham, Theophilus Cummings was there, along with his daughter and son-in-law. Avery and Sarah sat together on a small, threadbare divan, while Benjamin and Cummings were each ensconced in wing chairs that showed the nicks and scars of hard use. Polly stood behind her husband's chair, and she was the first one to greet Elliot.

"Hello, dear. Did you have any luck?"

Elliot hesitated before answering, well aware of the five pairs of eyes watching him intently as he took off his tricorn and hung the hat on a nail driven into the wall near the door. It was clear they had gathered to find out how successful he had been in his quest.

Finally Elliot said, "We don't need luck. We're going to make our own."

Theophilus Cummings snorted in derision, his sallow features looking more pinched than ever these days. "What the deuce do you mean by that?" he demanded.

"The ship that brought us here is still seaworthy, isn't it?" Elliot asked, ignoring Cummings and looking at his father.

Benjamin Markham nodded slowly. "Of course it is. Markham and Cummings ships are the finest vessels on the seven seas. You know that, boy."

A tiny smile tugged at Elliot's lips. Every so often, the old fire could be heard in Benjamin's voice, even though the once-powerful frame had grown gaunt. Benjamin's face was more lined these days, too, and his thick white hair had begun to thin, as if the malaise that gripped his spirit had affected his physical body as well. But at moments like this, something of the old Benjamin Markham could be seen and heard.

"I want to use that ship, Father," Elliot said.

"The last time you were on a Markham and Cummings ship, it was the *Carolingian*. Have you forgotten what happened?" Benjamin said, frowning.

Elliot flushed. Of course he had not forgotten. The *Carolingian*, a Markham & Cummings vessel, had been used by the British government to transport munitions to Boston a year or so earlier. The British had hoped to resupply their forces in the city without alerting the patriots; but colonial ships had hijacked the *Carolingian*'s cargo, an operation masterminded by none other than Elliot Markham and Roxanne Darragh. During their harrowing escape, Roxanne had chosen to reveal her identity as a patriot agent, but Elliot had played an innocent dupe, a role he was still trying to live down.

"This is different," he insisted. "This is completely my idea. I want to take the ship to Canada, load it with food and other supplies, and bring it back here."

"Ridiculous!" snapped Theophilus Cummings. "It can't be done."

Elliot swung toward him, forgetting for the moment the respect due Cummings as his elder and his father's business partner. "Why the hell not?" he asked sharply.

"Elliot!" Polly exclaimed.

Benjamin leaned forward in his chair to growl, "Watch your tongue, lad. I'll not have you talking to my old friend and partner that way!"

Sarah and Avery glared at him, too, and Elliot felt the weight of disapproval from everyone in the room.

"I'm sorry, Mr. Cummings, but this is important. It could be our salvation, and I don't see why you're throwing up obstacles."

"Our shipping line is practically ruined," Cummings said, his voice trembling. "I won't have another of our vessels sent to the bottom of the ocean on some fool's errand."

"But it's not a fool's errand," Elliot insisted. "Before the war, ships traveled between Canada and the colonies all the time. There's no reason why it can't be done again."

"What about rebel ships cutting off the trade?" Avery asked. "I've heard that there have been several naval engagements between British ships and colonial pirates."

Elliot shrugged. "It's true, there's a slight risk of that, I suppose. But isn't it a chance worth taking to see that our people have enough food to eat and clothes on their backs?"

"How noble of you, Elliot," Sarah said dryly.

"I'm not trying to be noble," he said, flushing again. "I just want to help."

Sarah's lips curved in a sardonic smile. She was as beautiful as ever, he thought, and from the way she was treating him now, no one would have guessed that she had paid him a visit in Boston—before the siege forced them to leave—and had tried to seduce him, claiming that her marriage to Avery had been an awful mistake. Elliot had managed to deflect her attentions then, and she had been cool toward him ever since.

Benjamin was frowning, and he rubbed his jaw in thought. "It's true that our ships used to stop at ports in Canada," he said. "And it would not be difficult to find a captain and crew who know the route along the coast. But Avery's right; there's a chance of running into trouble from the rebels."

"We're at war, Father," Elliot said. "We take a chance every time we get up in the morning."

Benjamin leaned back in his chair, and Polly rested a hand on his shoulder. Elliot waited anxiously for his father's decision, knowing that although Benjamin's respect for him had grown somewhat in recent months, there were still those years of conflict between them, years when Elliot had resisted the idea of going into the family business to the point of having to be almost dragged into the office of the shipping line for his infrequent visits. And now here he was asking for the opportunity to take one of the ships hundreds of miles through waters that could prove hostile and dangerous.

Finally Benjamin sighed and said, "Food supplies are growing desperately short, I'm told, and we'll get no relief from those so-called patriots. They're too busy gloating over their momentary advantage." He looked up and met Elliot's eyes. "So I suppose your idea has merit. If you think you can actually do this, you should try."

Before Elliot could reply, Theophilus Cummings said coldly, "And I suppose *I* have no say in this decision, Benjamin? I thought we were partners."

"Of course we're partners, Theophilus. But the boy has a good idea, and it appears he even has the guts to go through with it. I think he deserves a chance."

Cummings glowered at Elliot, and the younger man knew well the source of the hostility. Cummings had never forgiven him after Sarah had broken off their engagement. As Cummings saw it, Elliot had caused his daughter pain, and that was an unforgivable sin, even though the whole thing had been an unfortunate misunderstanding. Cummings would never see him as anything but an unreliable scoundrel.

"I won't have it," Cummings snapped after a moment, and Elliot's heart sank. There had been a time when Benjamin Markham would have opposed his partner and overridden his objections, but whether Benjamin still had that inner conviction was a question Elliot could not answer.

"It would be for everyone's good," Elliot said quickly, hoping that Cummings could be persuaded to come around. "And if someone doesn't do something about this problem soon, people are going to start dying."

"Elliot's right, Theophilus," Polly said. It was rare for her to take part in a business discussion, but this went beyond mere business. It was rapidly becoming a question of survival. Polly went on, "I don't like to see him taking chances either, but if it has to be done . . ."

Cummings stood up, paced back and forth for a moment, and then turned to glare at Elliot again, his arms crossed over his thin chest. "If I agree," he began, "it will be with one proviso."

"Anything," Elliot said immediately, seizing the slender chance.

"You can take the ship . . . if Avery goes with you."

It would have been difficult to say who was the most surprised person in the room at that moment. Elliot, his parents, and Sarah all seemed stunned, but Avery looked positively thunderstruck. His mouth opened and closed several times, and his eyes widened until the whites were showing all around the pupils.

Elliot found his voice first. "Avery's no sailor."

"Neither are you," Cummings shot back, "but you're going."

"Someone has to arrange for the purchase of the supplies."

"Avery's father was one of the leading bankers in Boston, and he's been groomed for a business career for years," Cummings pointed out. He sniffed. "I should think Avery is more qualified to negotiate such an arrangement than *you* are, Elliot."

"No!" Avery said frantically as he stood up and looked around, wild-eyed. "Wait just a moment! I'm sure Elliot can. After all, it was his idea . . . and I can't just go sailing off. . . . As he said, I'm no sailor!" He swallowed hard, knowing that he sounded like a coward, and went on quickly in an effort to save his dignity, "I just don't think it's a good idea, and although I appreciate the confidence you've shown in me, Theophilus, I don't believe I should be a part of this venture. Assuming, that is, that it ever comes about!"

There was a rare gleam of amusement in Benjamin's eyes as he said, "I have no objection to Avery accompanying Elliot on the voyage, Theophilus. That way we'll each have someone to look after our interests, eh?"

"Exactly," Cummings said. "That was my thought."

"But I can't leave Sarah," Avery protested.

She smiled up at him and said, "That's all right, Avery. I can manage just fine by myself for a short time. And as Elliot pointed out, this trip is for a good cause."

Even Elliot could see the humor in this unexpected turn of events, but he was almost as dismayed by Cummings's stipulation as Avery was. The prospect of spending several weeks on board ship with Avery Wallingford was unappealing, to say the least. But if that was the only way he could secure the blessing of his father and Cummings for the trip to Canada, Elliot supposed he could tolerate the situation.

"I can't—I just can't—" Avery stammered again, shuddering. He looked around at the people in the room, all of them watching him intently, and abruptly burst out, "All right! I'll go along, blast it! But I'm going under protest."

"Protest all you want," Cummings said. "Just don't let that hotheaded young . . . man . . . do anything foolish that'll get our ship sunk. After the Crown has crushed this ill-advised rebellion, we shall need all of our vessels to get the line going again."

"The ship won't sink," Elliot promised. "We'll get through with the supplies."

"You know, son, I believe you will," Benjamin said. He stood, walked over to Elliot, and clasped his hand firmly.

Elliot returned his father's handshake and smile, and at that moment he felt better than at any time since the Tories had been chased out of Boston. He turned and looked at Avery.

"We'll see to the outfitting of the ship tomorrow, and as soon as we can, we'll set sail for Canada!"

Avery just nodded weakly.

Chapter Four

The man stalking back and forth in the hallway of the London building that housed the Ministry of War wore the uniform of a major in the Fifth Lancashire Grenadiers, but that hardly told the true story of his service in His Majesty King George III's army. Alistair Kane was much more than a mere major, just as the man he was waiting to see was more than an assistant deputy minister of war, even though that was Cyril Eldridge's title.

Kane felt his impatience growing. He was a tall, well-built, handsome man with a thick shock of dark hair and a narrow mustache above his wide mouth. To all appearances he was a sterling example of an officer of the Crown, and he had always devoted himself to serving the king in any way he could—until Roxanne Darragh had come into his life. Now he could think of nothing but possessing her.

The door to Cyril Eldridge's office opened, and a clerk said, "Major Kane? Minister Eldridge will see you now."

"Bloody well about time," Kane muttered. He strode into the office, his black tricorn tucked under his left arm, his sheathed saber bouncing lightly against his leg as he walked.

The man behind the desk was a physically unimpressive specimen in his early forties, with pale skin, narrow features, and thinning grayish-brown hair. He wore a dark brown suit and was signing a document with a quill pen as Major Kane stopped in front of the desk and glared at him. Cyril Eldridge did not seem to notice the major's glower, nor did he appear to be in any hurry to acknowledge Kane's presence. Only when Kane cleared his throat impatiently did Eldridge glance up.

"Ah, there you are, Major. I trust your voyage from the colonies was not too unpleasant."

"It was a bloody disaster," Kane snapped. "I'm a soldier of the Crown. I am not accustomed to running away like a hare with a pack of hounds after it."

Eldridge leaned back in his chair, lifted a hand languidly, and rested his chin on it. "General Howe had no choice but to evacuate Boston," he said. "Once that damned Washington got his hands on enough cannon, it was inevitable he would pound the city into submission. Better to leave when you did, Major, than to wind up a prisoner of the rebels."

Kane's mouth was a taut, thin line as he said, "Perhaps you're right, Minister, but that doesn't mean I have to revel in our defeat."

"One strategic retreat does not mean a defeat, Major." Eldridge laughed humorlessly. "I would have thought you'd know that, an experienced officer such as yourself. Could something else be galling you?"

Kane looked over his shoulder at the clerk, who stood just inside the door, and said nothing until Eldridge motioned the man out of the room. Only when the thick door was closed securely did Kane reply to Eldridge's question.

"I've heard rumors that the girl escaped from you," he said harshly. "Is that true?"

Eldridge abandoned his negligent pose and sat up straight. His voice was every bit as harsh as Kane's when he said, "She was rescued by young Reed, with the help of my cousin Bramwell."

Kane blinked in surprise. "You mean Lord Oakley?"

"The *late* Lord Oakley. Bramwell died opposing me and my men."

The major felt a grudging respect for Eldridge. They had worked together for over a year now, Eldridge formulating espionage and intelligence policies for the Crown, Kane implementing those policies as the top British intelligence operative in the colonies. Now, with the British evacuation of Boston, Kane had returned to England, and this was his first meeting with the man to whom he had entrusted the captured patriot secret agent, Roxanne Darragh. Eldridge had a reputation for ruthlessness, and obviously it was well deserved if he had killed his own cousin for getting in the way. But Roxanne was no longer a prisoner, and any information she possessed about the rebels' espionage activities had escaped with her.

"Were you at least able to pry any useful information out of the woman before she got away?" Kane asked.

"Miss Darragh proved surprisingly stubborn, and as

long as Bramwell was alive, he prevented me from using *effective* means of persuading her to cooperate. But don't look so smug, Major! As I recall, Miss Darragh was your prisoner in Boston for quite a while, and your efforts to interrogate her proved as futile."

Kane stiffened and returned Eldridge's frown. He did not like to be reminded of the time when Roxanne had been his captive. Not only had she refused to answer his questions, she had also spurned the love he found himself feeling for her. Kane had known quite well it was unwise to allow himself such romantic feelings for a prisoner, but he had not been able to help himself.

To this day, he desired Roxanne Darragh with a passion that burned distractingly bright within him. Sooner or later he would have her, he had vowed.

All the way across the Atlantic, on the ship that had brought Kane and many of the British troops home from Boston, the major had taken solace from the fact that he would soon be seeing Roxanne again. He had expected Eldridge to have her safely tucked away somewhere, and in the back of his mind had been the notion that once she came to know him better, she would return his feelings.

But when he arrived, he had been told that the girl was no longer in custody, and it had taken until today to secure an appointment with Eldridge, the man who would have the answers to his questions. Now those questions had been answered, but he was no more satisfied than he had been before.

"There's no point in hashing over the past," he said. "What we must concern ourselves with is the future."

"I quite agree," Eldridge said, relaxing a little. "What do you propose we do about the situation?"

Kane hadn't expected to be asked his opinion so forthrightly, but he did not hesitate with his answer. "No doubt Reed and the Darragh woman will try to return to the colonies. I think I should go there as well."

"You intend to neglect your duties to settle a matter of personal business, Major?" Eldridge asked, lifting an eyebrow.

"Not at all," Kane said sharply. "Reed and the woman are both spies and traitors. They should be arrested not only because of the valuable information they surely possess, but also as a lesson to others who would defy the Crown."

"There are thousands of rebels defying the Crown at this moment," Eldridge pointed out. "We cannot simply arrest all of them, Major. That is why we are at war with the colonies."

Kane flushed angrily. "You don't have to explain the concept of warfare to me, Minister. I understand perfectly well what is happening in the colonies. I still say that Reed and the woman should be apprehended if at all possible. And to be quite honest about it, I am too valuable an asset to the king to be tarrying here in England. I need to be in the colonies where I can do some good for the Crown."

Eldridge laced his hands together on the desk and said, "I agree, Major. I agree with both your points. Reed and Darragh must be caught, and you're the man to do it. One of His Majesty's warships is setting sail for the colonies tomorrow, and you shall be on it. I have your orders right here." He held up an envelope sealed with dark red wax into which had been pressed an imprint from his ring.

Feeling a surge of excitement, Kane took the orders. "Thank you, sir," he said. "I shan't disappoint you."

"No, you certainly shall not. Because I'm going with you."

Kane blinked in surprise. "*You,* Minister?" He was unable to restrain the startled response.

Eldridge smiled thinly and coldly. "That is correct. I have my own reasons for wanting to find Miss Darragh. Or, I should say, Lady Oakley."

That came as an even greater shock to Kane. He demanded, "What do you mean?"

"I mean that that redheaded colonial slut married my cousin Bramwell Stoddard before she escaped," Eldridge replied, his iron control slipping, his voice trembling with rage. "Bramwell arranged things so that the whelp she is carrying will inherit his title and estate."

Staggered by the news that his beloved was not only married but with child, Kane groped toward the nearest chair. "My God! Roxanne is— But who is the father?"

Eldridge gestured distractedly. "What does it matter?" he said angrily.

Kane wiped a hand across his face as his shock subsided. He stared at Eldridge. The picture was becoming clear to him now. Just as he had personal reasons for pursuing Roxanne Darragh, so did Eldridge. "If not for Roxanne and the child," he said slowly, "*you* would be heir to the Stoddard estate."

"I could easily blame you for this, Major," Eldridge snapped. "You were the one who sent the Darragh woman over here and set this outlandish chain of events in motion."

"There was no way I could have guessed that she would marry your cousin."

"No, I suppose not. But that is the situation we must deal with. We each have our own goals, Major. Do you agree with my suggestion that we combine our resources to deal with the problem?"

Kane did not hesitate. "I agree we should work together."

"Very good," Eldridge said, reaching for another document on his desk. "Now we must deal with the question of where Reed and the woman will go."

"Back to Boston, I should think, since the city is now under rebel control and is their home."

Eldridge shook his head. "True, Darragh is from Boston, but Daniel Reed is not. He had relatives there, the Markhams, but he himself was born and raised in Virginia, on an inland plantation."

"Does he still have family there?"

"According to the information that my investigation has turned up, Reed's parents still live on their plantation."

"What about Reed's brother?"

"Vanished," Eldridge replied. "Along with that Buchanan ruffian. It's supposed that they went west together after the rebels captured Ticonderoga. My information is that they were sighted in Saratoga shortly after that, but they have not been seen since. I think Daniel Reed wanted his brother safely out of harm's way as the war intensified."

"You could be right," Kane said slowly. "But that's beside the point."

"Not really," Eldridge said. He stood up and walked over to a wall map of the colonies. Running a fingertip along the western frontier, he continued, "If Reed felt strongly enough about his brother's safety to send the boy west, he might want the Darragh woman out of harm's way as well."

"You're not suggesting that they're heading for the frontier, are you?"

Eldridge reached over and speared the colony of Virginia on the map with a slender forefinger. "Not at all. But remember, the Reed family plantation is in this area, where there has been no fighting. And since the woman is with child, Reed would want to take her someplace where she could give birth and have someone there to help her."

"Safe in the bosom of his family, eh?" Kane mused. "You could be right, Minister. It's a logical conclusion for Reed to reach."

Eldridge tapped the map, indicating an area between New York and Boston. "This will be the center of activity in the war. Reed may intend to return to the area, but he wouldn't take the woman back there. He'll leave her where he thinks she will be safe. I'm sure of it."

Kane agreed. Eldridge's theory was a virtual certainty as far as he was concerned. "So we're going to Virginia, to that plantation?"

"If Reed and the woman *aren't* there, we'll be able to pick up their trail at the very least."

"What excuse will you use for leaving London?" Kane asked. "Won't it be considered rather unusual for a deputy minister of war to travel all the way to the colonies, especially under the circumstances?"

"Let me worry about that," Eldridge replied curtly. "Concern yourself only with finding Reed and the woman once we get there."

"Yes, sir." Kane straightened, picked up his tricorn from the desk, and tucked it under his arm. "Now, if you'll excuse me, Minister, I'll begin making arrangements for our journey."

"You do that, Major," Eldridge said dryly.

Kane saluted, turned on his heel, and left the office. This meeting had been full of unexpected developments, but the important thing was that he was going after Roxanne.

And when he found her—when that damned Daniel Reed was dead—then things would be different. She would come to love him sooner or later, child or no child.

Cyril Eldridge waited until the major had gone, then turned to his desk and picked up a small dagger that lay among the stacks of papers. He whirled around, his narrow face distorted with anger, and stabbed the dagger's point into the map, between the *r* and the *g* in the carefully lettered *Virginia*.

Kane was pitifully transparent, he thought, especially for such a skilled espionage operative. The man's reason had deserted him when it came to the Darragh woman. Kane was in love with her, and he was undertaking this mission for only one real motive: to reclaim Roxanne Darragh as his own. Military objectives had nothing to do with it.

Eldridge could understand that. He, too, had personal reasons for going after Roxanne. He drew in a deep breath. The child she carried when she escaped from England represented the last obstacle in Eldridge's path to the vast Stoddard estate and the title of Lord Oakley. And the solution to the problem was simple. The child had to die, and the mother with it.

Kane wouldn't like that when he found out. But, Eldridge thought with a smile, if necessary Kane could be sacrificed as well. The major would serve his purpose and then die a noble death in the service of his king and country. At least that was the tale Eldridge would tell when he came back to England to claim his rightful inheritance.

And who would argue with the new Lord Oakley?

Chapter Five

The party at the Reed plantation showed every sign of being a success. As darkness settled that warm spring evening, the guests began to arrive, most of them in wagons, coaches, or phaetons, a few on horseback. The big house was more brightly lit than it had been in months, with every window full of the warm glow of lamplight. Colored lanterns hung in the branches of the trees spreading over the front yard, and the sounds of music and laughter filled the evening air as servants took charge of the vehicles brought by the guests, who then strolled through the open front doors of the house.

Inside, quite a crowd was on hand. As Quincy stood in one corner of the ballroom and looked around, he spotted people he had not seen in years. There were the

Remingtons from Richmond, and the Duprees and the Williamses and the Richardsons and old Miss Eugenia Callison and Harvey and Micah Danvers and . . . well, in general, more people than he had been around in a long time. Many of them had known him since he was a youngster, and he was growing tired of the comments about how hard it was to believe that he was all grown up, married, and about to become a father. Did they think he didn't *know* that?

Geoffrey Reed had said that they would not invite as many guests to this party as they might have before the war, but Quincy thought there were quite enough people here, thank you.

"Well, what do you think, son?" Geoffrey asked as he approached Quincy and clapped a hand on his shoulder. "Quite a celebration, eh?"

"Yes, indeed," Quincy agreed.

"Where's that young wife of yours? I haven't seen her all evening."

Quincy lifted his gaze toward the ceiling. "Mariel's still upstairs. She wasn't feeling very well, but she said she'd be down in a little while. It's sort of difficult, you know, in her condition—"

Geoffrey lifted a hand. "Say no more. I remember how your mother was when she was carrying you and Daniel. It's a hard thing on a woman, being in the family way. Worthwhile, though, wouldn't you say?"

Quincy smiled but didn't answer. He felt a bit uncomfortable talking about such things with his father. Their conversations over the years had had more to do with hunting and fishing and the efficient management of the estate than, well, *babies*.

He was saved from having to continue the discussion by a tall, red-haired gentleman who ambled over to join them, brandy glass in hand. His silk shirt, blue coat, and cream-colored breeches were well made and expensive but not gaudy. "Good evening, Geoffrey," he said, then extended his hand to Quincy. "And it's good to see you again, young man."

"Thank you, Mr. Jefferson," Quincy said as he shook hands with the politician and gentleman farmer who had made his home nearby on the Rivanna River.

"How are you, Tom?" Geoffrey asked. "And how's that house of yours coming along?"

Thomas Jefferson's smile broadened. "The construction of Monticello is proceeding apace, as they say. We're actually living in the house now while the work on it continues."

Quincy recalled that the construction of the huge mansion Jefferson called Monticello had been under way when he and Daniel went north to Boston several years earlier. Evidently it had still not been completed. In addition to being a farmer and a statesman, Jefferson was something of an amateur architect and had designed the house himself. The rumor around the county was that Monticello would be quite a showplace . . . when and if it was ever finished.

"You're probably not getting much done since you've spent so much time in Richmond and Philadelphia the past year," Geoffrey said.

"Affairs of state are far more pressing than personal business these days," Jefferson said. "I had to come home for a while, though, when Martha and little Jane were both taken ill."

"We were all greatly saddened when Jane passed away," Geoffrey said solemnly.

"It was a hard thing," Jefferson said softly. "Only eighteen months old. She was a precious child." He squared his shoulders. "But while I still think of her each day, the affairs of state must come first now. That's why

I've been raising money to take to Philadelphia when I return for the reconvening of the Continental Congress. Fighting a war, even an undeclared one, is an expensive proposition."

Thomas Jefferson and Geoffrey Reed continued discussing the conflict with the British, but Quincy paid little attention to their words. He had seen the war first-hand, had dodged enough redcoat musket balls to last him a lifetime. He was thinking instead about what Jefferson had said about the death of his baby daughter. Clearly the child's passing had had a profound effect on the man, and even now, months later, Quincy had seen the flash of utter pain in Jefferson's eyes when he spoke of the loss.

Suddenly a terrible fear swept through Quincy. What if something happened to the baby Mariel was carrying? He remembered the times on the trail when they had spoken quietly together in the wagon at night, talked about their plans for their family, and how Mariel had taken his hand and placed it on her stomach so he could feel the baby shifting and then kicking inside her.

Even though the child was not yet born, Quincy knew he loved it. He was completely sure of that. It was already a vital part of his life. And he wasn't sure he could stand it if something happened to either Mariel or the baby or, God forbid, both of them. Quincy swallowed hard.

A moment later, a murmur of sound drew his attention. He turned to see what had caused the slight commotion and saw his wife and his mother, arm in arm, descending the curving staircase at the far end of the room. Mariel and Pamela looked lovely, and Quincy could understand why all eyes in the room were drawn to them.

"We've reason to be proud, eh, lad?" Geoffrey said, beaming.

"Indeed, Father, that we do."

The two men walked across the ballroom to greet their wives.

Mariel wore a pale blue gown that complemented the color of her eyes and fell in soft folds over her prominent belly. She was covered from her shoulders to her hips by a beautiful lace jacket designed to cover her dress and further hide her advanced state of pregnancy. Pamela wore a green silk dress trimmed with an abundance of lacy white ruffles, and both women carried stiff lace fans, for the spring night was warm.

As Quincy and Geoffrey reached them, the musicians Geoffrey had hired for the party began to play a minuet, and the men swept their ladies into their arms. Quincy took Mariel's hand and slid an arm around her back, being sure to keep some distance between their bodies as they began to dance. More than once Mariel had told him that she was not fragile, that he could touch her without worrying about harming her or the baby, but Quincy remained cautious.

"How are you feeling?" he asked in a low voice.

"Much better now," she replied, a beautiful smile lighting her face. "Your mother made me some herb tea, and it helped."

"I'm glad. Everyone came tonight to meet you."

Mariel blushed prettily. "Surely not. They are here to welcome you home, Quincy."

"*And* to see the girl I brought back with me," he replied with a grin. "Don't worry about it. I'm sure you meet with the guests' wholehearted approval."

They danced through several numbers, and Mariel was surprisingly light on her feet considering her condition, although Quincy wisely kept that comment to him-

self. Then, not wanting to tire her, he found her a place
to sit on a padded bench in a corner of the big room.

"Wait here and I'll fetch you some punch," he told
her.

"That would be nice. The evening is rather warm."

It was downright hot, Quincy thought as he made
his way across the crowded room to the long table covered with a snowy white cloth on which sat the punch
bowl and a sparkling array of crystal cups. One of the
servants, resplendent in red livery, stood behind the table and filled the cups for the guests. All this finery was
rarely used, Quincy knew; the Reed plantation was a
working farm, with fields planted in tobacco, cotton,
wheat, and corn, and most of the time everyone rolled
up their sleeves and pitched in. Geoffrey Reed had only
a few slaves. Most of the laborers on the plantation were
freed people of color. It was a matter of both ethics and
efficiency for Geoffrey: Free men worked harder and
took more pride in what they accomplished than slaves
did, to his way of thinking, and the prosperity of the
Reed plantation was proof enough for him that he was
right.

As he approached the table, Quincy saw Murdoch
Buchanan standing there, talking to the servant on the
other side of the punch bowl. The man was glaring at
Murdoch, and there was a darkly ominous expression on
the face of the big Scotsman as well. Murdoch was
dressed not in his usual buckskins but in a dark suit that
Geoffrey had rustled up somewhere; Lord knew where a
suit of clothes big enough to fit the massive Murdoch
had been found. As Quincy came up beside him, he put
a hand on Murdoch's arm.

"What's wrong, my burly Scottish friend?"

Murdoch pointed a blunt finger at the liveried servant. "This here fancy fella is trying t' give me nothing

more than a wee cup o' this punch," he complained. " 'Tis fit for a lady, mayhaps, but no' a man. Besides, he will no' allow me t' add some o' me own special ingredient t' the mix."

"The gen'leman means he wants to po' some whiskey into the punch bowl, Master Quincy," the servant said in a deep voice. "I tole him he couldn't do that with all these ladies present. He wants somethin' stronger than this here punch, he can go outside with the other gen'lemen who done brought flasks with 'em."

"Junius is right, Murdoch," Quincy agreed with a grin. "You can't put whiskey in the punch."

"This will no' be much o' a party, then," he said, snorting in derision. "Won't even be any good fights if everybody stays sober."

Quincy was trying to figure out how to explain to Murdoch that while this part of Virginia was certainly not as high-toned as Richmond or Norfolk, or as stuffy as Boston, it wasn't quite the same as the frontier to which his friend was accustomed. Suddenly a loud burst of exclamations drew his attention. He turned and looked toward the double doors that opened into the hallway that led to the front of the house.

A man stood there, a lean individual of medium height with thick brown hair touched with gray under his pushed-back tricorn. He had his hand under the arm of a red-haired woman who stood somewhat unsteadily beside him. He supported her as he looked around and said in a loud, shaken voice, "We need some help here."

"Daniel!" Quincy cried, unable to believe what he was seeing.

Less than a year had passed since they had parted, but still, Daniel had changed quite a bit. Both Murdoch and Quincy pushed quickly through the startled crowd toward Daniel and Roxanne. Murdoch's brief clash with Junius was completely forgotten.

Pamela let out a cry when she saw her older son, and she and Geoffrey reached Daniel's side at the same time as Quincy and Murdoch.

Daniel smiled wearily at her and said, "Hello, Mother. I hope we haven't ruined the party." Then he turned to his brother and, with tears in his eyes, reached out to clasp Quincy's arm.

"Quincy! I didn't expect to find you here. But it's the answer to my prayers. It's good to see you again, so very good."

"Daniel, what—" Quincy began, and then his eyes moved down Roxanne's figure to a very familiar sight: the swollen belly of a woman in the advanced stages of pregnancy. Quincy blinked in surprise and decided it wouldn't be a good idea to ask Daniel what in the world he had been doing since they had parted in Saratoga all those months earlier.

But Murdoch wasn't quite so tactful. In his usual blunt manner, he said to his cousin, "Roxanne, how'd ye get in such a state?"

"You don't really want me to answer that, do you, Murdoch?" Roxanne responded, smiling weakly.

Murdoch blinked, and Quincy saw a surprising sight. The big Scotsman was actually blushing. But that did not stop Murdoch from stepping forward and hugging Roxanne. Then he helped Daniel lead her to a sofa, where she sat down slowly and carefully.

Daniel looked up at his parents. "Mother, Father, allow me to present Mrs. Roxanne Stoddard."

"You've heard me speak of Roxanne," Quincy added to Geoffrey and Pamela. "She's Murdoch's cousin, and she helped rescue me from jail when we were in Boston."

"Welcome to our home, Mrs. Stoddard," Geoffrey said graciously. "If there's anything we can do to make you comfortable, please let us know."

Pamela cast a glance at her husband, then sat down beside Roxanne on the sofa. "I think the best thing we can do for Mrs. Stoddard, Geoffrey, is to summon Dr. Fletcher and Granny Strickland."

"Please, Father," Daniel said. "There's no time to waste."

"Of course," Geoffrey said. He motioned to one of the servants behind the table, who immediately took off the powdered wig and bright red coat he wore.

"Alonzo," Geoffrey ordered, "take one of the carriages to Granny Strickland's cabin right away and fetch her back with you."

The servant nodded and hurried out, while Geoffrey located Dr. Fletcher among the guests. The portly, red-faced physician was already pushing toward the front of the crowd. Along with the midwife, Granny Strickland, he had delivered many of the babies in the county, Daniel and Quincy among them.

Daniel, Quincy, and Murdoch stood shoulder to shoulder to keep the crowd back from the sofa as Dr. Fletcher sat beside Roxanne and took her hand.

"We'll take good care of you, my dear," he promised. Casting a glance at Pamela, he went on, "I assume we can use one of the bedrooms upstairs?"

"Oh, of course!"

"Then I think we'd best get the young lady up there right away," Fletcher said, a note of concern in his voice.

Quincy heard that concern, and judging from the anxious expression on his face, so had Daniel. Daniel looked tired as well, and Quincy wondered where they had come from. The journey must have been a long one.

Mariel moved forward, introduced herself to Roxanne, and along with Pamela, Dr. Fletcher, and several maids, prepared to take Roxanne upstairs.

Suddenly Roxanne reached out and clasped Daniel's hand. "Wait," she said. "There's something I have to do first."

"Young lady, I hardly think there's time for anything else—" Dr. Fletcher began.

Roxanne ignored him. Daniel knelt beside her, and as she peered into his eyes she said urgently, "I was foolish, Daniel. I can see that now. It's only right that we be married. There's . . . there's no way of knowing what the future will bring, and it's not fair to our child that I put Bramwell's wishes above what's best. The little one deserves to have both mother and father when he comes into the world."

Quincy was not sure what was going on or what Roxanne was talking about, but he saw the look of relief and love that appeared on his brother's face.

Daniel tightened his grip on Roxanne's hand and said quietly, "Thank you. I promise I'll be a good husband to you and a good father to the child."

"No need to promise that," Roxanne told him, leaning her head over to rest it against his. "I know you will."

Geoffrey Reed stepped up, a frown on his face. "Excuse me for interrupting, but am I to understand that a wedding is about to take place?"

"Is there a parson here?" Daniel asked, looking deep into his father's eyes.

Quincy glanced around and spotted a face in the curious crowd. "Parson Timmons!" he called. "We need you here, sir."

The balding, lanky clergyman strode across the room and asked the elder Reed, "What is going on here, Geoffrey?"

There was a bemused smile on Geoffrey's face as he answered, "It seems that we need someone to perform a wedding, Parson. My son Daniel, who has appeared by some miracle of fate, and Mrs. Stoddard would like to get married. And since it will be a few minutes before Alonzo gets back with Granny Strickland, if we hurry, perhaps we'll have time for the ceremony."

Timmons's eyebrows lifted as he looked at Roxanne, seated on the sofa. There was no mistaking her condition, and Timmons said dubiously, "I don't know about this. The church can't condone—"

"Surely the church would have no objection to a man marrying a respectable widow," Daniel said sharply. "Mrs. Stoddard's husband passed away several weeks ago."

"That's not very long," Timmons protested.

Quincy moved up on one side of the minister, and Murdoch stepped up on the other.

"They dinna have much time, Rev'rend," Murdoch said ominously, "and since Roxanne be me cousin, I'd be careful about casting doubts on her character."

"I didn't mean anything by it," Timmons said quickly. He hefted the black book he always held in his hands. "I have my Bible right here. I'd be glad to perform the ceremony."

"Thank you, Parson," Geoffrey said. "I thought you'd see things our way." Geoffrey still looked a bit confused by this sudden, unexpected turn of events, but he was handling it well, as was Pamela, who sat down beside Roxanne and took her hand.

Quickly, everyone was moved out of the way, and Parson Timmons took his place in front of the young couple. Dr. Fletcher was still frowning in disapproval at this delay, but Murdoch gently steered him to one side.

Quincy put a hand on Daniel's shoulder and squeezed hard in encouragement, remembering his own wedding.

Roxanne sat up as straight as she could on the sofa, biting her lip for a moment against the pain, then turned a smiling face to Daniel as Parson Timmons began, "Dearly beloved, we are gathered here on this, ah, unforeseen but happy occasion—"

"Stick t' the Good Book, Parson," Murdoch growled.

Quincy, who was holding Mariel's hand, lowered his head so that his grin wouldn't be too obvious. Wasting no more time, Parson Timmons plunged ahead with the ceremony. In a matter of moments he was pronouncing Daniel and Roxanne husband and wife, and Daniel leaned over to brush his lips against Roxanne's. Cheers and applause erupted from the party guests. Quincy smiled at Mariel and kissed her softly.

Then Dr. Fletcher stepped in again. "Now that that's over," he said, "I really must insist that we get the young lady upstairs—"

Roxanne let out a low cry, and Daniel bent over her anxiously. "What is it?"

"I . . . I think the doctor's right, Daniel," she replied weakly.

Pamela and Mariel moved in again, taking charge. Pamela spoke crisply to the maids who had been waiting, then gently and carefully helped Roxanne to her feet and led her toward the stairs. Daniel watched them go, a helpless expression on his face.

Geoffrey looked worried, too, but he turned to the gathering and held up his hands for attention. "No need to stop the party," he said in a loud voice. "We just have more reason for celebrating now, with the marriage of my son Daniel and the lovely Roxanne!"

He motioned to the musicians to begin playing

again, and soon the guests were dancing, talking, drinking, and circulating once more, many of them discussing the evening's unexpected excitement. Meanwhile, Geoffrey took Daniel's arm and drew him aside. Quincy and Murdoch joined them near the foot of the stairs.

Geoffrey embraced his older son and slapped him on the back. "Lord, I never expected to see you tonight, Daniel, let alone to witness your wedding!" he exclaimed. "I'm delighted you're here, though. Welcome home!"

Quincy hugged Daniel as well, and Murdoch pounded him on the back, staggering him a little.

"Where have ye been all these months?" Murdoch asked.

"I was in Boston for a while," Daniel replied. His features grew solemn. "Roxanne was captured by the British and held prisoner there, but before I could find her, they shipped her to England."

"England!" Quincy echoed in amazement. "How did she get back here?"

Daniel smiled wearily again. "I went over there and found her."

"You've been to England?" Geoffrey sounded flabbergasted, and Quincy and Murdoch mirrored his surprise.

"That's right," Daniel said. "And to France, as well. In fact, it was a French ship that brought us here. We were bound for Norfolk originally, with medical supplies for the patriots donated by the French government, but when we found that the redcoats had burned the city, we sailed on to Portsmouth and barely slipped ashore ahead of them. Then we rented a wagon and came here, as we had planned all along."

"What's this business about Roxanne being married to someone else?" Quincy wanted to know.

"She was," Daniel replied, his face even more serious now. "While she was in England, she thought I was dead, and she married a man named Bramwell Stoddard. He owned the estate where she was being held."

"He was her captor?"

"Not really," Daniel said with a shake of his head. "It's a complicated story, Quincy. For the time being, let's just say that Stoddard helped both of us escape from the British. He died helping us, in fact."

"This is an incredible story, son," Geoffrey said. "I'm sure you have much more to tell us, but right now you look exhausted. How about something to eat and drink, and then you can get some rest."

"That sounds fine to me," Daniel agreed. "But I don't know if I can sleep. I don't *want* to sleep." He lifted his eyes toward the second floor. "With Roxanne up there about to give birth, I need to stay awake. I've been worried for days that we wouldn't get here before she went into labor. We almost didn't make it."

Geoffrey hesitated, then said, "This may be a rather indelicate question, Daniel, but about this child . . . You said Roxanne was married to that man Stoddard in England, but—"

"The child is mine," Daniel said quietly.

"I won't give you any lectures about morality," Geoffrey said with a frown. "At any rate, it appears to be much too late for that." He shrugged, and his frown was replaced by a faint smile. "Besides, I rather like the idea of another grandchild. I must say, though, I would have sooner expected something like this from Quincy than from you, Daniel."

"Thank you, Father," Quincy said dryly.

Geoffrey waved a hand. "I meant nothing by the comment, lad. It's just that both my sons have surprised me recently. Your lives have taken turns I never would have expected."

"War plays tricks with fate," Daniel said.

Quincy was about to agree when there was another stir among the guests. The Reeds and Murdoch turned to see Alonzo escorting an elderly woman through the foyer and up the stairs to the second floor. Granny Strickland, the midwife, had arrived. Her cabin was less than a mile from the Reed plantation, and Alonzo had gotten there and back quickly with the carriage.

Turning to Daniel again, Quincy said, "You didn't get a chance to meet my wife before she went upstairs, Daniel. Her name is Mariel."

"And she's about t' have a wee bairn, too," Murdoch added, causing Quincy to flush.

"It seems the past months have been eventful for everyone," Daniel said, smiling at his brother. "I thought you and Murdoch were going out to the frontier with Cordelia and her father after we left Saratoga."

"We did."

Quincy explained how Mariel and her brother, Dietrich, had joined their small group of pilgrims and that Cordelia Faulkner and her father had remained behind in the settlement on the Ohio River after Cordelia's wedding to the blacksmith Ulysses Gilworth.

"Mariel wanted to come back to a more civilized area," Quincy concluded, "so we headed here, thinking it might be safe from the war."

"The war is going to spread everywhere before it's over," Daniel said grimly. "The British won't give up easily, and they won't be forced into a settlement. I'm convinced of that now. Public sentiment in England is evenly divided on the subject of the war, but the king doesn't seem to care about that. His ministers don't, either. There's going to be plenty of blood spilled—"

Before Daniel could continue his bleak prophecy, he was interrupted by a voice calling from the top of the stairs. Dr. Fletcher stood there, and as the musicians fell silent and the crowd in the ballroom turned expectant eyes toward him, the old physician pulled a handkerchief from his pocket and mopped his sweating face.

"We have a . . . complication of sorts," he said.

Quincy saw the fear strike Daniel's eyes, fear for both Roxanne and the child. Quincy recognized it because he had experienced the same feeling.

Daniel bolted up the stairs. "Is something wrong with Roxanne, Doctor?"

"It's not Mrs. Stoddard," Fletcher said. "I'm afraid it's Mrs. Reed."

"Pamela!" Geoffrey exclaimed. "My God, what's wrong?"

The doctor shook his head. "The youngest Mrs. Reed, I should have said." He looked straight at Quincy. "Young man, *your* wife has gone into labor, too."

Quincy's eyes widened as he tried to comprehend what Fletcher had just said. "I . . . I don't understand! It's not Mariel's time, not for another month—"

"Babies sometimes pay no attention to the calendar." Fletcher looked at the four men clustered at the bottom of the stairs and went on, "Geoffrey, perhaps you should send everyone home. It looks as if we're in for a long night."

"You're right. I'll see to it immediately."

Quincy heard his father's voice trail off, but he could not tell if Geoffrey had actually stopped speaking or if his brain simply no longer understood the words. His mind echoed with what Dr. Fletcher had just told him.

Mariel was about to have their baby, whether they were ready or not. . . .

Chapter Six

Murdoch Buchanan prowled up and down the long hallway, his hands clasped behind his back. He had shed the coat and cravat he was wearing earlier in the evening, unbuttoned the top two buttons of the white shirt, and rolled up its sleeves. He was a bit more comfortable, but he missed his buckskins.

Daniel, Quincy, and Geoffrey were sitting in armchairs in a small alcove at the end of the hall. Close at hand were the doors of the adjacent bedrooms in which Roxanne and Mariel were ensconsed. Dr. Fletcher and Granny Strickland had been hurrying from room to room for over an hour, and so far neither of the young women had delivered.

Murdoch had been sitting with his friends, but the atmosphere in the alcove had become so strained and gloomy that he had been forced to get up and stretch his legs for a bit, and that moment had turned into a lengthy bout of pacing. He wondered if he was annoying the others, but they seemed to be paying little or no attention to him.

For much of his life, ever since leaving Scotland in particular, Murdoch Buchanan had been a loner. He had had friends and comrades during his long hunts on the frontier, and he had relatives in Boston whom he had visited from time to time—Roxanne's family—but no one in years had become as close to him as Daniel and Quincy. A love of adventure and a thirst for freedom had led Murdoch to cast his lot with them and the other patriots, but his relationship with the young men had grown into something more. They were as brothers to him, and now Murdoch knew how it felt to wait for the birth of a niece or a nephew, for that was what Daniel's and Quincy's children seemed like to him.

There was a staircase at the far end of the corridor, and as Murdoch approached it, a man and a woman appeared there. The woman had red hair a shade lighter than Roxanne's, and the man's curly hair was a reddish brown. He was solidly built and dressed in a brown suit and black tricorn, while the woman wore a plain gray dress and a bonnet. Both appeared to be in their twenties.

"Excuse me, sir," the man said to Murdoch, a familiar Scottish burr in his voice. "We're lookin' for Daniel Reed."

"Down at the other end o' th' hall," Murdoch told

him. "But I dinna think he wants t' be bothered right now. What do ye want, if ye dinna mind me asking?"

"I'm Hamish MacQuarrie," the man replied, "and this is my wife, Moira. We've been travelin' with Daniel and Roxanne. We tended t' th' wagon and th' team when we got here, and by th' time we got inside, everyone had left. We've been waitin' downstairs, but there's no one about. What's goin' on here?"

Murdoch stared at the man for a few seconds, then growled, "MacQuarrie, did ye say?"

"That's right. And who might ye be?"

"Me name is Murdoch Buchanan."

Hamish MacQuarrie's eyes narrowed. "Buchanan!" he repeated. "Of the Clan Buchanan?"

"None other."

Moira caught her husband's arm. "Dinna be doin' anything foolish now, Hamish," she cautioned.

"I'm just surprised to find the likes of a back-stabbin' Buchanan all the way over here in America!"

Murdoch clenched his fists, and the muscles in his brawny shoulders corded as he struggled to hold his instincts in check.

"And 'tis surprised I am that a cowardly MacQuarrie would dare t' show his face under the same roof as a Buchanan. I thought we'd run all o' ye back into yer holes."

"What's going on here?" Daniel called out, aware that the air was brittle with impending violence. He came toward them. "Oh, Lord, I'm sorry! With everything that was going on, I forgot about you and Moira, Hamish. Roxanne is about to give birth."

"She's in labor?" Moira asked. "I'm not surprised, the way she looked on the way here. Can I do aught to help?"

"Her room is right there," Daniel said, pointing.

"I'm sure the doctor and the midwife and my mother would be glad for a helping hand. You see, my brother's wife is about to have a baby, too."

Moira gave him a startled look, then hurried past the still-bristling Murdoch and vanished into the room where Dr. Fletcher and Granny Strickland were tending to Roxanne.

Daniel looked from Murdoch to Hamish and back again, then said, "Murdoch, Hamish and Moira have been good friends to Roxanne and me."

"Well, I'll take that into account, Dan'l, and I'll not kill this skalleyhootin' MacQuarrie under your father's roof," Murdoch grated.

"And since ye know this oaf of a Buchanan, I'll not take a pistol to him," Hamish responded. "But only as a favor to ye."

Daniel held up both hands as Geoffrey and Quincy, their attention drawn by the confrontation, walked down the hall to join them.

"Wait a minute, both of you," Daniel said to the Scotsmen. "Why are you at each other's throats?"

"There's bad blood between Clan Buchanan an' Clan MacQuarrie," Murdoch explained without taking his eyes off Hamish. "Always has been and always will be."

"Aye," agreed Hamish fervently. "Th' clans may have been dissolved, but nothin' will end the feud between the MacQuarries and the Buchanans until the last o' the Buchanans lies in his grave."

"It will no' be th' Buchanans who die out, laddie. I can promise ye that."

Murdoch and Hamish leaned a little closer together, and Daniel quickly slid between them. "Hold on," he said. "Quincy, give me a hand here. Take Murdoch down to the other end of the hall."

"Come on, Murdoch," Quincy urged, putting a light hand on the big man's arm. "Let's go sit down. With everything else that's going on, we don't need you and this fellow fighting."

Murdoch knew Quincy was right; the Reeds already had their hands full. Grudgingly he allowed Quincy to turn him around and lead him away to the alcove at the far end of the hallway.

Meanwhile, Daniel introduced Hamish to his father and explained how the young Scottish couple had worked for Bramwell Stoddard at Ilford Grange, Lord Oakley's ancestral estate.

"They befriended Roxanne," Daniel said to Geoffrey, "and they helped me as well. I told them that you might be able to help them get settled here, Father."

"I certainly can," Geoffrey said. He shook Hamish's hand warmly and went on, "I'm pleased to meet you, Mr. MacQuarrie. Looking for employment, are you?"

"Well, for the time being," Hamish replied. "Moira and I have given some thought t' havin' a place of our own."

"That's a worthwhile ambition," Geoffrey agreed. "In the meantime, how would the two of you like to work here? My wife has been saying that we need someone to take charge of the household, and once these babies are born, that'll be truer than ever. What about it? That wife of yours sounds like she'd fit the bill just perfectly."

"Ye'd have to ask Moira, but it sounds like a fine idea t' me," Hamish said. "We'll not take charity, though. We'll earn our keep, Mr. Reed."

Geoffrey chuckled. "I'm sure you will. You're going to be one of my overseers, Mr. MacQuarrie. There's quite a bit of responsibility involved, but I'm sure you can handle it."

"Aye, I'll do my best," Hamish promised.

"There's just one thing," Geoffrey continued. "If you stay here, can you get along with Murdoch?"

Hamish looked down the hall, his face taut. Forcing himself to relax a bit, he said, "If it means makin' a new start in America, I can. Yes, I can even put up with a Buchanan for that."

Geoffrey turned and motioned for Quincy and Murdoch to rejoin them, and as the big frontiersman strode up, Geoffrey said, "Mr. and Mrs. MacQuarrie are going to be working here on the plantation, Murdoch. I hope that's not going to be a problem."

Murdoch shook his head. "Yer boy has been talking t' me, Mr. Reed, and I suppose he's made me see we got t' put the old hates behind us. MacQuarrie and me, we got a common enemy now in th' redcoats, and we both want t' be free men in a free country."

"Aye," Hamish said. "Ye speak the truth, Buchanan."

"And what else did ye expect?" Murdoch asked with a snort.

"Don't start arguing again," Daniel said before Hamish could respond. "We've all got other things to worry about, so why don't the two of you shake hands?"

Both Murdoch and Hamish hesitated for a long moment, then Murdoch stuck out a big paw. Hamish took it immediately, and if the grips were a little firmer than usual—bone crushing, perhaps—neither man showed sign of it.

"That's fine," Geoffrey said.

He turned slightly and looked at the closed doorways of the bedrooms. The others followed his lead and were aware that the momentary crisis was over, settled in the face of the ongoing and more important one.

But unknown to each other, Daniel and Quincy

were asking themselves the same question as they thought about their wives: *How much longer can this go on?*

Sometime in the seemingly endless hours after midnight, Murdoch went to his room and came back with an earthenware jug of whiskey. He passed it around, and each of the men took a healthy swig of the fiery liquor. It helped to lessen the tension a little, but the atmosphere was still full of worry.

"Tell us about th' trip t' England ye made," Murdoch said as he urged Daniel to pass the jug along. "Tell us about th' other things ye've been doing since Quincy and me last seen ye."

To take some of the strain off the moment, Daniel launched into an account of his activities since parting from Murdoch and Quincy in New York. He told them about helping Elliot Markham break up the gang of criminals called the Liberty Legion in Boston; about the hazardous, midwinter trek across the Berkshire Mountains with Henry Knox to bring Ticonderoga's cannon back to George Washington; about the capture of the turncoat Dr. Benjamin Church, who had used his position as a patriot leader to spy for the British; and about the daring voyage to England to rescue Roxanne from Cyril Eldridge, the British spymaster.

When he was done, Quincy had a tale of his own to recount. He told of finding Mariel and gradually falling in love with her as the travelers overcame the traps laid for them by the Reverend Jason Sabbath, a crazed preacher who had stirred up the Mohawk Indians against the white settlers in western New York. With growing relish, he explained how Murdoch had defeated Sagodanega, the brutal Mohawk war chief, in hand-to-hand battle, winning the respect of Joseph Brant, the English-educated leader of all the Mohawks.

During the storytelling, the jug continued its rounds, and soon the men were laughing in spite of themselves as the potent liquor took effect. It was exactly what Murdoch had hoped would happen. It had been too long, he thought, since the doctor and the midwife, along with Pamela Reed and the MacQuarrie woman, had closeted themselves in the bedrooms. Something was wrong. Murdoch was sure of it, even though he tried not to dwell on that possibility.

Sometime before dawn Fletcher hurried from Roxanne's room into Mariel's, and a few moments later all the men in the hall heard the screams. Quincy bolted from his chair and might have run into the room if Geoffrey hadn't grabbed his arm.

"Let me go!" Quincy cried. "That's Mariel!"

"There's nothing you can do for her in there, son," Geoffrey pleaded. "Give me a hand with him, Murdoch!"

Murdoch's hand closed on Quincy's arm. "Steady, lad," he advised. "If ye want t' do something, say a prayer."

Quincy stood very still, his face contorted in a worried grimace. Gradually the screams from inside the bedroom died away, but no one could have said if that was a good sign.

A moment later the door to the other bedroom opened and Pamela emerged. She looked exhausted, her hair bedraggled and her party finery stained and rumpled. But there was a broad smile on her face as she approached Daniel and took his hands in hers.

"Roxanne . . . ?" Daniel whispered, his half-drunken state of a few minutes earlier completely vanished now.

"She's fine," Pamela told him. "And so is your son."

"My . . . my son?" Daniel echoed.

"You have a beautiful baby boy."

Daniel let out a whoop of joy as Quincy, Geoffrey, and Murdoch pounded him on the back. Quincy's fear for Mariel was quelled slightly by his happiness at the birth of his brother's child.

"Can I see them?" Daniel asked, still hugging his mother tightly.

"If you'll be very quiet. They're both asleep. It wasn't a particularly difficult birth, just long and tiring."

She escorted Daniel into the bedroom, motioning for the other men to stay out for the time being. Silently Daniel walked to the side of the bed and peered down at the woman he loved and the child they had brought into the world. Roxanne was pale, the scattering of freckles on her face more visible against her pallor. Her hair was matted with sweat. Their baby, wrapped in a blanket and cuddled on the bed beside his mother, was red and wrinkled, with a tuft of dark brown hair on top of his head.

Daniel thought they were more beautiful than he ever could have dreamed.

He watched them sleeping for several minutes, then, at his mother's light touch on his arm, turned and slipped out of the room with her. Quincy, Geoffrey, and Murdoch were waiting in the hall for another round of congratulations, but before they could begin, Dr. Fletcher appeared in the doorway of Mariel's room. The man's jowly face was grim.

"Better prepare yourself, lad," he said to Quincy. "I've got bad news."

"Mariel!" Quincy cried and started forward. "Oh, God, she can't be dead!"

"She's alive," Dr. Fletcher said, hurriedly moving to block Quincy from the door. "She's had a hard time of it, though. She wasn't ready for what she had to go through, and she's lost a great deal of blood. I'm sorry, Quincy, but she may not survive."

Daniel clasped an arm tightly around his brother's quaking shoulders, his own joy temporarily pushed aside.

With a sigh, the doctor went on, "The good news is that the babies are doing fine, just fine. I expect them to be all right."

Quincy blinked eyes that were damp with tears and swallowed hard. "B-babies?" he said as the doctor's words penetrated his stunned brain.

"That's right, my boy. Twins. A boy and a girl. Granny Strickland is tending to them, and I think you can see the babies in a few minutes. For now, though, you'll have to stay out and let your wife rest. The next twenty-four hours will tell the story on her."

"But I have to see her!" Quincy said wretchedly.

Fletcher was shaking his head when the door opened behind him and the old midwife said, "She's askin' to see her husband, Doctor. I think you should let him in."

For a second Fletcher looked irritated at having his judgment questioned; then he relented. "All right, but only for a moment."

Behind Quincy's back, Daniel, Murdoch, and Geoffrey exchanged a glance. They all had the same thought: The doctor might be allowing Quincy into the room because it could be his last chance to see Mariel alive.

With Fletcher and the midwife trailing him, Quincy quietly entered the bedroom. With a spryness that belied her age, Granny Strickland picked up two blanket-swaddled bundles from the bed and displayed them to Quincy. Both babies, wrinkled and fretting, had healthy tufts of dark hair on their heads.

Quincy blinked rapidly, overcome by worry and fear for his wife, happiness over seeing his children for the first time, and a horrible uncertainty about what the future might bring.

"Here's your son and your daughter, Master Quincy," the old woman said quietly.

"May . . . may I hold them?"

"Careful now." Gingerly Granny Strickland handed over the babies, making sure that Quincy had a firm grip on one before giving him the other.

Unable to distinguish between them, he stared hard first at one, then the other. He had heard that all newborn babies looked alike, but this was ridiculous. Slowly he became aware that there was a broad smile on his face.

"Quincy?" The voice was barely a whisper from the bed. "Are you there, Quincy?"

"I'm here, Mariel," he said, kneeling beside her. "And just look who I have with me."

She was pale, washed out, and her long blond hair was in disarray on the pillow. Her eyes were dull, and Quincy suspected that the doctor had given her some sort of nostrum for the pain. But her gaze focused on the infants in Quincy's arms, and a beatific smile spread slowly across her face.

"Our babies," she breathed.

Her eyes slid shut.

Quincy was terrified by the sight. He had lost her. At the moment that should have been the most wonderful of their entire lives, she was gone. . . .

Fletcher's hand squeezed his shoulder. "She's asleep, lad," he said. "She's just asleep."

Quincy forced his eyes away from Mariel's pallid face and saw the slow rise and fall of the sheet over her bosom. Her breathing was irregular, but it was *there,* and that was all that mattered. Mariel was still alive.

Quincy began to sob, barely aware that his mother was in the room, and she and Granny Strickland took the twins from him. Strong hands lifted him to his feet, and Daniel and Murdoch led him out of the room.

"She's going to be all right," Daniel murmured beside him. "You'll see."

"A pair o' wee ones," Murdoch said. "Ye be a lucky man, Quincy Reed."

"Yes," Quincy said, his own voice seeming to come from a thousand miles away. "A lucky man."

Chapter Seven

Elliot leaned on the aft railing of the Markham & Cummings ship and watched the Canadian port city of Halifax, Nova Scotia, recede into the distance. He felt a deep sense of satisfaction. So far, the journey had gone quite smoothly, and that was an accomplishment with Avery Wallingford along.

The ship had left New York a week earlier. Gathering a crew was the biggest obstacle Elliot had faced in his preparations. There were plenty of sailors in New York with nothing to do, but most of them wanted to be paid, and this was strictly a volunteer mission. Finally he had hit on the idea of promising the crew members an extra share of the provisions they would bring back, and in a few days he had managed to recruit enough men to sail the ship to Canada and back.

The captain, an old salt named Beaumont, had

turned down his extra share as a gesture of goodwill.
Elliot and Avery, of course, were not taking any extra
either, although Avery started to say something about
that very thing in one of their meetings before Elliot
fixed him with a stony stare, and he subsided into silence.

The voyage up the coastline and around the bulge
of Nova Scotia to Halifax had taken only a few days. The
weather was clear, the wind brisk, and they had not
sighted a single ship during that time. So far, Avery's
fears of American privateers had proved groundless.

Now the hold of the ship was loaded to the very top
with supplies and foodstuffs: sacks of flour, grain, sugar,
and salt; crates of salted meat; blankets; medical supplies; a few fruits and vegetables, although it was too
early in the season for most of them; tins of salted fish
from a Halifax cannery; and even some small toys for
Tory children and bolts of bright, colorful cloth for their
mothers.

The cargo Elliot and Avery were taking to New
York would help the loyalists through some of the bad
times to come. The depressing thing was knowing just
how quickly these supplies would run out. But doing
something was better than doing nothing, Elliot supposed. Maybe a regular supply route could be estab-
lished between New York and Halifax. The patriots
might not interfere with it if they knew the ships' cargoes
were meant for strictly humanitarian rather than military purposes. With his contacts in the American espionage network, Elliot was in a good position to pass that
word.

A footstep behind him made him look around.
Avery stood there, a wistful look on his face as he stared
toward the buildings of Halifax, which were rapidly

shrinking in the distance as the ship caught the wind and moved out smartly.

"It was good to be back in civilization again," Avery said with a sigh, "even if it was only for a short time."

"I'd hardly say that New York is uncivilized," Elliot replied.

Avery snorted in disgust. "No place that's full of traitors and rebels can be considered civilized. There are no scum like that in Canada. At least these people are still loyal to the king."

It was true that the Canadians had been very helpful. With the money Elliot had scraped together from the Tories in New York, he had been able to purchase more supplies than he had expected, and he was sure the Canadian merchants in Halifax had given him a good deal. Some of the provisions had even been donated free of charge, as a gesture of support for fellow subjects of the Crown.

They would have been shocked and horrified, not to mention confused, if they had known that Elliot was a patriot secret agent, dedicated to the overthrow of the king's rule in the colonies. As a matter of fact, Elliot thought, he was rather confused himself at the moment. The colonies and the mother country were at war, and he was trying to help both sides. But at what cost? he wondered. How high was the price to be paid in human suffering?

He shook his head. There was no point in pondering such questions. He could sort out his philosophy after the war was over . . . if he survived.

The return trip to New York would take several days, and Elliot hoped this leg of the voyage would be as easy as the first part. At midmorning of the second day at sea, however, a sharp cry rang from the lookout high

in the sails. Elliot was on deck at the time and looked up
to see the sailor pointing to the southeast.

Elliot hurried to the railing along with several members of the crew. His eyes scanned the horizon, but he
saw nothing but the ceaseless waves below a deep blue
sky dotted with white clouds.

"What is it?" he anxiously asked the seaman beside
him. "I don't see anything."

"Keep watchin', mate," the man replied. "Tom can
see farther from that crow's nest than we can down here,
but I reckon whatever he spotted'll be comin' in sight
soon."

From the bridge nearby, Captain Beaumont called,
"Come up here, Mr. Markham. You can use my spyglass."

Elliot turned away from the railing and walked to
the ladder leading up to the bridge. He took the steps
quickly and joined Beaumont near the wheel, the spokes
of which were gripped firmly by the helmsman. Beaumont extended his glass to Elliot, who trained it on the
sea to the southeast.

Sure enough, in a moment he spotted a small blotch
of white on the horizon that quickly resolved itself into a
sail. Soon he could see the vessel beneath that sail.

"Is she flying a flag?" asked Beaumont.

Elliot studied the ship intently for a moment, then
shook his head. "Not that I can see," he answered.

"Then she's not a British ship, else the Union Jack
would be flying." Just as it fluttered in the breeze high
above the deck of the Markham & Cummings vessel.

Elliot lowered the spyglass and looked at Beaumont. "American?"

"Mayhap," the captain said, shrugging his bony
shoulders. "I reckon we'll know if she fires on us. She's
certainly moving as if she intends to cut us off."

With a grimace Elliot returned the spyglass to Beaumont. Better for the captain to have a good view of the other ship, he thought. If there was trouble, Beaumont was going to have to be the one to get them out of it. Elliot was no sailor, and command was the last thing he wanted right now.

"Do what you have to do, Captain," he said grimly.

"Aye." He turned and bellowed to his crew to man the guns.

But the guns were few—a couple of four-pounders at the bow, a pair of eight-pounders amidships, and two more four-pounders near the stern. It would be hard to fight off an attack with only three cannon on each side. This ship had been built as a cargo vessel, not a warship.

Elliot returned to the forward port railing. He could see the other ship with his naked eye now, and luckily it didn't seem to be a warship either. While it was not lumbering through the waves as slowly as the Markham & Cummings vessel, it seemed only slightly faster.

That small edge in speed was probably going to be enough to allow the other ship to intercept them, however, Elliot judged. The distance between the ships was lessening with each passing minute as the other vessel angled toward them.

Elliot turned and looked around the deck, searching for Avery. As the representative of Theophilus Cummings, Avery had a right to know what was going on. He was nowhere to be seen, though, and Elliot started toward the forward companionway. Avery was most likely in his cabin, and that was where Elliot would look first.

A sharp rap on the cabin door brought an irritated "What is it?" from Avery.

Elliot leaned close to the panel and said, "It's me, Avery. You'd better come up on deck."

A second later, the door was jerked open violently. Avery stared wide-eyed at Elliot and demanded, "What is it? A storm? A rebel ship? Oh, God, I knew coming on this trip was a mistake!"

"There could be a patriot ship closing in on us," Elliot told his distraught companion. "We don't know if there's going to be a battle, though. They might just take a look at us and move on."

"I don't believe that for a second, and neither do you. They're going to sink us, I just know it!"

"We won't go down without a fight." Elliot's voice was firm and more courageous than he actually felt. In truth, the prospect of exchanging cannon fire with the mysterious ship made him rather queasy.

"I'm staying here," Avery said without hesitation. "I'm not going to go up there and be blown apart by a cannonball."

"I've made it clear to Captain Beaumont that he's in complete command of the ship. Is that all right with you?"

"Of course. Why are you even asking me such a stupid question?" Avery's voice shook, and he was paler than usual.

Elliot smiled faintly. "You came along as your father-in-law's representative. You have to look after his interests, remember?"

"The old man's interests can go to blazes! I just want to get back to New York alive." Suddenly Avery reached out and tightly grasped Elliot's arm. "Do you think we should just surrender to this other ship and have done with it?"

The same thought had crossed Elliot's mind, but only for an instant. If the vessel was an American ship, its crew would no doubt steal the cargo and either keep the Markham & Cummings ship for themselves or sink it. Either way, they would all become prisoners. But when Elliot thought about the desperate situation of the people they had left behind in New York, he knew there was no way in the world he was going to give up the supplies without a fight.

"We're not going to surrender," he said flatly. "If you brought along a pistol, I'd advise you to load it."

With that, he turned on his heel and left Avery, frightened and quaking, in the doorway. Elliot felt contempt for his former friend, but he also felt a surprising surge of sympathy. It was true that Avery had not wanted to come on the voyage; he had been forced into this situation, and now he would have to live or die with the rest of them.

When Elliot reached the deck, he was shocked at how much closer the ship had come during the short time he had been below. He could see it plainly with the naked eye, and what he had suspected before was now confirmed: There was no flag flying above the other ship. They were pirates; he was sure of it.

At that moment flame blossomed from a gun emplacement on the other vessel. Elliot heard the distant boom of the cannon and at the same instant heard the rushing sound of the ball passing over the bow of his ship. Water spurted high above the surface to starboard where the cannonball fell.

Elliot looked up at Captain Beaumont, who waved a hand casually.

"A warning shot," the captain called. "Nothing more. And we're going to reply in kind!"

The old sailor shouted an order, and the eight-pounder on the port side thundered as the gunner touched off its powder charge. The weapon's maneuverability was limited, but the crew members assigned to the cannon had managed to angle its barrel enough so that the shot came close to the attacking vessel. The sailors let out a triumphant whoop as the cannonball splashed into the water only yards from the enemy.

"That'll show the bastards we mean business," Beaumont said savagely. "Reload!"

Elliot tried to count the cannon emplacements on the other ship but gave up after reaching eight. Clearly, he and his companions were outgunned. The other ship was faster, too. Elliot felt his heart sink in his chest as he realized that the odds of getting out of this predicament were very slim indeed.

Going to Canada for supplies had been a good idea, he told himself. But he had needed luck on his side, and evidently the lady had decided to be fickle.

A volley of cannon fire from the other ship crashed through the bright, sunny day.

The engagement quickly took on the quality of a nightmare for Elliot. Beaumont's crew fought back gamely, loading and firing the cannon as quickly as they could manage. The noise was deafening, and a thick pall of gray smoke hung over the ship, stinging Elliot's eyes and making him cough violently. He could have gone below, but the knowledge that he had gotten these men into this mess kept him on deck.

The Markham & Cummings ship suffered two hits, but both were above the waterline. A few moments later, a cannonball caught one of the sailors scurrying along the deck and smashed into his body. Elliot saw the man die and felt a surge of sickness. He just made it to the railing before he heaved up his breakfast. Sorrow gripped him along with the retching pain; he felt as if the dead man's blood were on his hands.

But he would have the blood of even more innocents on his hands if he turned his back on the starving Tories in New York. Once the idea of going to

Canada had occurred to him, he knew he would have to follow through with it or be unable to live with himself.

Being a wastrel was certainly easier on the conscience, he thought with a grimly ironic smile as he straightened from the railing and wiped the back of his hand across his mouth. In the old days, he rarely gave a thought to whether someone else would live or die. Those days were gone, thank God, and had been for two years. Elliot slipped a pistol from inside his coat. He might die, but he would die a free man with a patriot's love of country, doing what he thought was best.

The two ships were closer together now, so close Elliot thought they might ram each other. Little damage had been done by the cannon fire, and he decided that the Americans must not be very good shots. Either that or they wanted the ship for themselves and were deliberately trying not to inflict enough damage to send it to the bottom of the sea. Either way, Elliot counted himself lucky that he was still alive. He lifted his pistol and sighted on one of the crewmen on the enemy ship.

A sudden jolt threw him off his feet before he could fire. As he scrambled up, he saw that the two vessels had indeed run together, and the rebels were leaping over the railing of their ship onto the deck of the other and fighting hand to hand.

He surged to his feet and fired the pistol at a saber-wielding privateer. The shot missed, but it drew the man's attention, and the length of cold steel slashed through the air toward Elliot's head.

A gun cracked, and the man holding the saber staggered backward, mortally wounded by the shot. Elliot snapped his head around and saw an ashen-faced Avery Wallingford standing at the top of the stairs that led to the forward companionway. He was holding a smoking pistol in his hand.

Elliot was astounded. In the past Avery had tried to have him killed, and now when he could have stood by and watched Elliot cut down by the enemy, he had joined the fight on Elliot's side.

The motive was unimportant. He threw Avery a nod of gratitude and reloaded his pistol. It wasn't easy, though, with the chaos around him on the deck.

Suddenly, the rebel boarders turned and ran, vaulted over the railing, and leapt aboard their ship. Those who didn't make it plummeted into the water between the vessels, but they quickly grabbed ropes dropped over the side by their comrades and scurried up like monkeys. The ships peeled apart; the privateer veered off to the northeast.

"They've given up the fight!" Beaumont shouted from the bridge.

Elliot grasped the railing to steady himself and shook his head in puzzlement. Why had the rebels abandoned their attack? As far as he could tell, they had been winning the battle handily. Another few minutes and the ship would have been theirs.

Then he looked at the sea to the south and saw three ships flying the Union Jack. British warships! They had approached unnoticed during the battle, and when the patriot commander had seen them, he must have ordered an immediate retreat.

Two of the British ships turned after the privateer and fell in behind it in pursuit. Before the day was over there would probably be another naval battle, but this time the American vessel would be the one outnumbered and outgunned. Elliot felt a twinge of regret. Now that the battle was over, his reason was returning, and he hated to think about the men on the privateer being killed or taken prisoner.

But those were the fortunes of war, and today fate

had smiled on Elliot after all. He looked up to see Captain Beaumont approaching.

"Lucky, we were," the captain said without preamble, echoing Elliot's thoughts. "Only three men killed, and the damage to the ship is minor."

Elliot wiped a hand across his face. Now that the battle was over, he was aware that he was sweating in the warm spring sunshine.

"I hope we don't run into any more of those privateers," he said.

"Aye, I share that sentiment, Mr. Markham. Still, we gave a pretty good account of ourselves for a crew not trained in the arts of war."

Elliot didn't try to fool himself. They had been only minutes away from utter disaster. There was no point in saying that to Beaumont, however, so he kept quiet as the captain pointed out a small boat being rowed over from the British warship.

A lieutenant in His Majesty's navy was in the small boat, along with two seamen, and when the young officer had come aboard, he extended his captain's compliments to Elliot and Beaumont and conveyed an offer of an escort down the coast. Beaumont accepted gladly.

"We won't be able to accompany you all the way to New York," the lieutenant said, "but we can stay with you far enough that I don't think you'll have to worry about any more of those rebel privateers."

"You've our sincere thanks, Lieutenant," Beaumont said. "Pass that along to your captain."

"I will, sir, you can rest assured."

When the lieutenant returned to his vessel, the crew of the Markham & Cummings ship set about repairing the damage incurred during the battle. It would have been easier to do the repairs if they could have put in to shore somewhere, but Elliot wanted to get back to New

York as soon as possible. The crew would just have to manage.

Elliot hadn't seen Avery since that moment during the fighting when Avery had shot down the saber-wielding assailant. He went belowdecks and knocked on the door of Avery's cabin. The sound of someone being violently ill told him that Avery was inside.

A few moments later, Avery appeared. He looked terrible, his face devoid of color and his features pulled into gaunt, haggard lines.

"What is it?" he demanded in a surly voice.

Elliot took a deep breath. "I just wanted to thank you for saving my life."

"You don't think *I* want the responsibility for this ship, do you?" Avery shook his head. "Don't thank me, Elliot. Just remember that you owe me a favor now, and one of these days I'll collect on it."

"Anytime," Elliot replied tightly. He didn't like the idea of being in Avery's debt, but he had to admit he liked the thought of being dead even less.

Avery shut the door. Elliot went to his cabin, telling himself that if the supplies in the hold kept one child in New York from starving, then the battle had been worth it.

The ship sailed into New York Harbor under an overcast sky and docked at a wharf along the southern tip of Manhattan Island, near the cluster of buildings that formed the main part of the city. Word of its return spread quickly among the Tory community, although the loyalists tried to be discreet. With the patriots in control of the city, it was possible that they would try to steal the cargo, so the loyalists decided not to unload the ship until nightfall.

Benjamin and Polly Markham, along with Theophilus Cummings and his daughter, Sarah, were waiting for Elliot and Avery when they reached the Markham house. Benjamin pumped Elliot's hand and slapped him on the back in a display of emotion that Elliot rarely saw these days.

"Welcome back!" Benjamin said enthusiastically.

"We heard there was trouble," Polly said quietly, hugging Elliot. "Are you all right?"

"We're fine," he replied, extending his answer to include Avery. "We had an encounter with a rebel privateer, but it was frightened off by some British warships that happened to be nearby. The whole thing didn't really amount to much."

Elliot exchanged a quick, meaningful glance with Avery. They had agreed to keep the details of the sea battle to themselves. It was Elliot's firm intention to make another trip to Canada later in the year to replenish their supplies, and if too much was made of the fight with the Americans, the others might force him to abandon the idea.

Sarah gave Avery a perfunctory hug and kiss, then turned to Elliot. "I thought about you every day," she said, "and I prayed for you every day, too. Both of you, of course," she hastily amended at the sight of Avery's frown.

"Thank you," Elliot said. He hoped Sarah wasn't getting any ideas about him again. She had tried to seduce him once since her marriage, an incident that had led to an abortive duel with Avery, even though Avery hadn't known exactly what had happened between his wife and Elliot. In the past Elliot's scruples had not stopped him from bedding an occasional married woman, but not *this* one.

Theophilus Cummings approached Elliot and

looked intently at him. "Was there much damage to the ship?"

"Her hull was holed in a couple of places above the waterline," Elliot replied. "Captain Beaumont had the crew repair the damage immediately, as best they could. They can finish the job now that the ship's back in port."

Cummings snorted. "You came close to losing the ship, isn't that true?"

"That question is open to interpretation," Elliot replied coolly. "What matters is that we made it back safely, and we brought enough supplies with us to last a while."

"I suppose you'll want to go to Canada again," Cummings said with a frown of disapproval.

Elliot replied honestly, "I've given it some thought."

Benjamin stepped in. "We'll talk about this later. Right now, I think we all need a drink. I managed to lay my hands on a bottle of fairly decent brandy just for this occasion."

Elliot was touched that his father had gone to so much trouble, not to mention puzzled as to where Benjamin had gotten a bottle of brandy. But he certainly wasn't averse to having a drink, now that the hazardous mission was over. Benjamin brought out the brandy and Polly fetched glasses for everyone.

When everyone had a full glass, Benjamin lifted his and said, "To my son Elliot . . . and to Avery Wallingford as well. We owe them a debt of gratitude."

"To Elliot," Sarah said. "And to Avery," she added as she lifted her glass. Her father grudgingly echoed her sentiments.

When they had drunk the toast, Polly said abruptly, "I almost forgot, dear. A man brought this for you several days ago." She reached into the pocket of her apron and brought out an envelope, which she handed to Elliot. He took it, his brow furrowed in puzzlement.

"Did you know the man?" he asked.

"I had never seen him before. He just asked if I would give that message to you, and I said I would, of course."

Elliot turned the envelope over. It was sealed, but the wax bore no identifying mark on it.

"Aren't you going to open it?" Sarah asked, clearly impatient to find out what was in the message.

"I suppose I should," Elliot replied slowly. He put his glass on the table, pulled the wax away from the envelope, and took out a folded piece of paper. It took only a glance to see what was written on it, and then he grimaced and shook his head as he crumpled the note and thrust it negligently into his pocket.

"It's nothing. Just a note from an acquaintance, tactfully asking if he can borrow some money. I'm afraid he's going to be disappointed."

"I should think so," Benjamin said. "We all need everything we can put our hands on these days. It's not like it was before the war, when we could afford to be generous."

Elliot murmured his agreement, and the talk moved on to other subjects, primarily the sea voyage to Canada and back. Behind his calm demeanor, Elliot's brain was a mass of confusion. The crumpled paper in his pocket was not a message from a friend wanting to borrow money; that had been a bald-faced lie.

The only writing on the paper had been a boldly inked numeral 5, the number by which Robert Townsend and Benjamin Tallmadge, organizers of the patriot espionage network, knew him. The message was from them, and it could mean only one thing.

The patriot spymasters had need of him once again.

Chapter Eight

Tramping through the thick woods near the Reed plantation, Daniel paused and leaned on the butt of his flintlock, resting a moment after the morning's hunting. The game bag that hung from a strap over his shoulder had a plump pheasant in it, the only thing he had shot so far. He wondered how Moira MacQuarrie, now assisting with household duties, would prepare the bird, and he was looking forward to finding out at dinner.

Near Daniel, Murdoch Buchanan had also come to a stop. The big frontiersman was in his buckskins once again, with his coonskin cap perched on his rumpled thatch of red hair. As he stood there, long-barreled flintlock rifle cradled easily in the crook of his left arm, eyes scanning the thick, bushy foliage around them, Daniel thought Murdoch was everything a woodsman was supposed to be. With him along, Daniel would have been willing to go anywhere in the wilderness with the knowledge that they stood an excellent chance of returning alive.

Several yards behind them, Quincy stood with his back against the trunk of an elm tree. His eyes were dull and his expression melancholy. Clearly this hunting trip had not fulfilled its real purpose, which was to get Quincy's mind off the struggle for life Mariel was waging in her room at the plantation house.

It was the day after the birth of Geoffrey and Pamela Reed's three grandchildren, and all three infants were doing very well. Granny Strickland had spent the night at the house to help care for the babies, and Dr. Fletcher had come by early that morning in his carriage to check on them. He had pronounced them all in good health. Roxanne was also feeling well; she was still weak but was regaining her strength with each passing moment, and Daniel had spent a wondrous hour that morning with her and the baby, whom they had named Joseph Bramwell Stoddard Reed.

Unfortunately, Daniel's joy was mixed with sympathy and concern for his brother and his brother's wife. Their twins—Thomas and Elizabeth—were smaller and weaker than his strapping Joseph, but Dr. Fletcher was confident that the babies would be fine. A wet nurse had already been brought in, and from what Daniel had heard both Thomas and Elizabeth seemed to have healthy appetites. He, too, was sure that they would thrive.

Mariel's health was a different matter entirely.

Dr. Fletcher had left her room that morning shaking his head, a glum expression on his face.

"Your wife is still very weak," he had told Quincy. "All we can do is continue to wait."

"Wait," Quincy had echoed bitterly.

Daniel remembered all too well what it had felt like when he did not know if Roxanne was alive or dead. Quincy had to be feeling that horrible uncertainty that ate away at a person's soul. Daniel remembered how his mind had been taken off Roxanne's plight by his involvement with his cousin Elliot in the task of smashing the Liberty Legion. Looking back on it now, he was thankful he'd had something with which to occupy himself during that bleak time.

So he had suggested the hunting trip into the woods where Quincy and he had spent so much time when they were growing up. He hoped the outing would lift Quincy's spirits, and Murdoch had jumped at the chance to get into the forest again with a rifle under his arm. Together they had talked Quincy into coming along, though he hadn't wanted to leave the house while Mariel's life hung so precariously in the balance.

"Your mother is with her, son," Geoffrey had told him. "And I'll be right outside the door. If there's any change, I'll send one of the boys for you right away."

Quincy had finally acquiesced, and the three men set off, heading north from the house, across the fields, then into woods so thick that the sun was shielded and it seemed to be eternal twilight beneath the spreading branches.

Like Daniel, Murdoch had shot a pheasant, and he had also downed a couple of plump squirrels. Quincy had yet to fire his rifle. He had not said much since leaving the house, replying only in monosyllables whenever Daniel or Murdoch asked him a direct question.

It had been a while since they had fired a shot, and the woods were full of birdsong and the rustlings of small animals. Daniel was happy just standing there and listening to the sounds, sounds he had heard so often as a boy and a young man growing up in this area. After everything that had happened in the past few years, he appreciated this peaceful respite more than he would have thought possible. It was hard to contemplate returning to the war—even though he knew that soon he would have to leave to report to General Washington. After all, he *was* a member of the commanding general's staff.

"We'd better be starting back," Murdoch said, breaking the silence. "We've come a mite farther than we intended."

"You're right," Daniel said. "If I recall the landmarks correctly, we're not far from the river. Not only that, but Mr. Jefferson's estate is nearby."

"I've heard talk o' this Monticello. Supposed to be quite a house, it is."

"It should be," Daniel said. "He's been working on it for long enough. Would you like to take a look?"

"Aye, I would no' mind seeing th' place. 'Twould be something t' tell me friends back out on th' frontier, providing I ever get there again."

Daniel had no doubt of that. Circumstances might lead Murdoch to stay in the East for a time, but sooner or later the rugged Scotsman would always return to the frontier. It was in his blood.

"What about you, Quincy?" Daniel asked, turning to his brother. "What say we take a look at Monticello?"

Quincy shrugged. "I suppose it would be all right, but I don't much like going any farther away from the house."

"We'll take the road back," Daniel promised. "It's longer, but we can make better time that way. Mr. Jefferson might even lend us some horses."

"All right. If that's what you and Murdoch want to do, I'll go along."

There was a decided lack of enthusiasm in Quincy's voice, Daniel thought, but maybe a visit with Thomas Jefferson would perk him up. Jefferson was such a vital individual that he had that effect on people.

"I talked t' this fella Jefferson at th' party last night," Murdoch said as the three men resumed their trek through the woods. "He seems t' be a good man. Ye would no' know from talking t' him that he be such an important man."

"It's hard for me to think of him that way," Daniel said. "I've known him all my life, it seems like. To me, he's always been just a gentleman farmer who lived nearby. But I'll say this: The colonies are lucky to have such an intelligent man helping to guide their course."

Quincy contributed nothing to the discussion, and Daniel knew his brother's mind was back at the Reed plantation.

After a twenty-minute walk, Daniel spotted a flash of white through the trees and pointed.

"That's the dome over the second floor," he said. "It rises high enough to be seen for quite a distance around."

They pushed on, more of the massive redbrick structure becoming visible through the thinning foliage, when Murdoch suddenly held up a hand to stop them. Daniel and Quincy both stood stock-still and made no noise. They were accustomed to following Murdoch's orders when they were in the woods. After a moment Daniel heard the sounds that had alerted Murdoch to the fact that they were not alone in the forest.

Somewhere nearby, men were moving through the woods, making considerably more noise than Murdoch, Daniel, and Quincy. In addition, as the men drew nearer, Daniel could hear them talking in loud, coarse voices, although he could not make out the words. Judging from the sounds, the other group was passing about fifty yards to the right of the three men.

"Who might that be?" Murdoch asked in a whisper.

"I don't know," Daniel said. "But they don't sound like the kind of men you usually find out here."

Indeed, although it was all instinct on his part, Daniel felt uneasy about the other group, as if they were intruders in the woods.

Evidently Murdoch felt the same way, because there was a deep frown on his craggy face. "They dinna sound like woodsmen t' me," he said, still keeping his voice low enough so that it couldn't be heard more than a few feet away. "How about we take a look at 'em?"

Daniel nodded curtly. He had been thinking exactly the same thing.

Murdoch motioned them forward. Daniel glanced over at Quincy and saw a flicker of interest in his younger brother's eyes. Quincy's curiosity had been aroused by this development, and Daniel felt encouraged by that.

The three men glided through the woods almost soundlessly. If Murdoch had been alone, Daniel knew, the frontiersman would have moved as silently as a shadow, but the Reed brothers lacked his experience. They made a few small noises, but nothing that would alert the other men, who were still talking loudly.

Murdoch stopped again, crouched behind a bush, and motioned for Daniel and Quincy to get down as well. As they knelt, concealed by the brush, the men tramped past only a few yards away. Daniel expected them to go on, but a harsh voice suddenly growled, "That's far enough."

Breathing shallowly, Daniel, Quincy, and Murdoch waited.

"That's it," the same voice said. "Monticello. Damned ugly place, ain't it?"

"The gent must have a lot of money to throw up a castle like that," another man commented.

"More than that," the first voice replied. "Word is, he's been raisin' cash to take back to Philadelphia, to help Washington and the army fight those damned lobsterbacks. I reckon he's got a small fortune on hand."

"A fortune we'll relieve 'im of, eh, Jethro?" asked a third voice with a chuckle.

"Aye," declared the first man, the one called Jethro. "We can put that money to better use than old Washington."

Daniel and Murdoch exchanged glances. They knew that Thomas Jefferson had been raising funds for the war effort, and obviously word of his activities had reached this group of scoundrels. Daniel had no idea who the leader, Jethro, was, but he knew the man sounded utterly ruthless.

Murdoch inclined his head, indicating the denser woods to their right, behind the group of would-be thieves. As Jethro ordered, "Everybody check your weapons and make sure they're loaded and primed," Daniel and Quincy followed Murdoch's lead and slipped through the undergrowth, moving more slowly to avoid making any warning noises. Without saying a word, they knew they had to do something to thwart this robbery attempt.

When Murdoch was satisfied with their position, he gestured for his companions to stop. They were on a slight rise, looking down at the huge clearing where Jefferson's mansion was being constructed.

Parting the brush, Daniel was able to see nearly a

dozen men waiting in the trees at the edge of the woods. The leader was a burly, broad-shouldered man with close-cropped brown hair under a tipped-back tricorn. His hard and ruthless look matched his voice, and the others were all cut from the same cloth. They were as nasty a band of cutthroats as Daniel had ever seen.

He lifted his flintlock and cocked an eyebrow at Murdoch. The big Scotsman nodded grimly, loosened the brace of pistols in his belt, and raised his rifle. Next to Daniel, Quincy readied his weapon as well.

"Don't aim to kill," Daniel whispered. "Perhaps we can frighten them off."

He settled the butt of his rifle against his shoulder and eased his finger around the trigger. He nestled his cheek against the smooth, polished wood of the stock and peered over the long barrel, finally bringing the sights to rest on the ground between the feet of one of the men.

"Ready?" he hissed. "Now!"

The three flintlocks boomed almost as one. Dirt and leaves kicked up between the feet of Daniel's target. A few yards away, a branch cracked and leapt into the air less than a foot from the head of another man as the ball from Quincy's rifle clipped it. The gang leader's black tricorn spun off his head, a neat hole bored in its low crown. Daniel knew that had been Murdoch's shot; he was the only one capable of such marksmanship.

Or perhaps Murdoch had been aiming for the man's head, despite what Daniel had said.

Either way, the volley was very effective. With curses and frightened shouts, the men scattered through the woods, only a few of them turning and looking for the source of the shots. As they did, Murdoch leaned his rifle against a tree and pulled out his pistols, touching off both of them in a twin explosion that routed the slight resistance.

Daniel and Quincy finished their hurried reloading and fired their rifles again, sending the balls after the retreating bandits, who were fleeing eastward along the edge of the woods, away from Monticello.

Two of the thieves, including the leader, hesitated long enough to turn around and fire their rifles toward their unseen assailants, but the shots came nowhere near Daniel, Quincy, and Murdoch. Murdoch had reloaded his rifle, and he fired again, though the distance to his target was close to two hundred yards. The ball peeled a strip of bark from the trunk of a tree only a couple of feet from the leader, who promptly turned his back and ran for his life.

Murdoch let out a hearty laugh. "Those boys will no' stop running for a while," he said. "They were as surprised a lot as I've seen in a long time."

Daniel agreed with that, but there was no time to discuss it. He looked toward Monticello and saw not only Thomas Jefferson but several of the estate's slaves as well, heading toward the woods carrying muskets and pistols. The gunfire had drawn their attention.

"Let's go," Daniel said with a jerk of his head. "I don't want to have to explain to Mr. Jefferson what all the shooting was about."

He couldn't have said why he wanted to avoid Jefferson. There was nothing wrong in what he and Murdoch and Quincy had done. In fact, by routing the would-be thieves they had performed quite a service for the man. But Daniel had become accustomed to acting without any fuss being made over him, and he wanted none now.

He and the others faded into the woods, leaving Monticello behind. They headed toward the Reed plantation, their tentative plan to borrow horses from Jefferson forgotten. If Quincy and Murdoch wondered why Daniel wanted to keep their part in this affair a secret, neither of them said anything.

Murdoch chuckled a few times about the way the leader of the gang had jumped when his hat had gone sailing off his head.

"You *were* aiming for the man's *hat,* weren't you, Murdoch?" Daniel finally said.

"Oh, aye, o' course. After what ye said, I knew ye'd be upset if I had done otherwise."

From the broad grin on the frontiersman's face, Daniel wasn't sure whether to believe him or not, and he decided it would be better to let the matter drop. The robbery attempt had been foiled before it could begin, and that was what was important.

Quincy became more impatient as they neared the Reed plantation, striding out in front of Daniel and Murdoch, and when they finally came within sight of the house, he let out a startled cry at what he saw.

Dr. Fletcher's carriage was parked in front of the house. That morning the doctor had said he would come back to check on Mariel in the late afternoon, and the fact that he was here now, just past the middle of the day, meant that he had been summoned. The summons must have been an urgent one.

Those thoughts flashed through Daniel's mind and must have gone through Quincy's at the same time because the younger man broke into a run toward the house, his face set in grim, anguished lines. Daniel followed him, hard put to keep up, the game bag with its pheasant banging against his leg as he ran.

"Mariel!" Quincy howled as he reached the steps leading up to the porch.

Someone must have seen them coming, because the

front door opened and Geoffrey Reed stepped out quickly, grabbed his younger son by the shoulders, and stopped him abruptly.

"Calm yourself, lad! There's no need to be upset."

As he and Murdoch approached the porch, Daniel looked at his father and saw the broad smile on Geoffrey's face. He felt a wave of relief wash over him. If anything had happened to Mariel, Geoffrey would not have been grinning as he was, almost as broadly as he had when he saw his grandsons and granddaughter for the first time.

"Mariel—" Quincy began again.

"Mariel is fine," Geoffrey said, maintaining his grip on Quincy's shoulders. "She woke up and asked for her babies, and then she wanted some food and something to drink. Dr. Fletcher is with her now, but he came out of her room long enough to tell your mother and me that he's very encouraged."

As if to confirm what Geoffrey was saying, the elderly physician chose that moment to stroll out the open front door of the house.

"Ah, there you are, Quincy," he said. "I'd go up and see that pretty wife of yours if I were you. She's been asking for you."

"She . . . she's going to be all right?" Quincy's voice trembled with joy and relief.

"I think so. Oh, she's still very weak, mind you, but in my judgment she's on the road to recovery. As long as she gets plenty of rest and care, she should be fine."

Quincy pulled free of his father, and this time Geoffrey let him go. As Quincy dashed into the house, Geoffrey and Dr. Fletcher chuckled.

"I'm glad you called me, Geoffrey," Fletcher said. "Seeing the expression on that lad's face was worth the trip out here. If you can keep him from tiring out Mariel by fussing over her, she'll be all right."

"Thank you, Doctor," Geoffrey replied. "I'm sure Pamela will keep Quincy from getting carried away."

The two men shook hands, and then Fletcher headed for his carriage.

Geoffrey looked at Daniel and Murdoch and asked, "How was your little hunting expedition?"

"We bagged a couple of pheasant and some squirrels," Daniel replied.

"Not t' mention a gang o' thieves."

Geoffrey frowned, and Daniel felt a brief touch of annoyance at Murdoch for breaking the news so bluntly. But it didn't really matter; Daniel had intended to discuss the situation with his father anyway, and now was as good a time as any. Better, perhaps, since the rest of the household was caught up in Mariel's recovery, and the conversation concerning Thomas Jefferson's problems could remain discreet.

"Some men were going to attack Monticello and steal the money Mr. Jefferson has collected for the war effort," Daniel told Geoffrey. "We ran across them in the woods and threw a scare into them. They fled before they could do anything else."

The frown on Geoffrey's face deepened. "I've been worried about just such a thing happening. Tom hasn't kept quiet about what he's doing. Of course he couldn't very well keep it a secret that he's been raising money. I gave him some myself. I don't know how much he's gathered, but I imagine it's quite a lot."

"A small fortune, one of those bandits said. When is Mr. Jefferson returning to Philadelphia?"

"Later this week, he told me," Geoffrey replied. "What is it, Daniel? What are you thinking, son?"

"I've got a feeling those men won't give up so easily,

Father. They want that money, and just because they didn't get it today doesn't mean they won't try for it again."

"Aye," rumbled Murdoch. "They be a sorry lot, Mr. Reed."

Geoffrey rubbed his temples in thought. "You're probably right. I suppose I should have a talk with Tom. He's not planning on taking anyone with him on the trip to Philadelphia except old Bob, that manservant of his. He's asking for more trouble. The only thing is, Tom Jefferson is so proud and stubborn that warning him could make him more determined to go ahead with his plan."

Daniel suddenly realized why he had wanted to keep Jefferson from finding out what had happened in the woods that morning. Instinctively he had known what his father had just said was true. Jefferson would have thanked them for foiling the robbery attempt, but knowing about it would not have led him to alter his chosen course of action.

"We've got to do something to help Mr. Jefferson," he said now, "otherwise all that money intended for the revolution could wind up in the hands of those thieves."

"You're right, of course," Geoffrey said. "But I'm not sure what we can do."

Daniel smiled faintly. "I have an idea. . . ."

Chapter Nine

After receiving the cryptic message from Tallmadge and Townsend, Elliot held himself ready.
Two days later another note was brought to the
house by a ragged man who could have been a successful
Tory businessman in Boston before the British evacuation forced him to flee. Given the patriot spymasters'
ironic sense of humor, the man was a fitting messenger:
It would be just like them, Elliot thought, to use a loyalist desperate for a few coins to deliver their messages.

He tore open the missive and passed it off to his
parents as just another note from his acquaintance who
wanted to borrow money. Then he read it again in private. All it said was: *The docks—eight of the clock tonight.*

As the last light of the late sunset was fading and
night was settling over the city, Elliot Markham strolled

along the street next to the wharves at the southern tip
of Manhattan Island.

He wore a plain dark suit and shoes, and a simple
black tricorn sat on his head. The only reminders of the
fop he had once been were the white shirt with its frills
and ruffles and the fine silk cravat. A man had to allow
himself a few luxuries, he thought.

Thick clouds were scudding in from the sea, and
Elliot glanced up at them as they slowly obscured the
stars that were winking into life. There might be a
shower later, he mused. He hoped his business with Tallmadge and Townsend would be concluded by then.

The note he had received had contained no instruc-
tions or information about how he would be met, only
the location and time. He told himself to be patient and
ambled down the street. When he reached the end of
the dock area, he turned around and strolled back in the
direction he had come from. Even at this hour there was
activity around the wharves: A ship was being unloaded,
another was being repaired by lantern light, and an occasional wagon rumbled over the cobblestones. Most of
the warehouses that lined the streets in this vicinity were
closed and dark, but light and noise spilled from the
taverns.

Elliot walked to the edge of the street next to the
water and leaned his forearms on the railing that ran
along it. He stared out over the darkening harbor and
wished Tallmadge and Townsend would hurry up. The
air was warm, fetid, and heavily laden with the smells of
the sea, none of which Elliot particularly liked.

"Good evening," a voice said from beside him.

Elliot jumped. He hadn't heard the man approach,
and as he turned to see who had spoken, he saw not one
but two shapes looming out of the gloom. He tensed.
This was a rough section of town, and the two men might

be robbers instead of the espionage masterminds he was to meet. His hand slipped toward the butt of the pistol concealed beneath his jacket.

"No need for that, Operative Five," said one of the men.

Now that they were closer, Elliot could make out their shapes. One was tall and lean—that would be Benjamin Tallmadge—while the other was short and stocky, and Elliot recognized him as Robert Townsend.

"I'm here as you instructed," he said in a quiet voice. "What do you want of me?"

"You sound rather unfriendly, Markham," Tallmadge said with a humorless chuckle. "Not regretting your little arrangement with us, are you?"

"Of course not. Why would you even ask such a thing?"

"It's just that we've heard about your trip to Canada on that ship belonging to your father and his partner," Townsend said. "There was an encounter with one of the Continental Navy's vessels—"

"The Continental Navy," Elliot broke in with a chuckle. "Isn't that a rather pretentious name for a bunch of privateers?"

"They do valuable work," Tallmadge replied tersely. "And they're as devoted as we are to the cause of liberty for the colonies. You fought them, Markham. Good men died. You can't blame us for wondering about your loyalties."

Elliot glanced around. No one was within a hundred yards, which meant their conversation was private and safe. He allowed some of the anger he was feeling to edge into his voice.

"I'm no military man, and you know it. The only reason I went to Canada was to try to get enough supplies to keep my family and friends from starving."

"By family and friends, you mean Tories," Tallmadge said, contempt strong in his tone. "Loyalists. Traitors to the cause of freedom."

"Call them what you will," Elliot snapped. "They're not soldiers. They're as much victims of this war as anyone."

Townsend moved quickly between Elliot and Tallmadge.

"There's no need for argument," Townsend said, trying to play the peacemaker. "All we need to know, Elliot, is whether you're willing to continue to help us?"

"I'm here, am I not?" Elliot returned.

"There's nothing more deadly than taking a viper to your own bosom," Tallmadge said. "If we suspect you're going to betray us, Markham—"

Elliot's hands clenched into fists. "I'm a man of my word, damn it! At least I seem to have become one, whether I like it or not. . . . Now, what is it you want of me?"

Both Tallmadge and Townsend hesitated, and finally Townsend said, "As you may have suspected, we've moved the center of our espionage operation here to New York, now that Boston is firmly in patriot hands. And it's a good thing, too, because we've heard rumors of some sort of British plot based in this area."

"Plot?" repeated Elliot. "What sort of plot?"

"We don't know," Tallmadge said with a shake of his head. "We were contacted by someone who claims to have some important information concerning British schemes against the patriots in New York. The Tory community here is still a hotbed of unrest and defiance, you know, most of it stirred up by Mayor Matthews and his cronies."

Elliot had seen little evidence of unrest or defiance in the time he had been here. In fact, most of the Tories in New York seemed to be concerned with day-to-day survival. None of them had the time or energy to engage in conspiracies. However, Elliot knew that the hatred many of the Tories felt for the patriots ran deep—it certainly did in his father—and he supposed it was possible that some sort of plot could have been hatched.

"What do you want me to do?" he asked.

"Your job will be to meet this person, get whatever information he has, and bring it back to us," Tallmadge said crisply. "Do you think you can do it?"

"Of course. I'll just be a messenger, another layer of deception between you and your informant."

"Precisely." Tallmadge's voice was cold.

Townsend spoke up again, his tone a bit friendlier than his companion's. "It shouldn't be a dangerous job, Elliot. Of course it *could* be a trap, I suppose, designed to draw out any patriot secret agents in the area."

"That's why I'll be running the risk instead of you two," Elliot said dryly.

Townsend shrugged.

"I'll do it. What do you know about this informant?"

"Nothing other than his name," Tallmadge replied. "He's called Casey, and you're to meet him in a dram shop known as Corbie's Tavern. Do you know it? I'm told it's in an area called the Holy Ground."

Elliot had heard plenty about the Holy Ground during his time in New York, but he had not frequented any of its establishments. It was the most notorious section of New York City, rougher and more dangerous than the area around the docks. Full of alehouses, gambling dens, and brothels, it was the center of vice for the entire city.

"I can find the place," he told Tallmadge and Townsend. "I've plenty of experience in sniffing out taverns. When does the meeting take place?"

"Tonight," Townsend said. "Casey will be waiting for you at ten o'clock."

Elliot frowned. "You were rather sure of yourselves, and of me, weren't you?"

"We were hoping we could rely on you, despite your recent . . . activities on behalf of the Crown."

Glaring at Tallmadge in the near dark, Elliot started to explain his actions once more, then abandoned the idea. He had followed his own conscience, and if Tallmadge didn't like that, it was just too damned bad.

"Remember what we told you," Tallmadge went on. "I suppose we can feel a certain respect for what you did, Markham, but if it goes beyond that—if there's any indication that you've turned on us—we'll have no choice but to deal with the situation."

"Have me killed, you mean."

"I'm afraid it would be necessary, Elliot," Townsend said regretfully.

With a genuine—if slightly bitter—laugh, Elliot shook his head and said, "Don't worry. I won't betray you. Once I have the information from Casey, how do I get in touch with you?"

"You don't," Tallmadge replied. "Write it up in code and leave it with the baker named Simmons. Do you know his shop?"

Elliot nodded; the bakery was nearby.

"Address the message to Mr. Haversham," Townsend added. "Simmons will know what to do."

Once again Elliot nodded his understanding, and without any farewells Tallmadge and Townsend faded away into the night. Elliot waited until they were gone, then turned his steps toward the Holy Ground, knowing that it might take him a while to locate Corbie's Tavern.

Coded messages, false names . . . When you came right down to it, Elliot thought, espionage was nothing more than a child's game played for high stakes, sometimes the highest stakes of all. But still a game . . .

Corbie's Tavern, one of many in the area, was a squalid building made of thick wooden beams. There was little to distinguish it, and lights were so few and far between in the maze of narrow streets called the Holy Ground that Elliot was afraid he might have the wrong place. As he neared the vice district he asked passersby for directions, keeping his hand on his pistol the entire time to deter any attempts at robbery.

As he neared the building he saw a sign swinging from a post, and by the faint glow of a lantern he made out the name *Corbie's* carved into the wood. Confident that he was in the right place, he opened the door and stepped inside.

Elliot's senses were assaulted by foul odors and raucous noise. The noxious fumes were a mixture of spilled ale, rotten food, tobacco smoke, and human waste and sweat—the normal stench of a low-class tavern, multiplied several times beyond what was customary. Corbie, whoever he was, had spent little time, if any, cleaning out the place. The loud noises were typical, too—angry conversations, bawdy songs, the trill of a fife, the coarse laughter of the harridans who worked as serving wenches, obscene haggling over the price of a jot of ale. Elliot had heard it all before, but again, it was louder and more grating on his nerves than usual. This place was even worse than Red Mike's in Boston.

Elliot took a deep breath, regretted it, then plunged through the crowd toward the bar, wondering how in the world he was going to find Casey in this madhouse.

It took him several minutes of cautious maneuvering to reach the bar. He had to be careful not to jostle anyone because in a place like this, a simple bump could lead to an angry curse, followed by the thrust of a dagger or the crack of a pistol. Finally, though, Elliot stood in front of the scarred and pitted hardwood counter, raised his voice over the din, and ordered a mug of ale from the cadaverous-looking bartender.

The stuff slopped over the rim of the mug as the man slid it in front of Elliot, adding to the puddle of spilled ale already on the bar. The bartender didn't let go of the mug's handle until Elliot had dropped a coin beside it. The money disappeared, snatched up deftly by a pale, long-fingered hand, and with his other hand the bartender pushed the mug toward Elliot.

Not surprisingly the ale was barely drinkable, bitter and sour and thin. Elliot sipped it and waited for the bartender to come by again on his rounds up and down the length of the bar. When the man was close enough, Elliot leaned forward and asked bluntly, "Is Casey here tonight?"

The man gave him a blank stare, and Elliot dropped another coin onto the bar. It rattled on the hardwood, and again the pallid hand darted forward like a bird of prey. The bartender still didn't say anything, but he jerked his pointed chin toward the back of the room.

Elliot looked toward the rear of the tavern. The crowd extended to the booths that ran along the far wall, and he had no idea if any of the men he was looking at was the one called Casey. Then he noticed that one of the booths was empty. Maybe the bartender had been telling him to go and sit down.

Turning back to the man, Elliot lifted an eyebrow and said, "The booth?"

The bartender nodded gravely.

"All right." Elliot shrugged as he picked up his mug. Carrying it carefully so that he wouldn't spill any ale as he made his way through the press of people, he headed toward the booth.

It was still empty when he reached it, and he wondered if there was something special about it. Given the crowd here tonight, it should have been occupied. Perhaps this man Casey was some sort of criminal who always did business here; if that was the case, the regular patrons would know to leave the booth empty. But that was just wild speculation, and as Elliot lowered himself to the uncomfortable wooden bench on one side of the table, he told himself to be patient.

He hadn't been seated for more than a minute when a female voice, close to his ear, asked, "Lookin' for a good time, are you, mate?"

Elliot turned to look, and the view that met his eyes was the bountiful cleavage of a young woman leaning toward him in a low-cut gown. She was slender, but her breasts were surprisingly large and heavy, their skin smooth and lightly dusted with freckles, as was her face. Her green eyes were heavily lidded in a practiced expression of seduction.

He knew immediately that she was a prostitute, no doubt one of many who frequented this place. Her ginger-colored hair was tightly curled and fell to her shoulders, and her lips were painted a bright red. The gown she wore was cheap, designed to show off her overly lush figure. She was not beautiful by any means, but there was a certain gaminelike attractiveness to her features.

There had been a time when Elliot would have been glad for her company, but now she was just an annoyance, one that he was going to shoo away like a persistent fly.

"I'm not interested right now, thanks," he said coolly. "I think you'll do better elsewhere."

"But there ain't nobody in the place as 'andsome as

you, guv," she protested. Without waiting any longer to be invited, she slid into the booth on the other side of the table.

"Gimme a sip o' yer ale."

Elliot grimaced and shoved the mug across to her. "You can have the whole thing if you'll just go away," he told her.

"Talk like that'll make a girl think you don't like 'er." The young woman picked up the mug and took a healthy swallow. When she put it down, she wiped the back of her hand across her mouth like a man and smiled brightly.

"Better'n usual," she said.

If the ale was better than usual tonight, Elliot would have hated to taste the normal run of the brew. He felt his irritation growing, but he kept a tight rein on his temper as he leaned forward.

"Look, I'm really not in the mood for company tonight—"

"Oh, we can change that in no time," the redhead said, reaching under the narrow table to grasp him in the most explicit of caresses.

Elliot gasped and blinked in surprise. Under the circumstances he could not prevent himself from responding to her touch. As he did, her eyes widened and she said with a wanton look, "Sir!"

Flustered and angry, Elliot said, "I want you to leave me alone—"

"You couldn't prove that by what I'm feelin'," she shot back with a wicked grin.

"I'm telling you—"

Smiling broadly, she released him and slapped her hands on the table, then leaned forward and whispered, "Careful, mate, or you'll hurt little Casey's feelin's."

"Casey?" Elliot exclaimed without thinking.

"Aye. And you'd be the gent Tallmadge and Town-send sent to see me."

Elliot couldn't have felt more stunned if someone had hit him over the head with a mallet. Tallmadge and Townsend had said that Casey was a man, but they had also admitted that they knew next to nothing about their would-be informant. Elliot was the first one to have a face-to-face meeting with him—or rather, her.

As far as Elliot could see, there was nothing he could do but plunge ahead. Keeping his voice pitched so low that only the young woman could hear it, he said, "I believe you have some information for me."

Again she gave him a mischievous smirk. "That ain't all I got for you, guv. You're comin' with me."

"No, I can't—"

"Then you can go back to yer friends and tell 'em you failed, because I ain't talkin' 'til I'm good an' ready."

Elliot took a deep breath. "What do you want?"

"Come with me and find out, why don't you?"

"I don't have any choice, do I?" he muttered.

Swiftly reaching under the table again, her hand squeezed his most private part. "Not unless you want me t' lead you out o' here by *this*."

"All right, all right, I'll go with you," he snapped.

"Now you're bein' reasonable." Casey let go of him, stood up, and put a haughty look on her face. "Just don't pay any attention to anything you might hear as we're leavin'. These blokes don't know it, but I'm a respectable young lady, I am."

Of course you are, Elliot thought, but he kept the sarcastic comment to himself.

There were hoots and catcalls from some of the patrons as Elliot got to his feet and followed Casey out of the tavern. Evidently she was quite well-known in the

Holy Ground. She grabbed his hand when they reached the door and then led him down the street.

Relieved that it was his hand she had grabbed, the thought that this might be a trap crossed Elliot's mind as the darkness closed in around them. A light rain had begun to fall, and the shadows seemed thicker than before.

Casey turned down an alley, still tugging Elliot's hand. "Come on," she said. "We'll be there in a minute."

He followed. There seemed to be little else he could do. This game, whatever it was, had to be played out to the end.

Casey paused at a dilapidated building and fumbled with a key at a door. The door opened, and she drew Elliot inside. He was glad to be out of the rain, but the darkness inside was so complete it was almost tangible, surrounding him and clinging to him like pitch. Casey seemed to know where she was going, though; judging by the echoes their footsteps made, she was leading him along what sounded like a narrow corridor.

"Watch yer step up here," she warned him, and a second later they were climbing a flight of stairs. Elliot put his free hand out and brushed it against the wall, trying to keep himself oriented. He felt vaguely dizzy.

They reached the top of the stairs and walked down a hallway. Casey opened another door, and light came from within. The illumination was the faint, flickering glow of a candle, but after the stygian darkness through which they had come, even that seemed blinding to Elliot. He paused and blinked several times to let his eyes adjust, then allowed Casey to tug him into the room and shut the door behind him.

Elliot looked around. The building smelled almost as bad as Corbie's Tavern, but the unpleasant scent was not as strong in this room. He noticed a vase of fresh-cut flowers on a small nightstand beside the bed, and the bed itself was rather narrow, with a carved wooden foot-board and headboard that bore plenty of scars from years of use. However, the thin mattress was covered with what appeared to be a clean sheet and a blanket, and the flowers provided a bright, cheerful touch to the room.

The bed dominated the narrow chamber, but there were also a couple of straight-backed chairs and a small wardrobe in the room.

Casey looked at Elliot. "What do you think?" she asked.

"Lovely," he said, his voice dry.

Her full lower lip came out even farther in a pout. "You don't have to make fun of me, Mr.— What is your name, anyway?"

"Just call me Elliot."

"Elliot," she repeated, the pout replaced by a smile. "That's a pretty name. It suits you."

"Thank you."

"Oh, you're welcome." And with that, she reached down, grasped the hem of her gown, and peeled it up over her head. She was nude beneath it. She tossed the gown aside and stood there, letting Elliot look at her.

It would have been impossible *not* to look at her. The freckles he had noticed on her face and breasts covered most of her body, although they were much lighter, so faint in places they could barely be seen. The triangle of hair at the juncture of her thighs was the same ginger color as that on her head. Her thighs and hips were slim but gracefully curved, and her large breasts did not seem so out of proportion once the rest of her body was revealed. Her nipples were large, dark brown circles that hardened under Elliot's gaze.

He tore his eyes away from them. He had come to the Holy Ground on a mission, not to bed some doxy, no matter how earthy and appealing she was.

"This isn't necessary," he growled. "Just tell me what I came here to find out."

Casey grinned at him. "We got to go through with it, Elliot. We got to do what comes natural, just in case anybody's skulkin' 'round outside the room. Wouldn't want 'em to hear us talkin' 'bout things we shouldn't, would we?"

Elliot swallowed hard. There was no point in denying the effect Casey had on him. It had been a long time since he had been with a woman, and in the past he had always gotten a great deal of pleasure out of taking wenches like her to bed. He'd never had to worry about pretenses. What went on was a simple matter of satisfying appetites.

She stepped close to him, so close that the tips of her breasts brushed his chest. Her fingers found the laces of his pants and untied them.

"Come on," she said. "I'll whisper what you want to know in your ear."

"All right, damn it," he grated, unable to control himself any longer. "If that's the way you want it."

It was his duty as a patriot, after all. . . .

Elliot carefully slid his arm out from under Casey's shoulders as she snuggled against him in the bed an hour later. She was snoring softly. He slipped out of bed, stood up, and stretched weary muscles. Casey had not only been quite inventive, she had also seemed tireless. Finally, though, they had been sated.

As promised, she had conveyed to him in whispers the information he was to pass along to Tallmadge and Townsend. It was rather vague. According to Casey, Corbie's Tavern was a gathering place for many of the Tories who violently opposed the patriot cause, and she had heard that some of them were forming a secret organization to be known as the King's Militia. Casey had no idea what they were planning to do, but she was certain they intended to strike at the patriots, and soon. She had promised to try to find out more.

"And when I do . . . you're the only one . . . I'll tell, Elliot," she had whispered in a shaky voice.

He hoped he remembered everything she had told him, he thought as he quickly and quietly got dressed. The circumstances of their conversation hadn't been exactly conducive to strict concentration.

And there was still the question of Casey's trustworthiness. She might be baiting a trap, with the intention of uncovering the rebels' intelligence efforts in New York. Somehow he doubted it, though. He had a feeling she was exactly what she seemed to be: a free-spirited trollop who believed that the colonies ought to be independent and wanted to do whatever she could to help in that cause. After all, thought Elliot, a whore could be a patriot just like anyone else. Everyone had his or her part to play in this revolution . . . even former wastrels like himself. He and Casey, in fact, had quite a bit in common.

He looked at her again as she slept, and a smile played across his face. Then he let himself out of the room, fumbled his way down the hallway and the stairs, and left the building through the alley door. The rain had stopped, he saw when he reached the street, and even the Holy Ground seemed a bit cleaner now.

He would be coming back. Elliot was sure of that.

Chapter Ten

Daniel paused in the doorway of the bedroom, both surprised and touched by the scene before him. He had knocked on the door and called out to Roxanne, and she had told him to come in. When he opened the door, he found her sitting in a rocking chair, her robe pulled back to reveal one breast that was being heartily sucked at by their infant, Joseph. Daniel felt a brief moment of embarrassment, and he hesitated.

"Come in and shut the door, Daniel," Roxanne said. "There's nothing wrong with you being here for this."

"No, I suppose not," he agreed as he stepped into the room and shut the door quietly behind him. He walked to the rocker, taking pains not to startle the baby. With a slight frown of concern on his face, he said to Roxanne, "Should you be up this soon? It's only been a few days since Joseph was born. He can always go to the wet nurse."

"Don't be ridiculous, Daniel. Joseph is my son, and I'm perfectly capable of feeding him. I know conventional medical wisdom says that a woman should stay in bed for at least two weeks after giving birth, but I don't believe in that. Women who work in the fields don't have that luxury, and it doesn't seem to hurt them."

He reached out and lightly brushed his fingertips over the baby's fine-spun dark hair. It was almost impossibly soft. Everything about the child was a surprise to some extent, because Daniel had never been around a newborn before except for Quincy, and those memories were lost in the dim past. The thought that this perfectly formed, tiny creature was his son was almost too much for Daniel to comprehend.

Just as it was hard to comprehend that he was going to have to leave Roxanne and Joseph, even though mere days had passed since the baby's birth.

"I've come to talk to you about something," he said to her, forcing the words out past the love and affection that threatened to block his throat. "It's important."

Roxanne looked up at him, hearing in his voice just how serious this conversation was to be. As she did so, Joseph finished sucking and began to fret. Roxanne glanced down at him again, then slid a hand out from under him and picked up a cloth from the table next to her.

"Here," she said, handing the cloth to Daniel. "Put that over your shoulder and take the baby."

"Me? Take the baby?"

"Of course. You're his father, so you'd better get used to holding him."

Roxanne's tone told Daniel that she would brook

no argument, so he took the cloth and draped it over his left shoulder. Carefully he took the tiny bundle that Roxanne held up to him.

"Keep one hand behind his head," she cautioned as she tucked her breast back inside the robe and closed the garment. "Lift him and lay him against your shoulder. . . . Yes, that's it. Now pat him on the back."

Joseph was still crying, but the noises subsided as Daniel cradled him and patted his back. He found himself swaying instinctively from side to side. Joseph quieted even more.

"He's really a very good baby," Roxanne said.

"I know he is." Daniel swallowed hard. Holding Joseph like this made it even more difficult for him to say what he had come to tell Roxanne. It was impossible to postpone the discussion any longer, however.

"I'm going to miss the little lad," he said softly.

Roxanne looked at him sharply. "Where are you going?"

"I have to report to General Washington," Daniel said. "I'm sure he's wondering what's become of me."

"Where are you going?" Roxanne repeated.

"To Philadelphia," replied Daniel. "To the Second Continental Congress."

Her eyes widened in surprise. "But you're not a delegate to the Congress," she objected. "Thomas Jefferson represents this area."

"I know," Daniel said quickly. "And I'm not really going to the Congress. I'm going to keep an eye on Mr. Jefferson. It's something of a complicated story."

"You had best tell me about it," Roxanne urged.

Daniel did so, beginning with the robbery attempt at Monticello that he, Quincy, and Murdoch had foiled several days earlier. As he talked, he kept patting Joseph, and he was interrupted after a few moments by a belch that was truly monumental for such a small individual. After that, the baby settled down against his father's shoulder and went to sleep.

"There's no doubt in my mind that the robbers will try again to steal the money Mr. Jefferson has collected for the patriot cause," Daniel concluded. "My father has had men keeping an eye on Monticello without Mr. Jefferson's knowledge. We've discussed it, and it seems much more likely the thieves will wait to make another attempt until Jefferson is on the road between here and Philadelphia. Someone has to go along to protect against that."

"So you've appointed yourself the guardian of Jefferson and the money," Roxanne said.

"Quincy, Murdoch, and I should prove capable bodyguards."

"Oh, I've no doubt of that." Roxanne stood up and held out her hands for the baby. Daniel gave him to her, transferring the precious weight carefully, and Roxanne carried the infant to the bassinet in the corner of the room. She placed him on the pad and covered him with a lightweight blanket, then faced Daniel.

"I know what you're thinking," he said before she had a chance to say anything else. "You believe that I have no business leaving you and Joseph so soon after he was born."

"On the contrary," she said, crossing her arms over her chest. "I believe that it's your duty as a patriot to do everything you can to protect that money, so that it can go toward the defeat of the British and the establishment of freedom for the colonies."

Daniel blinked. He knew that she was fiercely devoted to the cause, but he had expected motherhood to assert itself.

But then her chin began to tremble slightly, and her

eyes grew damp with tears. Without saying anything else, she ran across the room and into his arms and rested her head against his chest.

"It'll be all right," he assured her in a whisper. "I wish I didn't have to go."

"That . . . that's not why I'm crying, you great bloody fool," she said without looking up at him. "I know you don't want to leave. *I* don't want you to leave. But you have to! The sooner this war is over, the sooner life can go on normally for all of us."

In his heart Daniel doubted that life would ever be normal again for any of them. Still, they had to cling to that hope. He found himself embracing his wife and patting her back much as he had patted his small son.

After a few moments she looked up at him and said, "I just wish I could go with you. I've always hated staying behind. You know that."

Daniel did indeed. He remembered how Roxanne had remained in Boston when he was forced to flee the city. She had become deeply involved with espionage activities, and it had earned her the enmity of the Crown. At least this time, ensconced here on his family's plantation, she would be out of danger.

"I tried to talk myself out of going," he said quietly. "But after I discussed the situation with my father and Murdoch, I knew I had no choice. Father rode to Monticello earlier today and talked to Mr. Jefferson, ostensibly about some agricultural questions, and he found out that the journey to Philadelphia will begin tomorrow. Mr. Jefferson isn't taking anyone with him other than a slave, a personal servant called Bob."

"That's foolish. He should have a troop of militia with him."

"Father suggested that, but Mr. Jefferson wouldn't listen. He said the militia was needed here at home in case of trouble from the redcoats." Daniel smiled thinly. "He's a headstrong man, Mr. Thomas Jefferson."

"You mentioned Quincy going with you. Is he breaking the news to Mariel?"

"I haven't asked Quincy yet. I want him at my side, but I hate to suggest that he leave Mariel and the babies after all the trouble she had. Murdoch and I will handle things by ourselves if need be."

"You have to ask him, Daniel," Roxanne said sternly. "Quincy would never forgive you if you and Murdoch went off without telling him."

"I suppose you're right."

Roxanne stepped back out of his embrace. "Come along. I'll go with you."

"You should rest."

"I feel perfectly fine. Joseph is sleeping soundly, and there's no reason I can't walk down the hall."

"Well, all right. I have to admit, I'll be glad for the company. I don't know how either one of them will react."

Holding hands, Daniel and Roxanne stepped out of the bedroom and crossed the hall to Mariel's door.

"It's Daniel and Roxanne. May we come in?"

Quincy opened the door himself, a grin on his face. He was looking more like his happy-go-lucky old self as Mariel grew stronger by the day.

"Come in, come in," he said. "Where's Joseph?"

"Asleep," Roxanne told him. "What about Thomas and Elizabeth?"

From the bed, where she was propped up on several fat pillows, Mariel smiled and said, "Oh, they're awake, I assure you." Both babies were lying on the bed beside her, each with a fist crammed in its mouth.

Daniel approached the bed with Roxanne and marveled at how much the three babies looked alike. There was no denying the Reed family resemblance. He rubbed the infants' cheeks softly before turning to his brother and clapping him on the shoulder.

"You've a great pair of youngsters there. Do you suppose they'll scrap as much as we did growing up?"

Quincy laughed. "I'll be disappointed if they don't. They wouldn't be proper Reeds without a few fusses along the way."

Roxanne sat lightly on the foot of the bed. "You look as if you're feeling better, Mariel."

"Much better, thank you. With Quincy here to see to my every need, how could I not recover quickly?"

"Well, that's one of the things we're here to talk about," Daniel said, then saw Roxanne flash him a warning look. It might have been better to ease into this discussion, he thought belatedly.

But Quincy had already sensed that something was up. "What is it, Daniel? What do you mean by that?"

"Remember that robbery attempt a few days ago at Monticello?"

Before Quincy could reply, Mariel asked, "Robbery? What robbery?"

"It was nothing," Quincy told her quickly. "Just some highwaymen who planned to hold up our neighbor Mr. Jefferson. You don't need to be concerned about it, Mariel."

"I'm afraid there's more to it than that, Quincy," Daniel said. "I've talked it over with Father and Murdoch, and we're agreed there's likely to be another attempt to steal that money, probably while Mr. Jefferson is on his way to Philadelphia. Someone is going to have to go along to protect him."

Quincy's frown deepened. "And you're thinking that should be the three of us, I take it?"

"Oh, Quincy, no!" cried Mariel, her pallor returning.

"We have a duty to the cause of liberty—" Daniel started to say.

"Hang the cause of liberty!" Quincy interrupted hotly. "I've already given my share of blood and pain to the cause! I took a bullet in the leg in Boston, and I risked my life and the life of the woman I love out on the frontier to stop the redcoats from using the Mohawks against us. We've *all* suffered for the cause. When is it ever going to be enough?"

Daniel had not expected Quincy to react so strongly, but he had a ready answer to his brother's question.

"It will be enough when the colonies are free, Quincy, and not before."

Quincy stared at him for a long moment, then turned away sharply and shuddered. "I can't go now," he said in a choked voice without looking at Daniel. "I won't leave Mariel and the babies. You can run off and desert your wife and son if you like, Daniel, but I can't."

"Quincy!" exclaimed Roxanne. "That's not fair, and you know it. Daniel isn't deserting us. I don't want him to go, but he has to. We can't let that money end up in the hands of thieves."

Mariel reached out from the bed and clasped her husband's hand. "Please, Quincy, do not be upset. I have not known Daniel for long, but I know he would not do this unless he thought it best."

"Best for him, maybe, but not for me," Quincy declared. He took a deep breath, then blew it out in a sigh. He turned to Daniel and said, "I'm sorry. I had no right to snap at you like that, Daniel. But you have to understand—"

"I do understand," Daniel broke in. "I was prepared for you to say no, Quincy. Murdoch and I can go, and I'm sure we can handle any trouble that comes up. It's all right, it really is. One of us should be here to help Father, anyway. You're right—I think you should stay behind. Believe me, I respect what you have already done for this country, my brother."

"I'm glad you see it that way. And I'm really sorry that I can't go with you."

"Don't worry about it." Daniel put a hand on his brother's shoulder. "Just take care of Mariel and those two little babies, you hear?"

Quincy managed a faint smile. "I will."

Daniel held out a hand to Roxanne. "We'll leave you alone now."

"Quincy and I will talk about this further, Daniel," Mariel said.

"Nothing to talk about," he assured her with a smile. "You just get some rest."

Daniel led Roxanne from the room. As they left, he glanced back and saw, from the look on Mariel's face and Quincy's slumped shoulders, that he had brought an added burden into his brother's life.

When they had returned to Roxanne's room, she said, "Quincy has changed. He's not the firebrand he used to be."

"He's been through too much hardship," Daniel said heavily, "and seen too much of the war."

"Less than you," Roxanne pointed out. "You were at Bunker Hill and in the mountains with Knox."

"I still can't hold it against him. He has to do what he thinks is right for his family, and Mariel and the twins are the most important part of that."

"I know." Roxanne slipped her arms around his waist and leaned against him again. "You're a lucky man, Daniel Reed, to have such an understanding wife."

"You're not telling me anything I don't already know," he said as he put a hand under her chin, tipped her head, and kissed her soundly.

Saying good-bye to Roxanne and Joseph was not something Daniel was looking forward to, but when the sun rose the next morning, it could no longer be postponed. He knew from his father's conversation with Thomas Jefferson the day before that the politician intended to start his journey early. Daniel slipped into Roxanne's bedroom just as the gray of dawn was beginning to fade.

She was already awake, he saw. With a smile she gestured toward the bassinet.

"Don't worry about disturbing me, Daniel," she said. "Joseph has already had his morning feeding and gone back to sleep. Come sit beside me." She patted the bed.

Daniel joined her. He was dressed in his traveling clothes: a homespun shirt, whipcord breeches, high boots, and a leather vest. He took off his black tricorn and held it awkwardly as he sat beside Roxanne. His flintlock, a brace of pistols, a powder horn, and a shot pouch were all waiting for him downstairs, but he would not bring such things into the room where his wife waited and his infant son slept.

"I wish I could say how long we'll be gone," he told her. "Perhaps only a matter of a few weeks."

"Aren't you going on to Boston after you reach Philadelphia?"

"Well, I hadn't quite decided yet. . . ."

"Then I shall decide for you," Roxanne said sternly. "You must report to General Washington, Daniel. You are not a deserter."

"You're right. I have to get back. The general may have another assignment waiting for me."

Roxanne reached under her pillow and brought out a piece of paper that had been folded and sealed with wax. She held it out to Daniel.

"Will you post this for me when you reach Philadelphia? It's a letter to my parents, letting them know that I'm all right and that they have a grandson."

"I thought you had already sent them such a letter. My father posted it for you, did he not?"

"Yes, but with the situation the way it is these days, so much confusion in the colonies, I want to send this one, too, just to make sure that one of the messages gets through."

"All right," Daniel said. He slipped the letter into a pocket inside his vest. "I'll take care of it for you."

"Take care of *yourself*. That's the most important thing you can do for me, Daniel." She leaned close to him and kissed him, and Daniel held her for a long while.

Finally he stood up and walked to the bassinet, kneeling beside it to peer in at the sleeping infant. He brushed his fingers along the baby's cheek and whispered, "I'll be back, Joseph. I'll be back." A tight band seemed to have cinched itself around Daniel's chest, and it grew tighter when he looked at his son.

Roxanne got out of bed, came to his side, and put a hand on his shoulder.

"Go with God, Daniel," she said.

Knowing that he had to leave quickly if he was going to leave at all, Daniel stood up, kissed her again, and strode from the room. He didn't look back as he went along the hall to the stairs and down to the foyer. His mother was waiting for him there, and Daniel hugged and kissed her as well.

"We will all pray for you, Daniel," Pamela told him.

Not trusting himself to speak, he picked up his weapons and ammunition and stepped outside. Murdoch was waiting for him, already mounted on a big chestnut stallion given to him by Geoffrey Reed, and Geoffrey was standing nearby, holding the reins of a black mare that Daniel knew to be a fine saddle horse.

But Geoffrey was holding another horse there as well, saddled and ready to ride, and Daniel turned in surprise as he heard a familiar footfall behind him.

Quincy strode out of the house, dressed much like Daniel and carrying his rifle.

"Well," he said with a rakish grin, "are we going on this adventure or not?"

For an instant Daniel felt as if he had been transported back in time. The Quincy he was seeing now was the same Quincy who had donned war paint and feathers in order to toss crates of British tea into Boston Harbor. The younger Reed exuded an air of confidence that bordered on recklessness.

It was an act, Daniel knew, a bit of bravado that Quincy was clinging to in order to find the strength to leave his wife and children. Mariel must have convinced him that going along to protect the money for the patriot cause was the right thing to do. Whatever Quincy's reason for changing his mind, Daniel was glad to have him along.

"I'm ready if you are, brother."

Quincy nodded. "Then let's go."

"Just one moment," Geoffrey said as he held out the reins to his sons. "Let me give you some advice."

"This is hardly the time for fatherly advice, don't you think, Father?" Quincy said.

"Hush, lad, and listen to me. I'm speaking as a fellow patriot now, not as your father."

"Go on," Daniel told him quietly.

"I've known Thomas Jefferson for many years. He's a brilliant man, no doubt about that, but he's also about the most stubborn individual you'll ever see. Tom feels that he and Bob can take care of themselves on this trip, and his pride won't allow him to accept the three of you as bodyguards."

"The same thought had occurred to me," Daniel said.

"What you're going to have to do," Geoffrey went on, "is trail him and keep an eye on him without his knowing it. Can you do that?"

Murdoch grinned broadly and said, "No offense, Mr. Reed, but th' day I canno' trail a politician is the day I'll be eating this old coonskin cap o' mine. We'll watch out for this fella Jefferson, dinna ye worry about that."

"We can do it, Father," Daniel added as he swung up into the saddle. He looked at Quincy and Murdoch. "Ready to ride?"

"More than ready," Murdoch replied.

Quincy summoned up a grin and nodded.

Geoffrey reached up and shook hands with each of them. "Good luck and Godspeed," he said fervently. "Come back safely, my lads."

With good-bye waves to Geoffrey and Pamela, who stood in the doorway of the big house, and to Roxanne and Mariel, who had come to the windows of their rooms on the second floor, Daniel, Quincy, and Murdoch turned their horses and rode away from the Reed plantation.

Thomas Jefferson, his servant, the Reed brothers, and their friend Murdoch Buchanan were not the only ones prepared for a journey that fine spring morning. Several miles away, at a roadside tavern, a dozen men waited. Some of them were drinking tea, while others were already swigging ale despite the early hour. They had eaten, and their horses were saddled and ready in front of the tavern.

A door at one side of the room opened, and the man who had led the aborted raid on Monticello swaggered out into the tavern's main chamber. He was followed by a buxom serving girl who was tugging her disarranged gown into a more decent position. Jethro Tyler stepped aside to let her pass and gave her a healthy swat on the rump. He laughed at the way the girl jumped, then turned to face his men.

"Any sign of Luther yet?" he asked.

"He's not shown up, Jethro," one of the group replied. Like the others, he had the look of a hardened highwayman about him. "Maybe you should've sent more than one man over there to keep an eye on the place."

Tyler glowered, insulted that one of his subordinates would imply a challenge to a decision he'd made. The man who had spoken muttered and leaned back on the bench where he sat, carefully averting his eyes from Tyler's glare.

"Jefferson may be on his guard now," Tyler said curtly. "I don't want half a dozen men blundering around Monticello, warning him that we're still after that money. Luther's a good man. He'll let us know when Jefferson leaves and how many bodyguards he takes with him." He gave a harsh laugh. "No matter how many it is, there won't be enough men to protect him. That money's as good as ours, boys."

If any of the bandits was reminded of the fact that Tyler had made the same promise just before the raid on Monticello, wisely none of them mentioned it. No one wanted to cross Jethro Tyler, a ruthless, dangerous man still burning with resentment at having failed to steal the money.

Tyler staggered behind the bar. It had been deserted by the tavern's owner, who had decided to let the gang have the run of the place rather than get himself killed opposing them. They would be gone soon enough, the proprietor had reasoned, and then he could set about repairing the damage they had done and replenishing the liquor they had drunk.

Tyler heard the sound of rapid hoofbeats outside as he tapped a keg of ale and filled a mug. The rider came to a stop and hurried in.

"Jefferson just rode out! And Jethro, he's only got one man with him, and a slave at that!"

Tyler swallowed half the ale in his mug and slammed it down on the bar. The news was better than he had dared to expect.

"Good job, Luther," he said. "We'll ride out in a bit and take the Philadelphia road."

"Why not leave now?" asked one of the other men.

Tyler shook his head. "I want to give Jefferson a good lead. We won't have any trouble catching up to him later. It'll be better if there's a bit of distance between us and this place when we take him."

"But what if he gives us the slip?"

"How's he going to do that?" Tyler demanded with a contemptuous snort. "There's only one real road leading north from these parts. Jefferson's going to follow it, because he won't want to waste any time getting back to the Continental Congress. Use your head, man."

"So we wait some more?" asked another of the cutthroats.

"We can all find something to do to pass the time," Tyler said, draining the rest of the ale in his mug, then looking around. His gaze fell on the serving girl who had left the back room with him. She was sitting on a stool in a corner, trying to look invisible but not succeeding. Tyler came out from behind the bar, strode over to her, and grasped her upper arm, left bare by the short sleeves of the gown.

"Come along, lass," he growled. "There's time for you to give me a proper farewell before we leave. Just be glad you don't have to say good-bye to *all* the lads."

With that, he pulled the girl to her feet and dragged her toward the door to the back room.

Soon he would be a rich man and wouldn't have to content himself with slatterns like this, Tyler thought. Soon he would wear silk and have the finest ladies and drink wine instead of cheap ale. Aye, a rich man he would be.

And if Mr. Thomas bloody Jefferson had to die first, well, that was just too damned bad. . . .

Chapter Eleven

As instructed by Benjamin Tallmadge and Robert Townsend, Elliot Markham wrote up what he had learned from Casey about the King's Militia —precious little though it was—then translated the message into the code used by the patriot intelligence network and left the coded letter at the bakery. He burned the original.

That done, there was nothing to do but wait to be contacted again, either by Casey or by Tallmadge and Townsend.

The ginger-haired prostitute seemed to be haunting his thoughts, and he found himself thinking of her again a few days later as he strolled down to the docks. Casey was an inspiring performer in bed, but Elliot didn't think that was the reason she was on his mind. At least, not

x

the only reason. He felt a genuine liking for her and hoped she realized how dangerous it could be to insinuate herself into the deadly cat-and-mouse games that made up the competing espionage efforts of the patriots and the British. A simple mistake could easily get her killed, but he couldn't worry too much about such things, he told himself. There was a job to do, and he intended to do it.

As Elliot walked he kept a wary eye on his surroundings, even though it was broad daylight. There was always a chance he might run into trouble, for he was known as a Tory, and many of the citizens of New York hated Tories with a passion. But he wasn't going to let anything keep him from reaching his destination.

It was time to make plans for a second voyage to Halifax, and Elliott was bound for the Markham & Cummings ship that had brought in the supplies from Canada. Captain Beaumont and a few members of the volunteer crew had remained on board after its cargo had been secretly unloaded and distributed among the loyalists in the city. Beaumont and his companions were there to make sure that none of the patriots tried to "liberate" the ship.

The leathery old sea captain was on deck when Elliot arrived at the wharf. Beaumont raised a hand in greeting and called, "Come aboard, Mr. Markham. It's good to see you again."

Elliot hurried up the gangplank and shook hands with Beaumont.

"How are you, Captain?" he asked. "Any trouble down here the past few days?"

"Nary a lick," Beaumont replied. "Some of the folks ashore probably wonder where we sailed to before, but they haven't come poking around to try to find out."

"That's good," Elliot said fervently, "because I think we're going to make the trip again soon."

Beaumont looked at him intently and asked, "How soon? The only reason I ask is that the lads don't have all the damage repaired yet."

"Not right away," Elliot told him. "But I'd like to sail again in another three or four weeks if possible."

"That won't be a problem." The captain grinned and waved a hand. "We'll have this fine old tub seaworthy again by then."

Elliot clasped Beaumont's arm. "I'm glad to hear it. Will you have any trouble getting a full crew?"

"I don't think so," the captain said with a shake of his head. "The word's got around amongst the loyalists in the city of the good we done last time, and I'm sure most of the lads will see fit to ship out with us again."

"All right. I'll speak to Mr. Wallingford, and we'll try to come up with the funds we'll need for another load of supplies."

"Will Mr. Wallingford be accompanying us again, sir?" Beaumont gave Elliot a dubious look.

"I suppose so. I hadn't really thought about it. Why do you ask, Captain? Is his presence going to be a problem?"

"Not for me or my crew, Mr. Markham, but I had the feeling there was a bit of bad blood between the two of you."

Elliot laughed, but there wasn't much humor in the sound.

"Avery saved my life during that battle with the rebel ship. True, we've not gotten along well in the past, but I'm hoping that's all over now."

"Well, I hope you're right, sir." Beaumont straightened. "I'll have the lads get busy on those repairs."

"Very good. I'll be in touch, Captain."

Elliot left the ship and walked uptown. As he made his way toward the Tory section of the settlement, he thought about the captain's question. Even with the success of the first voyage, the close call they'd had with the patriot ship would make Theophilus Cummings leery of committing the vessel to a second trip. Elliot was certain that Cummings would insist that Avery go along again, so he decided to stop by and have a talk with Avery, just to make sure that his former friend would be willing to undertake another voyage.

He went straight to the Cummings house, which was next door to the one he and his parents occupied for the time being. As he knocked on the door, Elliot hoped that Sarah wouldn't be home. He could tolerate old Theophilus and his wife, but the less he saw of Sarah the better.

Avery answered the summons, opened the door, and gave Elliot a dour look.

"Oh, it's you. What do you want?"

"I need to speak to you for a few minutes, Avery. Are Sarah and her parents at home?"

"As a matter of fact, they're all out at the moment. They've gone to church. I didn't feel up to it, however."

"Church? Is this Sunday?"

"You don't even know what day of the week it is? I thought you'd given up drinking that heavily, Elliot." A touch of Avery's old arrogance showed in his fleeting smirk.

"I've been rather busy lately," Elliot said as he stepped inside without waiting for an invitation, forcing Avery to move back to let him in. They stood in the middle of the shabby parlor, which was so different from the splendid rooms of the Wallingfords' Boston house. Like many other houses in which the fugitive Tories lived, this one was furnished in a manner that could hardly be called sumptuous. The floor was made of puncheons. There was a plain-looking table in one corner, along with several uncomfortable chairs and a thinly cushioned divan.

Elliot looked steadily at Avery, then said, "And we're both going to be busy in the future. We have to raise money for another trip up to Halifax."

"A-Another trip?" Avery repeated, blinking in surprise. His features paled slightly.

"That's right," Elliot responded. "You recall that we discussed the possibility. Those supplies we brought back the first time won't last forever, you know."

"Yes. Yes, of course. You're right, Elliot." With a sigh Avery went on, "You might as well sit down, if we have to talk about this."

Elliot ignored the ungracious tone of the invitation and sat down on one of the plain ladder-back chairs in the room. Avery sank onto the divan and rested his elbows on his thighs, cupping his chin in his hands. He gave Elliot a hangdog look.

"I don't suppose you could make this trip to Canada without me, could you?" he asked.

"To be honest, I don't see why not," Elliot replied, "except for the fact that your father-in-law is bound to want you to come along. My father might stand up to Cummings and insist that I take the ship whether you're involved or not, but I don't want to chance that. There's too much at stake."

"Yes, there is—our lives if we run into any more pirates in that ponderous old tub."

Elliot frowned. Avery seemed distracted, as if he was making his protest by rote. Elliot had no doubt that Avery did not want to make the voyage, but he sensed there was more to it than that.

"What's wrong, Avery?" he asked after a moment of hesitation. "There's more on your mind than pirates."

He could hardly believe these words were coming from his mouth. What reason did he have to be concerned about Avery Wallingford? True, Avery had saved his life, but that impulsive act had merely balanced out some of the misery that Avery had sown in Elliot's life over the past twelve months.

After a few seconds Avery said haltingly, "Yes, there is something on my mind . . . something I hardly know how to say to you, Elliot. With all the ill feeling between us . . ."

"We're partners of a sort, I suppose," Elliot told him grudgingly. "If you've something to say, Avery, just go ahead and get it over with."

"All right, I will. I can't go to Canada with you, no matter what Theophilus says. I can't leave Sarah here in New York."

"She has her parents to take care of her," Elliot pointed out. "Of course, given the circumstances, none of us is really safe—"

"That's not what I mean," Avery broke in. He stood up sharply, as if he could no longer remain still. He paced the room and nervously ran his fingers through his sleek dark hair. "I can't leave Sarah here because she's having an affair!"

Elliot tensed and held his hands up defensively. "I thought we settled this back in Boston with that so-called duel. What Sarah and I had between us is long since over—"

Avery swung toward him, an imploring look on his face. "I know that. I'm surprised you'll even listen to me after what happened, Elliot, but after all, we were friends once, and . . . and I don't think there's anyone else here in New York who might understand."

The man looked and sounded pathetic, Elliot thought. Given the circumstances, the background of hostility between them, Elliot should have been laughing at Avery's discomfiture. There had been a time, he realized, when he would have found this situation deliciously humorous. Now, though, he felt only pity for Avery, mixed with the usual contempt.

"Tell me all about it," Elliot sighed.

Avery continued to pace. "Sarah has been away from home a great deal ever since you and I got back from Canada. And in talking to her father, I gather that her absences began while we were gone. You know how Theophilus is, of course. His darling daughter can do no wrong." His tone was tinged with bitter acid. "And her mother is so empty-headed she might as well not even be here. So Sarah comes and goes as she pleases, with no one to challenge her."

"What about you?" Elliot asked. "Surely you've demanded to know what she's been doing."

"I didn't want to make things worse," Avery whined. "I . . . I've tried to keep the peace. She's so cold to me."

"Spy on her, then." Elliot allowed some of his old resentments to come to the surface. "You've always been good at sneaking around."

For just a second Avery glared at him. "I suppose I deserved that," he said. "But you're right, you know. That's exactly what I should do. That's what I'm *going* to do. And I want you to help me."

"Me? Help you?" Elliot could not contain the shocked exclamation. "Why in God's name would I help you spy on Sarah? Why would you even ask me such a thing?"

"It wasn't easy, I can tell you that," Avery said with a harsh little laugh. "But with all these rebels around the city, it's a dangerous place. You handle a pistol fairly well, and you're not totally useless in a fistfight. I just believe that two of us skulking around the city will be safer than one man alone."

Elliot supposed that Avery had a point, but to help him spy on the woman Elliot himself had once been engaged to marry . . . Well, that was almost too galling a prospect to contemplate.

"I don't think I can do it, Avery," he said.

Avery stalked over to him. "For the love of God, man, can't you see that I need help? When I saw that rebel pirate about to cleave you in half with his saber, I didn't hesitate to act."

Elliot's jaw clenched, then relaxed. "You have a point," he admitted reluctantly. "I suppose I do owe you a debt of honor. Don't forget, though, you tried to have me killed in Boston. One moment of gallantry will only buy you so much in return, Avery."

"Just come with me and help me find out what she's doing," Avery said fervently. "That's all I ask, Elliot."

"If I agree, what about the trip to Canada?"

"I can't answer that. I won't know until I'm sure where I stand with Sarah."

Elliot rubbed his jaw in thought. "It'll be a few weeks before we sail again, anyway. I suppose I can give you a hand . . . although I'll be damned if I ever thought I'd be saying such a thing to Avery Wallingford."

"Thank you, Elliot. This means a great deal to me."

Elliot stood up. "Let me know when you want me to accompany you. And in the meantime"—he pointed a finger at Avery—"you get busy raising money for the next voyage, and if you have any extra funds of your own hidden away, you'd best get them, too. I want to come back from Halifax with even more supplies than last time."

"All right, whatever you say, Elliot." Avery summoned up a smile. It had clearly been a tremendous effort for him to unburden himself and ask for assistance from a man he despised, but now that he had taken the first step, he seemed more at ease, more optimistic. He went so far as to clap a hand on Elliot's shoulder as Elliot turned toward the door.

"We'll get to the bottom of this, won't we?" Avery asked.

"We'll see," Elliot said noncommittally, trying not to flinch from Avery's touch.

Fate takes strange turns, he thought as he left the house. Only a year earlier, he had been engaged to Sarah, and now she was married to another man who suspected she was being unfaithful. And Elliot was going to help Avery find out the truth. If he had not been so depressed, he might have laughed.

Several days passed, and then, late one afternoon, Avery appeared at the Markhams' house. He said a cordial hello to Benjamin and Polly, then asked if he could speak to Elliot alone.

Elliot snagged his tricorn from the nail where it hung by the door.

"Come on," he grunted. "We'll take a walk down to the docks."

"Sarah's going out tonight," Avery said as they strolled along the lane lit by late-afternoon sunlight. "She didn't say where she was going."

"Did you ask her?"

"I was afraid to."

Elliot swallowed his disgust at the situation in which he had become entangled. No one had forced him to help Avery; it was his own fault that he was faced with the unpleasant prospect of spying on a young woman he had once loved.

"All right," he said. "We'll find out where she's going and who she's meeting. Do you think she suspects she might be followed?"

"I don't think she credits me with that much gumption," Avery said with a hollow laugh.

They had reached the docks, and Elliot saw Captain Beaumont on the deck of the Markham & Cummings ship. He waved at the captain, then turned to Avery.

"For now, just go home and try to keep things on an even keel. Don't do anything to make Sarah suspicious."

"I'll try," Avery said dubiously. Now that the time was at hand to carry out his threat to follow Sarah, he seemed to be having second thoughts.

"Do more than try," Elliot told him. "I'll see you later."

That evening, not long after nightfall, a knock sounded on the door of the Markhams' house. Elliot was expecting it, so he got up from the table where he and his parents had just finished a meager meal and went to answer the summons. When he swung the door open, Avery was standing there, dressed in a dark suit and black tricorn.

"She left a few minutes ago," Avery hissed. "Are you ready?"

Elliot reached for his hat. "I'll be back in a bit," he said over his shoulder to his parents.

"Who's that out there?" Benjamin growled with a touch of his old belligerence. "What are you up to, lad?"

"It's just Avery, Father," Elliot answered casually. "I won't be gone long."

Feeling like a little boy trying to cover up some mischief he was about to get into, he slipped out of the house before Benjamin or Polly could ask him anything else. Avery fell in step beside him as they walked quickly up the street, away from the harbor.

"This is the direction she went," he said. "We had better hurry."

There were few streetlamps anywhere in New York, but the area where most of the Tories lived was even darker than most. As they ran along the dusty streets, Elliot caught a glimpse of a figure passing through the tiny glow from a lamp several blocks ahead of them.

"Who's that?"

"I think it's Sarah," Avery replied. "It's difficult to tell at this distance, but that looks like her gown."

The finery that Sarah had brought with her from Boston had faded and frayed over the past few months, but it was still brightly colored enough to stand out from the shadows each time she passed through an area of light. Elliot and Avery gradually got close to her, and they were less than a block behind when Sarah reached a yard with a white picket fence around it. She opened a gate in the fence and turned in, following a stone walk up to a good-sized house.

Elliot and Avery tracked her progress by watching her silhouette against the lighted windows of the house, and Elliot put out a hand to stop Avery from going any closer.

"We can see enough from here," he whispered.

They moved into deep shadows under a tree beside the road, and Elliot was forced to tug on Avery's coat sleeve to get him to come along.

"Who lives there?" Avery asked. "I'm not familiar with that house."

"Neither am I," responded Elliot, keeping his voice pitched low. "But whoever owns it must be well-to-do. A house of that size is probably one of the oldest dwellings on the island."

Sarah must have been expected, because the door opened just as she reached it, spilling more lamplight onto the small porch. A man stepped out of the house to greet her, took her hands in his, then said something that Elliot and Avery could not hear.

Then the man leaned forward and kissed her.

Avery's breath hissed between his teeth, and he might have bounded out of the shadows and shouted in outrage had Elliot not clasped his arm firmly. Elliot's fingers tightened their grip as the man on the porch glanced up and down the street and then drew Sarah against him.

"Be still," Elliot hissed in Avery's ear. "You knew there was a good chance this was what we'd find."

"Who is he?" Avery asked in a trembling voice. "Who is that dog?"

Elliot had a fairly good look at the man's profile. He saw a strong nose and jaw, heavy eyebrows, and a sweep of thick dark hair. The man was rather handsome, Elliot supposed, or at least he would appear so to someone such as Sarah.

"That's Mark Hutchins," Elliot said to Avery. "I remember him from a meeting my father had with Mayor Matthews, right after we came to New York. Hutchins is one of Matthews's associates."

"Yes, of course," Avery breathed. "Theophilus and I were at that meeting as well. Hutchins is one of the leading Tories in the city." He gave a bitter chuckle. "Sarah is nothing if not ambitious. I'm surprised she didn't go after the mayor himself. I suppose his name occupies the next position on her list of conquests."

"You don't really know what's going on here, Avery," Elliot cautioned, but in the next moment Mark

Hutchins drew Sarah into the house, his arm around her shoulders, and shut the door behind them. It was all too obvious what was going on, Elliot thought.

"I know enough," Avery said, jerking his arm loose and raising his voice now that Sarah and her paramour had gone in. He reached inside his coat. "I know what to do about it, too."

Moonlight glittered faintly on the barrel of the pistol he had taken from beneath his coat.

"Put that away!" Elliot snapped. "Are you insane? What do you intend to do, break in there and shoot both of them?"

"I doubt that Sarah would hold still long enough for me to reload," Avery said. "But I can kill Hutchins, and then she'll have to live the rest of her life with the memory of her lover's death."

"And you'll be a murderer."

"Don't be ridiculous. A man is allowed to kill his wife's lover. Everyone knows that."

"Not when that lover is the second most powerful man in the city," Elliot said. "My God, Avery, we came here from Boston as fugitives, and it's only through the grace of men like Hutchins and Matthews that we were allowed to settle in New York. Do you want to turn everybody in town against us? Don't we have enough to worry about from the rebels?"

"But what can I *do*?" Avery asked, sounding completely wretched. "I can't just stand by and let that man have his way with my wife!"

"From what you've told me, that's probably already happened more than once," Elliot said, regretting that he had to be so brutally honest. "For now you're going to have to control your feelings until we figure out what to do next."

Avery stared at him in the gloom. "You mean you're going to help me?"

"I've come this far with you," Elliot replied grimly. "I suppose I might as well do what I can."

"Thank you, Elliot," Avery said fervently. "I never would have believed it, but you've become my friend again."

Lord save me from that, Elliot thought. But he did feel sorry for Avery, and the vestiges of affection he still felt for Sarah made him want to seek a resolution to this mess that would not hurt her too badly.

"Let's get out of here before someone notices us lurking around," he said.

At Elliot's urging, Avery put away the pistol and walked with him, muttering about how Sarah had betrayed him. Elliot paid little attention to his companion as he strode through the darkness, an ironic smile tugging at his mouth. It was not enough that he was still serving as a patriot secret agent and trying to help the Tory civilians at the same time. Now he had promised to sort out Avery and Sarah's marital entanglements as well. He supposed this was what was meant by the old saying about a choice of devils.

Chapter Twelve

Trailing Thomas Jefferson turned out to be a trickier proposition than Daniel Reed had expected. The road Jefferson was following led northeast toward Maryland, paralleling the Blue Ridge Mountains. It was the primary route through that part of the colony and ran almost as straight as an arrow to Baltimore and then on to Philadelphia. Daniel, Quincy, and Murdoch were forced to follow at a greater distance than they might have liked, and they ran the risk of not being close enough to come to the statesman's aid if he was attacked.

Luckily, they were not the only travelers on the

road. Even with the war against the British gaining momentum in the northern colonies, life was going on as usual in Virginia; farm wagons and carriages and men on horseback continued to use the road. With the other traffic as a form of camouflage, Daniel was sure that Jefferson would have a harder time spotting his three "guardian angels."

Still, the situation was worrisome, and by the time the pilgrims reached a small settlement on the banks of the Rappahannock River, Daniel was casting around in his mind for a better solution.

Two nights had passed since Jefferson and his servant, Bob, had left Monticello, and so far, there had been no trouble. Both nights the travelers had camped out, enjoying the warm weather of early summer. Daniel missed Roxanne and Joseph, and he knew that Quincy felt a similar longing for Mariel and the twins. But this adventure was good for the three men, Daniel decided. He and Quincy had both been through hell during the past year, traveling, fighting, experiencing both triumph and tragedy, suffering through periods of bleak despair. Being out of doors in such mild, pleasant weather and having a reasonably simple goal—keeping Jefferson and the money he carried safe until the politician reached Philadelphia—was a refreshing change.

In the late afternoon of the third day, faint strains of music floated to their ears.

Murdoch grunted and said, "Sounds like some sort o' celebration."

"Yes, it does," Daniel agreed. "But those aren't fifes and drums I hear. What sort of instruments are those?"

"I can't tell," Quincy said. "It reminds me of something, but I can't recall what it is." He frowned. "I remember there was a carnival camped on Boston

Common a couple of years ago, while I was still at the Latin School and you were attending Harvard, Daniel."

Now that Quincy mentioned it, Daniel recalled the colorful wagons that had served as transportation and home to some nomadic entertainers. He snapped his fingers and grinned.

"Gypsies!" he exclaimed. "They were Gypsies, Quincy, and that's a Gypsy flute and guitar we hear."

"Aye," Murdoch said. "That be Gypsy music, all right. I recollect th' wanderers visiting our village in Scotland when I was naught but a wee bairn. 'Twas said they'd steal yer babies an' leave one o' their own. The spawn of Romany, we called 'em."

"You don't sound like you're very fond of them," commented Quincy.

"I have nothing against 'em," Murdoch insisted, "only tha' they have a reputation as thieves an' liars." He grinned. "The women are mighty pretty, though."

"And the men are fast with their knives and hot-tempered," Daniel pointed out. "We'd best steer clear of the carnival while we're in this village up ahead. We've a job to do, and we can't be distracted."

"What if Mr. Jefferson goes to the carnival?" Quincy asked.

"That doesn't seem very likely to me," Daniel said. He reined in his horse when the three riders reached the top of a small rise and looked down at the village spread out on the banks of the river. He took a spyglass from his saddlebags and trained it on the settlement's main street. Half a dozen garishly painted wagons were parked on one end of the village green, but he was more interested in looking for Thomas Jefferson or the horses ridden by the politician and his servant. Luck was with Daniel. He spotted Jefferson entering a substantial stone and frame building with a sign over its door, and while Daniel was too far away to read the sign even with the spyglass, he felt sure the building was an inn.

"It looks as if Mr. Jefferson is searching for a room for the night. I thought perhaps he'd want to sleep in a bed again after spending the last two nights on the trail."

"This fella Jefferson is no' much of a frontiersman, is tha' what ye're saying?" Murdoch asked.

Daniel had to smile. "Thomas Jefferson is a great many things, but a frontiersman isn't one of them, at least not these days." He hitched his horse forward. "Let's ride down there. We can't risk taking rooms in the same inn, but perhaps we can stay close by."

There was a sizable crowd gathered around the Gypsy wagons. The music grew louder as they rode nearer, and the sound of enthusiastic clapping blended with the flute and the guitar. As they entered the village, Daniel caught a glimpse through the crowd of swirling red skirts and bare brown limbs as several young women danced to delight the spectators. Off to one side, a lean, swarthy man with a red neckerchief knotted on his head was putting on a display of knife throwing; the target at which he was aiming already bristled with blades.

Several tents dyed in alternating stripes of red, white, yellow, and green were set up between some of the wagons, and beyond the vehicles a rope corral had been put up for the glossy black horses that normally pulled the caravans. The carnival was colorful, noisy, and utterly intriguing to the citizens of this small Virginia village. On that afternoon with its bright sunshine and excitement, the bloody conflict with the British might as well not have existed.

And that wasn't altogether a bad thing, Daniel mused as he and his companions reined up in front of a tavern that rented rooms. Everyone needed a respite from their troubles now and then.

Daniel swung down from his horse, and as he did so he noticed that Quincy was looking along the green toward the Gypsies. There was a light of interest and curiosity sparkling in the young man's eyes, and Daniel wondered if he had made a mistake by declaring that they would not visit the carnival. After all, what harm could there be in watching some dancing and having your fortune told by an old Gypsy woman?

"Do you want to take a look?" Daniel asked his brother.

Quincy glanced at him in surprise. "I thought you said we shouldn't."

"Perhaps I was wrong," Daniel replied with a shrug. "Why don't I go in and get us some rooms for the night, and you and Murdoch can walk down the green and see what there is to see. Who knows, I might want to go later and have a look for myself."

Murdoch frowned darkly. " 'Tis no' sure I am o' this idea, Dan'l. Trouble follows these Gypsies, sure as me name's Buchanan."

"I don't think you're going to get into too much trouble in a peaceful little place like this. Go on," Daniel urged. "There's no reason we can't have a good time on this journey, as long as we remember why we're doing this."

"Well, that's certainly a different attitude than I'm used to from Daniel Reed," Quincy said with a laugh. "I was always the impulsive one, remember?"

"Things change, little brother." Daniel grinned. "Go on, both of you."

"Well, all right," grumbled Murdoch. "Come on, lad."

"You don't fool me, Murdoch," Quincy said as they walked off. "You're just as curious about all this as I am."

Daniel watched them for a moment as they strolled toward the far end of the green; then he turned and entered the tavern to see about securing lodging for the night.

Murdoch was still somewhat ill at ease as Quincy and he approached the Gypsy carnival. He could not have said why he felt that way; after all, he had faced redcoat troops and hordes of Indians in his time without flinching from the danger. What was there to worry about here?

Quincy, ignoring the knife-throwing exhibition, headed for the dancing first, and Murdoch let the young man lead the way. They joined the crowd of villagers gathered around the dancers. There were three girls and two boys dancing, none of them out of their late teens, all of them lithe and perspiring slightly from their exertions as they flung themselves through the elaborate moves of the Gypsy dance. An older man was playing the flute, and two men strummed guitars. Murdoch had to admit that the rhythms were infectious, and he found himself tapping his foot to the music as several onlookers, including Quincy, kept time by clapping.

The Gypsy girls danced in their bare feet, and their contortions sent their long skirts swirling up to reveal considerable expanses of tanned leg. The embroidered necklines of their peasant blouses swooped low enough to reveal even more skin, and as the thin fabric grew damp with sweat, it clung to their lush figures. Murdoch glanced around and saw the rapt expressions on the faces of the men watching the spectacle. The women were certainly having the desired effect, and men were throwing coins at the dancers' feet, bawdily expressing their admiration.

Murdoch's attention was drawn to a savory aroma

drifting through the late afternoon air, and he looked toward the wagons. A large iron pot had been set up over a fire built between two wagons, and the smell seemed to be coming from there. Quincy was completely wrapped up in the dancing, so Murdoch left him and ambled over to the cook pot. An elderly Gypsy woman was stirring its contents with a long-handled spoon.

"Would that be stew ye got cooking?" Murdoch asked her.

"Aye," she replied. "Would you like some?"

"Smells mighty good," Murdoch told her with a grin. "I would no' mind trying it."

"It will cost you a copper penny."

"I reckon I can manage that." Murdoch dug in one of his pouches and came up with a coin. He handed it to the old woman, who made it disappear into the folds of her long skirt with surprising deftness. She picked up an earthenware bowl from a stack sitting on the tailgate of the wagon, filled it with stew from the pot, and gave it to Murdoch along with a wooden spoon.

The stew was bubbling and steaming. Murdoch tried it cautiously, then nodded his approval with a wide grin.

"Tastes as good as it smells," he said. "I will no' ask ye what kind o' meat that is, though."

"A wise decision, backwoodsman," the woman said. "Do you wish your fortune told?"

"Ye read the palms, too, do ye?"

"Not me. Once I had the gift, but it has faded with time. Now my granddaughter Natalia is the one with the power to read the future."

"Maybe later," Murdoch said. "Right now I just want t' eat this stew."

By the time he drained the bowl, the dancing had broken up, and Murdoch gave the bowl and spoon back to the old woman, then went to fetch Quincy. The knife-throwing exhibition had ended, too, and a brief lull settled over the camp. Murdoch wondered what would happen next.

"Come have some stew," he told Quincy. " 'Tis mighty good."

"I want to see what the craftsmen have for sale," Quincy said. "I can eat later."

"Suit yourself." Murdoch followed along as Quincy inspected the goods laid out on colorful blankets. Most of the Gypsy artisans were either silversmiths or wood carvers, and there were some beautiful pieces on display.

Quincy negotiated with one of the men for a small silver teapot, finally haggling the price down to an acceptable level.

"I'll take this back to Mariel," he said with a smile as he and Murdoch moved on to see what else there was to amuse them.

A man emerged from one of the wagons and began to juggle an armful of brightly colored wooden balls. It was a dazzling display in the firelight, which had grown brighter as the sun set and dusk settled in. Quite a few of the villagers were lined up to sample the old woman's pot of stew, and Murdoch was glad he had eaten when he had the chance.

"Quincy! Murdoch!"

Murdoch glanced back to see Daniel catching up to them.

"I was just thinking about ye," Murdoch told him as he joined them. "Did ye find some rooms?"

"That I did, in the tavern where we left the horses. I haven't seen Mr. Jefferson, so I'm fairly certain he's still at the inn. He'll probably take his supper there and then retire for the night."

"Do you think he's safe?" asked Quincy.

"For now. We'll take turns standing guard later. There's a big tree right beside the inn, and we can use its shadows to conceal us from anyone trying to sneak into the place."

Murdoch agreed with the plan.

"Ye should get yerself some o' that stew the old woman is dishing out. Just dinna ask too many questions about what be in it."

"All right," Daniel said, grinning at the Scotsman. "Come on, Quincy, let's try it."

Murdoch was going to tag along with them, but a sudden commotion caught his attention. He turned to see a big man emerging from one of the Gypsy wagons. The man towered over the villagers around him, his broad shoulders well displayed under an embroidered vest. A bright red sash was belted around his middle, and he wore a pair of loose Gypsy pants and high black boots. His skull was as bald as an egg, save for bushy eyebrows and an astonishing sweep of mustache that curled up at each end. In one hand he carried a small round table made of such a thick chunk of wood that it had to be heavy, although he handled it as if it weighed nothing. There were two chairs in his other hand. As he glowered around at the crowd, clearing a small circle, he put the table in the center of the open space and the chairs on either side of it.

"Who will dare to challenge Gregor the Magnificent?" he bellowed in a voice that sounded like an outraged grizzly bear's.

Murdoch hesitated only a second before facing the mountainous Gypsy across the table. "Challenge ye t' what?" he asked.

"No one has ever defeated Gregor in the art of arm wrestling," proclaimed the big man, speaking with great bravura.

Murdoch supposed the arrogance was just part of the show, but it got under his skin. "Indian wrestling, we call it over here, mister," he told Gregor, "and I be a fair hand at the game."

Gregor gestured at the table with a hand the size of a small ham.

"Sit down and try your luck," he invited. "It will cost you only a copper penny."

"An' if I win?"

Gregor threw back his head and laughed as though the very idea was ludicrous.

"It will not happen, but if it does, you can have your choice of the articles my brother the silversmith has made."

"Fair enough." Murdoch pulled back the chair nearest him and sat down.

Gregor settled his considerable bulk in the chair opposite and planted his right elbow on the table. Murdoch did likewise. As big as Murdoch was, the Gypsy was a little taller and heavier. There was more to strength than sheer size, however, and Murdoch was confident that he had a good chance of defeating the man.

They locked hands in the center of the table, each man adjusting his stance and grip slightly, getting comfortable for what might be a long struggle. Onlookers surrounded them, and Murdoch heard some of them exchanging wagers. Gregor seemed to be the favorite, but quite a few members of the crowd were betting on Murdoch, too.

"Anytime you are ready, backwoodsman," said Gregor, his lip curling in a sneer.

Muscles rippled in the men's arms and shoulders as they threw their weight against each other. Their hands, locked together in the center of the table, swayed and quivered but didn't move more than an inch in either direction. It was clear they were evenly matched and this would be a contest of endurance rather than strength.

The noise from the crowd grew in volume as seconds ticked past and became minutes. Murdoch's hand began to dip toward the table, prompting cheers from the spectators who had wagered on Gregor, but then the frontiersman gradually forced Gregor's arm upright once more, bringing groans of disappointmemt from those who had thought the match was almost at an end. In fact, the tide had turned slowly in Murdoch's favor, and he saw Gregor's eyes widen slightly in surprise. It was doubtful that the massive Gypsy often encountered this much opposition. He probably crushed his opponents in short order.

But not tonight. Tonight Gregor was in for the battle of his life. Sweat bathed their faces as they strained against each other. Time had no meaning now, and the onlookers gathered around the table seemed to fade away into nothingness. Murdoch was unaware of anything but the struggle against Gregor, who stopped his progress and inexorably pushed the contest back into a stalemate.

Murdoch wondered fleetingly if they were still going to be sitting here grunting and straining come sunup.

The next instant, a gun blasted somewhere nearby.

The heavy boom brought startled yells from the crowd, and someone screamed.

Murdoch reacted instinctively. The muscles in his shoulders bunched and corded, and he slammed Gregor's hand down against the table. It wasn't a fair victory; Murdoch knew that. Gregor had been as surprised by the gunshot as everyone else. But Murdoch no longer cared about the contest. He stood up so quickly that his chair overturned, and he looked around to see what had happened. His right hand was numb and his arm was limp, so he reached with his left hand for one of the pistols tucked into his belt.

He spotted Daniel and Quincy standing nearby and knew they must have been watching the arm-wrestling contest.

"What was that shot?" he asked Daniel.

"I don't know, but it came from over there," Daniel replied, pointing to a knot of people struggling beside one of the colorful wagons.

The crowd was streaming in that direction, and Murdoch, Daniel, and Quincy joined them. The figures beside the wagon broke apart, resolving themselves into two separate groups, one of Gypsies and one of townspeople.

One of the villagers was holding his arm, and the sleeve of his coat was stained with blood. "The bastard cut me!" the man cried. "I'm bleeding to death!"

One of the Gypsy men brandished a knife, and in the firelight it was plain to see that the blade was wet with blood. Murdoch recognized him as the one who had put on the knife-throwing exhibition earlier.

The Gypsy said angrily, "You tried to kill Natalia. I had to stop you."

A woman dressed in the long skirt and peasant blouse of Romany stood behind the group of Gypsy men. They were protecting her, but from the fierce, furious expression on her face, it was difficult to tell if she wanted to be protected. She looked as though she wanted to attack the villagers herself.

"Let me have him, Anton!" she said to the man with the knife. "I will show him his future!"

"That's all I wanted in the first place," exclaimed the injured man. "She cheated me, damn it! She took my money and then wouldn't read my palm!"

"I read it, you dog!" the woman called Natalia spat back at him. "It said you would die within the year."

"That's a lie!" the villager yelled. "You never told me that!"

Natalia shrugged shoulders left bare by the peasant blouse she wore.

"I saw no point in it," she said.

The wounded man turned to his companions. "You know they're a bunch of lyin' thieves. We never should've let 'em camp here in the first place! Let's run 'em out of town!"

Angry shouts of agreement came from a few of his companions.

"We are not thieves!" said the man called Anton. He was still weaving his knife in front of him in an almost hypnotic motion, keeping the angry crowd at bay. "We want only to be left in peace."

This situation had the potential to become mighty ugly, Murdoch thought. The villagers were lining up on one side, the Gypsies on the other. If more violence broke out, it could turn into a full-fledged riot.

"Hold on there, blast it!" Daniel said sharply as he stepped forward, hoping to avoid a bloodbath.

The injured man, who was awfully loud for someone who claimed to be bleeding to death, swung toward him angrily.

"Who the hell are you?" he demanded. "What business is this of yours?"

Daniel hesitated, and Murdoch knew that he didn't want to reveal their true identities. To do that would be to chance Thomas Jefferson hearing about their presence here.

"It doesn't matter who I am," Daniel said. "Other than being an outsider who perhaps sees things a bit more clearly than you people. It sounds to me as if the

Gypsy woman was only defending herself. You *did* threaten her with a gun, mister."

"Only when she refused to tell my fortune and wouldn't give my money back!"

"As I said, I wished to spare you," Natalia put in. She spat on the ground. "I wish now I had not hesitated to tell you your fate."

"You could've given me back my money."

Natalia just stared coldly at him, as if she did not comprehend the concept of what he was saying.

"Here." Daniel held out a coin toward the wounded man. "Take it and go on about your business. This is over."

The villager reached for the coin, then stopped abruptly before taking it. He glared at Daniel.

"You got no right to come in here and lord it over us like you was ol' German George himself. Keep your money, you son of a bitch."

And with that, he swung his good arm straight at Daniel's head.

Daniel ducked and darted to the side, but one of the man's friends had launched a blow that caught him on the jaw. The impact sent Daniel stumbling backward against Quincy. Two villagers leapt at them and might have bowled into them if Murdoch's long arms had not shot out and grabbed their collars, and with a shout he brought the attackers' heads slamming together. They sagged, and he let them fall to the ground.

Daniel drove a fist into the belly of the man with the wounded arm. This had gone too far to stop now. The villagers were howling for blood, and the Gypsies surged forward, joining the fracas. Suddenly the area around the wagons was a madhouse of frenzied violence. Fists flew, but luckily no shots rang out. Murdoch and Gregor waded into the crowd, fighting on the same side. Their powerful arms and rocklike fists felled men right and left.

Daniel and Quincy were also in the thick of the fighting, but Murdoch was too busy to keep up with what was happening to them. He had his hands full as the villagers swarmed around him and tried to pull him off his feet. With a roar and a shrug of his wide shoulders, he flung several of them away.

At the sudden crash of a shotgun everyone froze. Several men strode into the middle of the crowd carrying fowling pieces. One of them called out authoritatively, "What the devil is going on here? What's all the ruckus about?"

"The damned Gypsies tried to cheat us, Constable Brooks," one of the townsmen cried. "Why don't you arrest the swarthy sons of bitches?"

The constable turned to Anton, who had dropped his knife during the struggle. There were bruises on the Gypsy leader's face, and the red kerchief on his head had been knocked askew.

"We meant to cheat no one," he declared. "We want only to conduct our business in peace."

"Their business is robbin' good honest folks!" shouted one of the townspeople.

Daniel caught Murdoch's eye and motioned slightly with his head. Along with Quincy, they moved into the shadows between the wagons. They didn't want to get involved in this dispute any more than they already had. It would be just fine if the constable overlooked them.

For the next few minutes, charges and counter-charges were flung back and forth between the Gypsies and the villagers. Finally the constable shook his head in frustration.

"This carnival is over!" he declared loudly. "You folks go back to your homes, and as for you Gypsies, I want you out of here at first light. If there's any more trouble, I'll throw the whole lot of you in the stocks!"

There was some grumbling from the crowd, but they began to drift away. The Gypsies huddled together by the wagons until the villagers were gone, and the constable gave them another warning, then strode off with his deputies.

Daniel waited until the authorities had left, then stepped out of the shadows with Murdoch and Quincy. The Gypsy leader looked at them in surprise.

"Are all your people all right?" Daniel asked.

"I believe this is so," Anton said slowly. "Thank you for trying to help us."

"We don't like unfair fights," Daniel said simply. "We'll be going now."

"You are welcome to stay and share our fire," Anton said.

Murdoch felt eyes watching him and looked over to see the Gypsy fortune-teller gazing at him. She was older than the dancers, in her late twenties perhaps, but no less beautiful. If anything, she was even more attractive because of an unblushing sensuality about her. Her hair was the color of midnight and fell in thick curls around her olive-skinned face. Her lips were full and red, her eyes dark and sparkling with mysterious fire. The thrust of her bosom against the peasant blouse was magnificent.

Daniel was telling Anton that they couldn't accept his offer of hospitality, and while Murdoch understood why, to his surprise he found himself wishing they could spend more time in the Gypsy camp. Perhaps he had been wrong about them all these years, he thought.

But regretfully he was not going to have a chance to find out. He and Daniel and Quincy had a job to do, and that came first. After saying their farewells, they headed along the green toward the tavern where Daniel had rented rooms for them.

"I thought you didn't like Gypsies," Quincy commented as he walked beside Murdoch. "You pitched in to help them fast enough."

"I did'na want anyone getting th' best o' that fella Gregor unless it be me," replied Murdoch. "We never really finished that Indian-wrestling match."

"And if they leave town at first light, you won't have a chance to," Daniel pointed out. "But I'm afraid we have more important things to worry about."

"Aye," Murdoch agreed grudgingly.

But he would have liked to know who would have won the contest, and he would have liked to see more of the woman called Natalia. . . . He grinned to himself, shook his head, and walked on into the night with his friends.

Chapter Thirteen

The sky was dark and starless behind a barrier of clouds that covered the Virginia coastline. The only illumination came from a faint phosphorescence that glowed on the waves as they rolled in toward the isolated beach. A dark shape moved over the water, gradually resolving itself into a small boat rowed by several British sailors. Farther offshore, lost in the gloom, was the warship from which the small boat had come to deliver its passengers.

Major Alistair Kane sat stiffly in the stern of the boat while the sailors manned the oars. The motion of the waves did not bother him, but if there had been enough light, Cyril Eldridge would have been seen to be positively green. He had been seasick ever since the warship had left England. Most men got their sea legs after a few days, but it had become clear that Eldridge would never become accustomed to the ship's pitching. He had spent most of the time hanging over the railing, and during the voyage his features had grown more pale and pinched than ever. All he wanted now was to set foot on dry land.

Kane pointed off to the south. "That's Cape Henry, although it's too dark to see it. Around the tip of the cape is Norfolk, which according to the captain of the ship has been burned almost to the ground by our troops. Portsmouth is several miles beyond Norfolk. Chesapeake Bay is to the north, although you can't see it, either."

"You don't for one moment believe that I really *care* about all these geographical details, do you, Major?" Eldridge all but groaned.

"I thought you might be interested," Kane said with a shrug of his shoulders. "This is your first visit to the colonies, isn't it, Minister?"

"Yes, blast it, and I wish I'd never had reason to come here." Eldridge clutched the bench on which he sat as the boat crested a wave. The sound of the water crashing on the beach ahead could be heard plainly.

"We'll head up the northern side of the James River once we've landed," Kane mused. "I hope the agent is waiting for us with the horses."

"I sent the message ahead of us on one of the faster ships," Eldridge said. "Everything should be arranged. I certainly hope that proves to be—ohhh . . ." His words trailed off in another moan.

"I'm anxious to find out just how strong the rebel forces are in this area," Kane said in an unsympathetic tone, for the benefit of the sailors who were rowing the boat. As far as the officers and crew of the British warship were concerned, Eldridge and he were on an espionage mission for the Crown. The two men had said nothing in the hearing of others about Roxanne Darragh or revenge or inheritances. Eldridge ignored Kane's comment, and Kane decided not to bother trying to make the man feel any better. *Let him stew in his own juices,* he thought.

A few minutes later, as he peered through the night, he was able to make out the beach. The sand formed a light-colored line in the darkness that grew as the oarsmen rowed the boat closer. Within a matter of minutes two sailors had hopped agilely from the boat and were pulling it up onto the wet sand.

Kane stepped out. Water splashed around the ankles of his high-topped military boots. The boots were the only part of his uniform he was wearing at the moment, and they were not so distinctive as to give away his true identity. Otherwise he was garbed in nondescript civilian clothes, just as Eldridge was. Neither of them looked like important Englishmen, and that was just the impression they wanted to give. The goal was to blend into the Virginia countryside while they searched for their quarry.

A man leading two horses appeared at the far end of the beach; the dark bulks of the animals appeared monstrous against the light sand.

"Yorkshire pudding!" the man called out.

"Kidney pie," replied Eldridge with a shudder. "God, I hate passwords."

"Part of the game," Kane commented. He was in good humor, glad to be back on this side of the Atlantic. "At least you're on dry land again, Minister."

"And don't think I don't appreciate it," Eldridge snapped. "Come along." He turned to the sailors and continued, "Tell your captain that you saw us delivered safely ashore. Beginning one week from tonight, you're to check this beach each night and send in a boat as soon as you see our signal fire. Is that understood?"

The lieutenant in charge of the detail gave Eldridge and Kane a crisp salute.

"Understood, sir," he said. "Good luck and Godspeed on your mission."

Eldridge mumbled a reply, but Kane said smartly, "Thank you, Lieutenant," as he returned the young officer's salute.

They waited until the boat had pushed off and slowly made its way against the tide, toward the warship, before taking the reins of the horses from the agent who had met them.

"How do things look here in Virginia?" Kane asked the man.

"Been no hostilities since His Majesty's troops burned Norfolk and then pulled out again," the British agent replied. "Most folks seem to think there'll be trouble sooner or later, but they don't know when. The Continental Congress is supposed to meet in Philadelphia in a few weeks, and it's generally figured that war'll be declared when they do."

"Let them come up with any sort of declaration they like," Eldridge said coldly. "In point of fact, they're already at war with us, and nothing they can do will make their treasonous actions legal."

The agent leaned over and spat on the beach. He was a lean, bearded man, probably a fisherman, Kane thought. "I guess treason's the least of the worries those gents have," the man said. "They've gone too far to turn back now."

"Aye, that's certainly true," Kane told him. "Thank you for meeting us with these mounts. You've done a good job, and it won't be forgotten when this revolution is put down."

"Just doing my duty to the Crown," the man said. "Where're you fellas headed from here?"

"Do you know where the Rivanna River is?" Kane asked.

The man pointed to the northwest. "Just follow the James. The Rivanna branches off from it a good ways inland. Folks who live along the river can tell you where it is."

"Thanks again," Kane said, making a conscious effort to suppress his British accent and sound American.

"Yes, thank you," Eldridge said, also trying not to sound too much like an upper-crust Englishman, although he was not as successful in the attempt as Kane. They could work on their accents as they made their way inland, Kane supposed.

They swung up into their saddles. Kane settled his tricorn on his head and heeled the horse into a brisk trot. Eldridge followed along behind, somewhat awkward in the way he rode.

The wind was blowing in strongly from the sea, and the clouds were breaking up, revealing patches of stars and finally the moon. Kane wondered if this was an omen; they had been blessed with darkness during the landing, and now they were being given light to guide them on their way. Off to his left, he could see the silvery illumination reflecting off the bay that formed the mouth of the James River. As long as he kept the river on his left hand, he would not get lost. He and Eldridge could follow it all the way across the Tidewater and into the rolling hills of the Piedmont.

Somewhere up ahead, across many miles of darkness, was the Reed plantation. Roxanne was there. Kane was sure of it. He could feel it in his bones, in the very core of his being. Each long-gaited stride of the horse beneath him brought him that much closer to the woman he loved—despite her betrayal.

The woman who would soon be his once again.

An icy shiver down his spine woke Daniel. He knew he had been dreaming, but the details were already fading from his mind. All he remembered was that the dream was about Roxanne and Joseph, and that they had been in danger, danger from which Daniel was helpless to save them.

He wiped beads of sweat off his forehead. When he looked around, he realized he was in the room above the tavern that he had rented the night before. Quincy, Murdoch, and he were still in the village on the shore of the Rappahannock River, and Quincy was asleep in the other narrow bunk. Murdoch was standing guard under the big tree next to the inn where Thomas Jefferson was staying. Murdoch had taken the last watch, relieving Daniel earlier in the night.

Daniel knew he would not sleep anymore after the disturbing dream, so he swung his legs out of bed and stood up, crossing to the room's single window and pushing back the curtain to gaze out. There was a line of grayish-red light on the eastern horizon, portending the rising of the sun. It would be dawn in less than an hour.

Jefferson was an early riser, Daniel knew. It was time Quincy and he were up and about as well, getting ready to travel.

Something caught his eye as he started to turn away from the window, and he looked down at the village green where the Gypsy wagons were parked. He saw movement around the vehicles and assumed the Gypsies were getting ready to depart, too, as they had been ordered to by the constable.

Suddenly an idea burst in Daniel's brain. He had

been trying to think of a way he and Quincy and Murdoch could keep an eye on Thomas Jefferson without being noticed by the statesman, and now he thought he knew. Quickly he pulled on his clothes and hurried downstairs.

He left the tavern and walked up the green toward the wagons. In the dim gray light the bright colors of the vehicles were muted, but there was quite a bit of movement around them, and as Daniel approached he spotted Anton.

"Good morning," he called as Anton finished hitching a team of horses to one of the wagons.

Anton turned sharply toward him, one hand darting instinctively toward the hilt of a knife tucked behind the sash around his waist. He stopped when he recognized Daniel.

"What do you want?" Anton asked without any greeting.

Daniel supposed that was understandable; he would not be very friendly if he were being run out of town, either.

"I was wondering if you could tell me where you're headed from here," Daniel asked, keeping his tone civil. "It wouldn't be toward Philadelphia, would it?"

Anton's eyes narrowed in suspicion. "Why do you wish to know?" he demanded.

"My brother and my friend and I don't want to cause you any trouble. But if you're going north toward Philadelphia, I'm hoping you might consent to let us travel with you."

Anton shook his head curtly. "No," he said without hesitation and then turned away, clearly intending to end the conversation.

Without thinking, Daniel reached out and grasped Anton's arm. "Wait a minute—"

Uttering what sounded like a curse in an unknown tongue, he jerked free of Daniel's grip, and the knife appeared in his fingers as if by magic.

"No one lays hands on me!" Anton blazed.

A massive shape stepped around the team of horses and reached out; a gigantic hand held Anton's shoulder in a tight grip.

"Only your brother," growled the man Daniel recognized as the huge Gypsy called Gregor. "Put the blade away, Anton. This boy has no wish to harm us. He and the other two helped us last night."

Gregor had changed since the previous evening. Gone was the arrogance with which he had greeted Murdoch's challenge, and Daniel sensed that was all part of an act.

Gregor greeted Daniel kindly, and Anton reluctantly put away the knife.

"My brother is sometimes too quick to anger," Gregor said in his rumbling voice. "But he is a good man and a wise leader. It is just that we have been forced to leave many villages in disgrace, and we are tired of it."

"I'm sorry you have to leave," Daniel said, "but it's important that I know if Quincy and Murdoch and I can travel with you. If you're headed north, that is. I still haven't gotten an answer to that question."

"We are going to Baltimore and then Philadelphia," Anton admitted grudgingly. "But we will not allow outsiders to travel with us."

"Please, just listen to me for a few minutes," he said. "It's important."

A woman pulling a shawl tight around her shoulders against the predawn chill strolled around the wagon. She was Natalia, the fortune-teller who had precipitated the riot the night before, Daniel recalled.

"Let the young man speak," she said to Anton. "I would hear what he has to say."

"I am the leader here!" Anton responded hotly. "You have no right—"

"I am your sister," Natalia snapped, "and Gregor is your brother. We have every right to be involved in any decisions regarding this band. You have forgotten that our grandfather still lives, Anton, and no one knows whether his power will be vested in you or Gregor when he dies."

"But we know *you* will not be our leader," Anton said.

"Let the young man talk," Gregor rumbled.

More Gypsies were wandering up to see what was going on, and Anton became aware that he had to do something to salvage his dignity. He turned to Daniel and nodded slowly.

"I will allow you to speak," he said in a magnanimous tone.

Daniel didn't care how pompous the man sounded; he just wanted to present his idea to the nomads. Over the next few minutes he told them about Thomas Jefferson's journey to Philadelphia and how he, Quincy, and Murdoch were trying to protect the politician without Jefferson being aware of their actions. He refrained from any mention of the money Jefferson was carrying, however, making it sound as if Jefferson was in danger simply because he was a leader in the patriot cause. After all, there was no point in tempting *anyone* by talking too much about the money.

He concluded by saying, "I thought that if we could travel with you, we could disguise ourselves as members of your band, and then Mr. Jefferson would never notice us. We could keep a close eye on him that way."

Anton shook his head jerkily. "Impossible," he

stated. "For non-Gypsies to pretend to be sons of Rom
. . . it cannot be done."

"Of course it can," Natalia said. "We owe these
men a debt of honor, Anton. They tried to defend us
from the villagers when no one else would."

"Yah," added Grcgor. "And I would like to have a
chance to try that big redheaded one again. Our contest
last night was cut short by the trouble."

Anton crossed his arms over his chest and frowned.
"Our people have been neutral in this conflict between
the Americans and the British. We have no interest in
who wins a war. All we want is to be left alone to live our
lives."

"That's exactly the way we Americans felt before
Lexington and Concord," Daniel said meaningfully.

Anton hesitated a moment longer, then sighed. "I
will not object to this plan of yours. But you will not
dishonor us, and you will be responsible for your own
safety."

"Of course," Daniel agreed.

"Go get your brother and your friend," Natalia told
him. "I will find clothing for the three of you."

"Thank you," Daniel said with a grin. "We'll be
back as soon as we can."

Anton glared at him. "Be here when we are ready
to leave or we will go without you," he warned.

Daniel hurried down the green. He stopped first at
the inn where Jefferson was staying and walked around
to the side where the large tree was. Murdoch stepped
out from the shadows under its spreading branches, his
flintlock rifle cradled in the crook of his left arm.

"What are ye doing here, Dan'l? I figured ye'd still
be asleep."

"I've been down at the other end of the green talking to the Gypsies. We're going to be traveling with them."

"Traveling with 'em?" he repeated, his bushy red eyebrows lifting in surprise. "Why would we want t' do tha'?"

"Because they're going to Philadelphia, and Mr. Jefferson isn't likely to notice three extra Gypsies."

A grin spread across Murdoch's rugged face. "Aye, that be a good idea, but I be a mite surprised them Gypsies went along with it."

"I talked Anton into it, with some help from Gregor and Natalia. You seem to have made a friend in Gregor."

"What about Natalia?" Murdoch asked with a chuckle.

"I'll leave finding out about that up to you," Daniel said dryly. "Have you seen any sign of Mr. Jefferson?"

"Not yet this morning, but that servant, Bob, has got their horses saddled and ready t' ride. I dinna expect it t' be much longer before they set out."

"That's all right. We'll be pulling out about the same time, I imagine. Come on, let's go roust Quincy out of bed."

Quincy was surprised at the plan but quickly became enthusiastic. "We'll be pretending to be Gypsies, you say?"

"That's right," Daniel said.

"Well, let's go." Quincy hurriedly pulled his clothes on. "We don't want them to leave without us."

When they reached the wagons, Natalia was waiting for them.

"Come inside this caravan," she said, holding open a door in the back of one of the vehicles, which were taking on their usual garish hues with the rising of the sun.

Daniel, Quincy, and Murdoch followed her inside the wagon and were surprised that it was furnished much like a room in a house, complete with bed, several chairs, and a tall cabinet from which Natalia took three silken shirts, two of them a bright red, the other a dark blue. The blue shirt was the largest, and Natalia handed it to Murdoch.

"This belongs to my brother Gregor," she told him, "but I think it will fit you. No one else in our band would have anything your size."

"Thank ye," Murdoch grunted as he took the garment. He kept his eyes averted, as if he was embarrassed to look directly at Natalia.

She smiled faintly and added sashes and kerchiefs to the garb she was handing out.

"Wear these as well," she told them. "Soon no one will be able to tell that you are not real Gypsies."

"That's what I'm hoping," Daniel said. "It's still a long way to Philadelphia, and a lot could happen between here and there."

"We will do everything we can to help you," promised Natalia. "And do not worry about Anton. He will come around."

Daniel pulled off his shirt when Natalia slipped out of the wagon and closed the door behind her. Quincy and Murdoch donned their Gypsy costumes as well, and the three men, smiling at one another and feeling somewhat foolish, left the wagon, swung up onto their horses, and prepared to leave town.

Ten minutes later the caravan departed, the wagon wheels creaking as they rolled along the rutted road.

Murdoch had spotted Thomas Jefferson and his servant leaving town only a few minutes earlier. Jefferson and Bob would make slightly better time than the group of wagons, but Daniel thought they should be able to keep up fairly well. He, Quincy, and Murdoch could always push ahead if they needed to, because they were on horseback rather than on the wagons. He doubted that anyone would notice three new Gypsies clad in the bright costumes of Romany with the group.

They headed north as the morning sun climbed the sky, north toward Philadelphia.

Chapter Fourteen

T he sun was setting as Elliot Markham strode quickly away from the harbor toward the area of New York where his parents lived. He had spent the afternoon talking with Captain Beaumont on the Markham & Cummings ship, and he had intended to be home before now.

More than a week had passed since Elliot and Avery Wallingford had followed his wife, Sarah, to her rendezvous with Mark Hutchins. Since then she had stayed home, but Elliot knew it was only a matter of time until she went back to Hutchins. However, he had yet to come up with any suitable plan for dealing with the problem, despite the fact that Avery was pressuring him to do something. Elliot hoped that Avery would be able to control his outraged ego; a confrontation with Hutchins at this point would serve little purpose. It would be better, Elliot had decided, to think of something that would make Sarah *want* to remain faithful to her husband. But knowing Avery as he did, that had proven an exceedingly difficult assignment for Elliot.

There was more than Avery and Sarah's marital difficulties and the upcoming trip to Canada on Elliot's mind this evening. It had been almost two weeks since his meeting at Corbie's Tavern with the prostitute called Casey, and in that time he had heard nothing from the ginger-haired informant. She had promised to try to find out more about the mysterious group known as the King's Militia and get in touch with him as soon as she had some information. He hoped that she was merely having a difficult time unearthing facts about the group and not that she had done something to make them suspicious of her.

Although he knew nothing about the King's Militia but its name, he was certain the organization's members would not hesitate to kill someone they suspected of being a patriot spy.

Elliot walked through the gathering shadows of twilight. He was borrowing trouble, he told himself. There was no reason to think that Casey was in any real danger, and anyway, she was nothing to him other than a possible source of useful information. True, she had been an energetic and enjoyable bed partner, but Elliot had never lacked female companionship. There was always another doxy to be had. But he kept seeing Casey's gaminelike face floating in his mind's eye.

"Hello, guv. Miss me?"

For a second Elliot thought he had imagined her voice. Then he stumbled, breaking stride as he realized that Casey was sauntering along the street with him. She wore a thin gown with a square, low-cut neckline and had a bonnet tied over her mass of ginger hair. Her freckled features were set in a roguish grin.

"Damnation!" Elliot exclaimed. "Where did *you* come from? I was just thinking about you."

"Well, that's mighty nice to know, that a swell gent like yourself can't get a girl like me out of his thoughts. As for where I came from, I was waiting in that alley back there."

Elliot grimaced in disgust at himself. He had walked right past the mouth of the alley without paying any attention to who might be lurking there. If it had been an enemy instead of Casey, he might be dead by now, shot from ambush. And deservedly so for letting his mind wander, he told himself.

"How did you know I'd be here?"

"Why, sir, I knew somebody would come along to help me out," she said in a loud voice as she linked her arm in his and let her hip bump softly against him.

Elliot realized she was putting on an act for the passersby, several of whom were now in earshot. She was pretending to be a common trollop on the prowl for a potential customer—a role in which she had undoubtedly had considerable practice, Elliot mused, then chided himself for such an ungracious thought. He had always treated even the lowest whore as deserving of *some* respect.

"I'm not sure I want to be bothered," he said, also for the benefit of anyone who might be listening, but the pedestrians seemed to be paying no attention to them, however, and he relaxed slightly.

Casey leaned close and said into his ear, "Agree with what I'm saying. I have some information for you."

"All right," Elliot consented, again loud enough to be overheard. He laughed and added, "That certainly sounds intriguing. Where would you like to go, my dear?"

"T' my place?"

"An excellent idea."

They soon found themselves in the vice district ironically known as the Holy Ground, and once again Casey led him down a dark alley and up the stairs to her room. There was still a bit of fading light in the sky from the sunset, but the illumination didn't reach into the dingy, twisting hallway.

Once the door of the room was shut behind them and Casey had lit a candle, Elliot demanded sharply, "What's going on here? How did you know where to find me?"

"No questions," she said with a seductive smile as she swayed toward him and pressed her hands against his chest. "Right now this is all I'm interested in."

She reached up with her mouth and kissed him. Elliot had sworn to himself that he would resist her temptations and put this relationship on a business level. That was before he felt the wet heat of her tongue parting his lips and sliding between them to flick maddeningly against his own tongue.

He returned the kiss and tightened his arms around her until her bountiful breasts were crushed against his chest.

When she finally took her mouth away from his, she inclined her head toward the bed. She looked so pensive that Elliot's resolve crumbled, and he could not resist her entreaty. Laughing, he moved toward the bed, keeping her locked in his arms so that she had to back up. When they reached the side of the bed, Casey fell backward onto the thin mattress and pulled Elliot with her.

He cupped one of her breasts with his hand, and he could feel the erect nipple prodding against his palm through the thin fabric of her dress. He squeezed lightly, eliciting a soft moan from her.

"How did you find me?" Elliot whispered.

Casey's fingers fumbled with the laces of his breeches.

"Much of New York is talking about someone bringing in a load of supplies for the Tories a while back," she replied, the words hissing between her teeth. "I heard rumors it was you and knew you might be found at the docks. I've been watching for you for days."

She tilted her head, and his lips nuzzled along the line of her jaw and then tasted the soft flesh of her throat.

"What have you found out?" he murmured as he grudgingly took his mouth away from her skin but kept his hands busy.

"There's going to be a . . . a meeting . . . of the King's Militia—ohhh!"

Elliot stifled her cry of passion by kissing her again. By now they were too inflamed to continue with the questioning.

For long minutes there were no sounds in the tiny room but the rustle of clothes being removed and the hushed cries and gasps of desire being satisfied. Elliot found himself lost in Casey and their lovemaking, all thoughts of the plight of the Tories, the King's Militia, and everything else concerning his double life forgotten in the tide of lust that carried him along. When they were finally sated and Elliot was stretched out on his back with Casey snuggled against him, it was several moments more before he regained sufficient breath to speak.

He turned his head and kissed her hair just above her ear, then whispered, "Tell me about this meeting of the King's Militia."

"I don't know what they have in mind," Casey replied breathlessly. "But I do know they plan to meet at a farm on Long Island. The place belongs to a man named Dawkins, and it's about a mile past Farley's Neck. Do you know the place?"

"I can find it," Elliot said confidently. "When is the meeting?"

"Tomorrow night."

He frowned. "You waited until rather the last minute to let me know, didn't you?"

"I told you, I've been looking for you for several days now," she said, sounding resentful of his chiding. "If I hadn't found you tonight, I would have come to your house."

Elliot pushed himself up on an elbow and peered down at her. "How do you know where I live?"

"I know a great deal about you, Elliot Markham," she said with an arch look. "While I might act like a common barmaid, my family has known better days. I even had my own tutor. I save my Cockney accent for the tavern; I'm a spy, remember?"

"A would-be spy," muttered Elliot, then went on hurriedly at her angry look, "You don't have any idea what the King's Militia is planning?"

"None at all. It took me over a week just to discover the information about the meeting."

"How did you find out about it?" Elliot asked curiously.

Casey smiled again. "Men talk more freely at times like this," she said.

For some unaccountable reason Elliot felt a surge of anger that made him sit up. "I don't have to hear about that," he said. "If you've nothing more to tell me, I'll be on my way."

"Wait!" she said as he started to stand up. She

reached out to grasp his arm. "You've forgotten something."

"Oh, yes. Just let me get my purse, and I'll find a coin for you."

Casey flinched as if he had struck her. "That's not what I meant. You're going out there, aren't you?"

"I've a feeling that it's important we know what these people are up to."

"Well, I wanted to tell you to be careful." She hesitated. "I don't want anything to happen to you, especially not on my account. I . . . I've come to enjoy these meetings."

Elliot coughed to hide the embarrassment he felt at the genuine concern he heard in her voice. He had no right to be resentful about her chosen means of survival, he realized. What mattered was her support for the patriot cause and her willingness to put her life on the line for it.

"I'll be careful," he promised her, "but the same caution applies to you. These are dangerous men we're dealing with."

"No more dangerous than what I'm accustomed to, sweet," she said lightly. Her hand rested on his bare arm for a moment, her fingers cool and smooth.

Elliot leaned over and brushed his lips over hers in a brief kiss, then began to pull on his clothes.

"You don't have to leave, you know," Casey said huskily. "That appointment of yours isn't until tomorrow night."

Elliot hesitated as he reached for his breeches. "You know," he said, a seductive smile appearing on his lips, "you're absolutely right. Tonight we have all the time in the world."

• • •

A ferry ran between Manhattan and the western end of Long Island, although it operated on a somewhat sporadic schedule these days due to the uncertainty of the times. Elliot was lucky and managed to catch the boat as it was leaving in the early evening of the following day. He led his horse on board and rode across the harbor with a dozen other passengers, two farm wagons with teams of mules hitched to them, and several saddle horses. Not surprisingly, the deck was awash with a mixture of harbor water and horse droppings, and Elliot was grateful for his high boots.

The trip took twenty minutes, and by the time Elliot led his mount off the ferry at the dock on Long Island, night had fallen. A lantern glowed over the doorway of the small office where the ferry owner conducted business, and Elliot tied his horse to a post at the front of the building.

"Excuse me, sir," he said through the open door, "can you tell me how to get to Farley's Neck?"

The lean, leathery ferry operator stood up from his desk and came to the door. "Farley's Neck, is it? What is it ye're wantin' with Farley's Neck?"

"I'm visiting relatives," Elliot lied, hoping that the man wouldn't ask for names. He didn't know a soul who lived on Long Island, and the only name he knew was Dawkins, the man who owned the farm where the King's Militia was supposed to meet.

"Ayuh." The man stepped out of the building and pointed down a road that ran northeast from the ferry landing. "Follow that road for about five miles. Ye can't miss the settlement."

"Thanks," Elliot said. He stepped to his horse and swung up into the saddle.

The ferry operator lounged against the side of the doorway and commented, "Lots of folks in Farley's Neck must have relatives visitin' 'em tonight. You ain't the first fella to ask f' directions."

"Is that so?" Elliot smiled genially. "Sounds like a popular place. Perhaps I'll move there."

"Ayuh," the Long Islander said dryly. "You do that, mister."

Elliot waved casually, then turned his horse and heeled the animal into a trot. As he rode along the lane he was glad for the moonlight that shone through the clouds and the lights from the farmhouses along the way, and he wondered if the other men looking for Farley's Neck were bound for the meeting of the King's Militia.

This end of Long Island had originally been settled by the Dutch, he knew, and many still lived here. This had been farmland for over a hundred years. To the south was a village called Flatbush, but he had never been there. In fact, tonight was the first time he had ever set foot on Long Island.

There were few travelers on the road. Elliot passed some farm wagons on their way to the barns from the fields, but he seemed to be the only person on horseback at the moment. According to the ferry operator, other visitors had asked for directions to Farley's Neck, and Elliot hoped the meeting wasn't already under way. He would draw more attention to himself by arriving late.

He would have guessed that a village with a name like Farley's Neck would be located near a narrow bridge of land spanning a body of water, but when he arrived at the settlement, he found it to be completely landlocked, several miles distant from Long Island Sound. Nor was there a pond or stream to be seen. Perhaps the name had come from some other, more grisly source. Not that it was important, Elliot told himself. All that mattered was finding the farm where the meeting would take place.

A lantern was burning over the doorway of a small general store, and a man was in the process of locking up for the night as Elliot rode up.

"Excuse me," he called to the man, whom he took to be the storekeeper. "Can you tell me where to find the Dawkins place?"

The man turned and looked at him with only slight curiosity. "Dawkins, ye say?" He rubbed his narrow jaw and frowned. "Dawkins, Dawkins . . . Seems like I've heard the name. . . ."

Elliot suppressed his impatience. He had to keep a civil tongue in his head or risk offending the man.

"It's a farm somewhere east of Farley's Neck. This *is* Farley's Neck, isn't it?"

"Oh, aye, this is Farley's Neck, all right." The man scratched his prominent chin. "Dawkins . . . Ye wouldn't be meanin' *Billy* Dawkins, would ye?"

"It could be," Elliot said, struggling to hold his temper in check.

"Well, why didn't ye say so? Billy Dawkins's farm is another two miles up the main road. Look for the big silo off to the south."

"Are there any other people named Dawkins who live around here?" Elliot asked, hoping there wouldn't be.

"None that I know of," the man replied. "But I thought it was Billy Dawkins ye said ye was lookin' for."

"It is," Elliot said quickly. "Thank you, sir."

"If ye be lookin' for anybody else, ye just come on back here anytime and ask me. I know ever'body on this here island."

"I'll do that," Elliot promised, then urged his horse into a trot again.

After he judged he had gone two miles, he began looking for the silo the man had mentioned. The moon shone clearly now, and Elliot had no trouble spotting the landmark. It rose into the night sky about a hundred yards from the main road. He found a lane leading toward it and turned his horse onto the narrow path. He saw lights burning to one side of the silo, and as he drew near he could tell that the illumination came from a large bonfire and many torches.

Well, this must be the place, he thought. With his muscles tensed, he rode to the edge of the brightly lit farmyard.

There were many horses tied there already, and at least a dozen men holding torches stood around the large open area surrounding the bonfire. For an organization that was supposed to be secret, they weren't going to much trouble to conceal their presence, Elliot thought. They clearly felt confident that they could assemble safely there.

He knew the men were watching him as he swung down from his horse and looped the reins around the tongue of an empty hay wagon where several other mounts had been tied. Then, spotting a pile of unlit torches stacked to one side, Elliot walked over, picked one up, and thrust it into the flames as though he had every right to be there. He knew that a man who acted as though he belonged stood a better chance of not being challenged.

With a friendly nod, Elliot joined the men. They returned his nod. A few of them looked vaguely familiar, and Elliot thought they might be Tories who had been forced to flee Boston at the end of the American siege.

Even if he was recognized, that was all right, he told himself. After all, he was known to be a Tory, too, and his father was well-known as a staunch supporter of the Crown. As far as the loyalists knew, he had just as much right to be at a meeting of the King's Militia as they did.

A man appeared in the open doorway of the large barn. "Come inside, men," he called. "We're ready to start."

Perfect timing, Elliot congratulated himself. He fell in step with the others, blending in with them, letting his torch sag just slightly so that it would be difficult to make out his facial features. The group trooped into the barn and joined another forty or fifty men already inside.

Elliot knew his situation was precarious, and he felt nervous. If anyone deduced his true calling as a patriot spy, he would stand no chance. These men could rip him to pieces, and he wouldn't be able to put up much of a fight. There was no reason they would know what he really was, though, he reassured himself.

The barn was smoky from the torches, but Elliot could see clearly enough as a man climbed onto the back of another empty hay wagon and held up his hands to get the attention of the crowd.

"Good evening, gentlemen," he called in a loud voice. "Thank you for coming. As you know, we are here to discuss the formation of a group dedicated to the support of the Crown and the crushing of the treasonous, unwashed rebels who have dared to oppose our beloved king!"

A cheer of agreement went up from the assembly, and Elliot joined in without hesitation.

The speaker, a ruggedly built man with a ruddy face and prominent nose, went on, "As some of you know, a small group of us have been planning a bold stroke against the rebels, and I give you now the man responsible for this daring initiative and the formation of our group!"

Elliot felt his pulse speed up. The ringleader of the King's Militia was about to speak, and with any luck the man would reveal the details of the group's plan. Elliot craned his neck slightly in order to get a better look at the man who stepped lithely onto the back of the wagon.

With a shock, Elliot recognized him immediately. The man was tall and handsome, with thick dark hair and eyebrows, and the last time Elliot had seen him, he'd had his arms around Sarah Wallingford.

The leader of the King's Militia was Mark Hutchins.

He shouldn't have been so surprised, Elliot thought when the moment had passed. After all, Hutchins was one of the leading Tories in the city, second only to Mayor David Matthews in influence. Hutchins was a financier, with shipping and mercantile holdings, and if the patriots won this war, he would be ruined. There was no more likely candidate to head up the formation of the King's Militia.

The men in the barn were cheering him, and Hutchins let them go on for several minutes before he held up his hands for quiet. Then he spoke in a deep, resonant voice.

"Thank you for coming here tonight. I know you are loyal subjects of the Crown, or you would not be here. Your lives are dedicated, as is mine, to the suppression of this illegal revolution and to the utter destruction of those who would practice treason and murder!"

A loud cheer rang out. Hutchins let it subside, then went on, "Mark the names well! Samuel Adams! John Hancock! Thomas Jefferson! Benjamin Franklin! And the spawn of the devil himself, George Washington!"

Shouts of outrage followed each name as Hutchins called it. The Tory leader raised his hands again as the angry sounds threatened to overwhelm him.

"These are your enemies, gentlemen! These are the

criminals who must be stopped, they and their traitorous ilk! And stop them we will!"

Now the shouts were of approval and agreement. Hutchins allowed the response to run its course before continuing.

"As some of you know, we have a plan to deal with this threat, to strike such a blow against the rebels that their damned revolution will never recover! Soon your other leaders and I will be ready to reveal the details of this plan and put it into action. But for now, know that we are devoting our hearts, our souls, our very lives to a cause that is just, the cause of law and divine order! We ask only that you share our devotion! Do you share that devotion?"

They shouted a mighty YES! And Elliot joined in wholeheartedly . . . at least on the surface.

Inside, he was seething with frustration. Hutchins's stirring speech was just that, a speech to enflame the emotions of his new followers. He was not going to lay out the details of his plan for all to hear, and from the sound of it, he did not intend to reveal the plan until it was time to put it into effect. Elliot would not have any time at all to counteract whatever devilish scheme Hutchins and his cohorts had hatched.

There was only one thing Elliot could do: He was going to have to continue his infiltration of the King's Militia and penetrate the group further. He was going to have to become one of the plotters' inner circle, and that was likely to be his most dangerous move yet.

Chapter Fifteen

"Step up here, sirs, if you would, and test the strength of these two giants!"

A pretty young Gypsy woman uttered the challenge to the group of villagers assembled in front of the wagon. Behind her, standing at each end of a stout log that had been trimmed of its branches, were Murdoch and Gregor. They had their arms crossed and wore haughty expressions, as befitted men utterly confident in their strength. Gregor was dressed as he had been during the arm-wrestling match with Murdoch, and the big Scotsman wore the dark blue silk shirt, loose pants, and bright red sash he had been given by Natalia. A black kerchief was tied around his head so that his red hair would not be too obvious.

Responding to the words of the Gypsy girl, several men stepped forward and climbed onto the log, balanc-

ing themselves carefully. The log itself would have been
a heavy burden for two men to lift, but with the added
weight of the villagers, it should have been impossible.

But Murdoch and Gregor were not normal men.
They stooped and wrapped their arms around each end
of the log, stiffening their backs as they set themselves.
Then they slowly uncoiled their legs. Their shoulder
muscles stood out in stark relief as they lifted the log and
its human cargo. The villagers wobbled somewhat and
put out their arms to keep their balance as they were
raised several feet above the ground. Gregor and Murdoch slowly straightened until they were standing upright again, the log braced between them. They grunted
with the effort, but the log remained rock steady, and
the villagers who had gathered to watch the amazing feat
of strength cheered and applauded.

"Step off to the tailgate of the wagon, gentlemen!"
the Gypsy girl called to the men on the log. When they
had climbed down and the log was free of its burden,
Murdoch and Gregor raised it high over their heads,
tossed it into the air, then caught it. More incredulous
gasps and cheers issued from the spectators.

Murdoch grinned at Gregor. He and the Gypsy
strongman had worked out this routine several days earlier and had performed it in two villages before this one.
Murdoch was not yet accustomed to the applause of the
crowd, however, and it still embarrassed him. At the
same time, he had to admit that he enjoyed the attention. He had spent much of his life since coming to
America alone, ranging over the frontier as a long
hunter, and he had always been satisfied with his own
company, but there was something to be said for the
camaraderie he felt among these wanderers.

The two big men lowered the log to the ground and
threw their arms up as they bowed to the crowd of villag-

ers. There was more applause; then most of the spectators moved on to see what other attractions this nomadic carnival held.

Gregor slapped Murdoch on the shoulder.

"We are a good team, you and I," he said. "Are you sure you cannot stay with us after we reach Philadelphia?"

"Our job'll be done then," Murdoch replied, not without a touch of regret. "I'll be heading back t' th' wilderness. 'Tis too much time I've spent in civilization th' past couple o' years."

"I suppose I can understand that," Gregor said. "We Gypsies like to roam wherever we please. Freedom is the most important thing to us."

"Aye, and t' me. That be why I joined up with Dan'l and Quincy t' fight th' damned redcoats."

"Politics mean little to me," Gregor said, shaking his head. "One government is as bad as another, I am thinking. But you are my friend, Murdoch, and I will do whatever I can to help you in your cause."

A week had passed since Daniel, Quincy, and Murdoch had joined the group of Gypsies. In that time, they had covered quite a bit of ground and would be arriving in Baltimore in two days. Thomas Jefferson had made the journey unmolested so far, but Daniel and Quincy took turns scouting ahead to keep an eye on the statesman, who seemed to be in no hurry to reach Philadelphia. Each evening, the caravan caught up to the village where Jefferson was spending the night.

It was possible that the thieves who had raided Monticello had not followed Jefferson, Murdoch thought, but his instincts told him there was still danger. He knew from his discussions with Daniel and Quincy that they felt the same way, and they would not relax until Jefferson had reached Philadelphia and turned over the money to the Continental Congress.

But Murdoch put those worries out of his mind. Jefferson was safely bedded down at a local inn, and Daniel and Quincy were watching the place. Murdoch would take his turn later. For now, he had something else to do.

He gave Gregor a friendly wave and departed as the Gypsy strongman brought out his table and chairs for the arm-wrestling matches that would follow. Undoubtedly some of the locals would feel confident enough to challenge Gregor, and just as undoubtedly they would lose. Murdoch and Gregor had never finished their interrupted match, and neither man seemed anxious to resolve the issue now. Their pride allowed them to believe that the contest would end in a draw.

Murdoch strolled along behind the Gypsies' parked wagons and paused when he reached a certain one. The wagon was as gaudily painted as the others, but it had the words MADAM NATALIA—KNOWS ALL, SEES ALL! PALMS READ! FORTUNES TOLD! painted in an arch over the door, which was open. Inside the wagon, the room was dim because the windows were hung with black drapes. A single candle burned on the table where Natalia sat. Her customer, a villager, sat across from her, hand extended on the table with his palm up so that Natalia could "read" what was etched there. She held the man's hand in one of hers, tracing the lines with one finger, and as she bent forward her low-cut blouse afforded the customer a tantalizing view of the deep valley between her lush breasts.

"You will lead a long life and win the heart of the woman you love," Murdoch heard her saying. "Success will follow you wherever you go. Your palm says it is so, and the palm never lies."

The villager gazed intently at her and accepted what she told him despite the fact that it was a blatant generalization designed to make him feel good about himself. Natalia was very good at sizing up her customers and telling them exactly what they wanted to hear. Murdoch had realized that right away, but she insisted she possessed some legitimate mystical powers. However, such things were too fanciful for the hardheaded Scotsman to believe in.

He waited until the customer's reading was finished and the man had gone away satisfied. Then he stepped up into the wagon, and Natalia broke into a genuine smile when she saw his brawny figure filling the doorway. Murdoch had to stoop to come in.

"Are there no more customers waiting?" she asked.

"No' right at th' moment," Murdoch told her. He thrust out his hand. "I thought maybe ye'd read me palm and tell me what th' future holds for me."

"Do you have a coin for me, sir?" Natalia's smile turned coy. "The veils of the future will not open unless you cross *my* palm with silver or gold."

Murdoch's hand closed around the slim fingers she held out toward him, and he pulled her out of her chair and into his arms with effortless ease.

"I have something else for ye," he growled, then brought his mouth down on hers.

Natalia returned the kiss and pressed herself against him. The attraction between them had been there from the first, and now their romance was in full bloom. Murdoch could barely believe what was happening, considering the way he had always felt about Gypsies, but Natalia had taught him that he had been wrong to mistrust them. Daniel had worried that Murdoch might make the men in the band jealous by pursuing

Natalia's affections, but so far there had been no trouble.

Murdoch wasn't concerned about that. None of the men in the group posed any threat to him physically with the possible exception of Gregor, and he was Natalia's brother and Murdoch's friend. Her brother Anton had put aside his hostility and accepted the relationship, too.

For a long moment Murdoch and Natalia embraced and kissed, and then Natalia snuggled her head against Murdoch's broad chest.

"I had a vision," she said in a quiet voice.

Murdoch had already learned to tolerate Natalia's "visions," even though he put no stock in them.

"What was it about?"

"You and me."

A grin spread across his rugged face. "I like th' sound o' tha' already. Was there any . . . romance involved?"

"Oh, yes," Natalia replied. "Much romance. And a house."

"A house?" he echoed.

"Yes, a house and a garden. And children. Many children."

"Hold on there just a minute—"

"I saw you settled down in that house, Murdoch," Natalia said as she looked at him imploringly. "And I saw your wife. A very beautiful woman she was, with ebony hair and dark eyes. A woman much like myself."

"Ye're making this up—"

"I am not," Natalia said sharply. "I would not lie about the truths that my visions reveal to me. My powers are a sacred responsibility, and I cannot use them on those I love except to tell the truth. We were happy together in my vision, Murdoch, so very happy."

He put his hands on her shoulders and moved her

back a step, shaken by what she had just told him. Not that he believed she could really foretell the future, but it was clear what she was getting at. She saw their relationship ending in marriage and children, and that was something Murdoch had not considered. He had not even wanted to consider it!

"Tha' will no' be possible," he told her quickly. "There be too many places t' see, too many things t' do. I am no' ready t' settle down with *any* woman, even one as lovely as yerself, Natalia."

"Are you saying that you will not marry me?" Her voice was cold.

"Well, no' *now*. Mayhap someday. . . . Who can tell what the future might bring?"

That was a mistake, and he knew it as soon as the words were out of his mouth. He winced at the angry look that appeared on her face.

"*I* can tell!" Natalia flared. "I just told you what the future will bring—if you are not so bullheaded and stubborn as to ignore my vision!"

"But Natalia, these visions o' yers—they might no' be right all th' time."

She let out a gasp of anger and frustration and reached for the nearest thing she could grab and throw, which was a small cooking pot. Murdoch ducked frantically as the missile flew toward his head.

"Hold on there!" he exclaimed. "Ye dinna want t' be doing tha'!"

"Do not tell me what I want to do, Murdoch Buchanan! You know nothing of what I want!" With that, she flung another pot at him and followed it with a hard sausage, which he batted aside before it struck. Natalia was cursing at him in a language he couldn't understand, and he thought fleetingly that his ignorance was probably a good thing. He reached out and flipped the sign on her door to say CLOSED, then kicked the wagon door shut so that passersby couldn't watch their argument. No point in letting them have a free show, he thought.

Natalia was still flinging things at him. He put up his arms to shield his face and took a couple of long steps toward her that brought her within reach again. His hands caught her wrists and kept her from throwing anything else, but he couldn't stop her from kicking him.

"Here now!" he said angrily. "Ye'd best stop tha'—"

"Make me!" she blazed at him.

"All right, I will, blast it!" With that, he jerked her toward him and planted his mouth on hers in a long and passionate kiss. Natalia struggled for a moment, then sagged against him and returned the kiss with equal fervor.

After several moments she pulled away and sighed. "I suppose we should not ruin the present by arguing about the future."

"Tha' be th' way I look at it," Murdoch replied as he ran his big hands down her back to the soft swell of her hips. Natalia's bunk was nearby and inviting, and they knew they wanted to forget the argument and take pleasure in each other once again.

"Oh, Murdoch, from now on we will argue only about the present," she said as she tugged the kerchief from his head and ran her fingers through his rumpled hair.

"Aye," Murdoch said, his voice hoarse with need. He bent slightly to place his arms more securely around her, then lifted her and buried his head in her shining dark hair that smelled sweetly of herbs. He carried her toward the bunk, and as he laid her down, his need was plain for her to see.

"Besides," Natalia said knowingly, getting in the

last word before they surrendered to their desires, "the future is already ordained, and there is nothing you can do to change it, Murdoch Buchanan. . . ."

Daniel kept his horse at a steady trot down the tree-lined road, and his eyes scanned the passing countryside for a good place to camp. It was late afternoon, and he had ridden about half a mile ahead of the Gypsy wagons, both to keep an eye on Thomas Jefferson and his slave and to find a good place for the caravan to spend the night.

Earlier in the day, the wagons had rolled across a bridge over the Potomac River, leaving Virginia behind and entering the colony of Maryland. The next day would see them arriving in Baltimore, but there did not seem to be any settlements along this stretch of road where the nomads could park their wagons on a village green and make some money from their entertainments.

Of course, the Gypsies were accustomed to camping out. Whether they were in a village or a field beside the road, they slept in their wagons and cooked over outdoor fires. But for the first time since the beginning of the journey, Jefferson and his servant were going to have to camp out, too, instead of spending the night at an inn or tavern. This worried Daniel. If a gang of thieves was trailing the statesman, they might look on this as their best opportunity to strike.

Daniel was about a quarter of a mile behind Jefferson, midway between the politician and the Gypsies. This coastal country was mostly flat, like the Tidewater in Virginia, but there were a few rises, and every time he reached one, Daniel paused and unshipped his spyglass to check on Jefferson. Satisfied that Jefferson and Bob were moving on steadily, Daniel forged ahead, too. When he saw Jefferson stop for the night, he would find

a place for the Gypsy wagons to halt. He didn't want the
caravan overtaking Jefferson, because the disguises he
and his friends wore might not stand up under close
scrutiny.

The sun was not far above the horizon when Daniel
saw Jefferson and Bob ride into a grove of trees beside
the road. There was probably a clearing that he couldn't
see from where he was, Daniel decided, and he reined in
and used the glass to keep an eye on the woods until he
saw a faint flicker of firelight through the trees.

Daniel was about to wheel his horse and ride back
to the Gypsy caravan when something caught his eye,
and he stiffened in his saddle. The red rays of the setting
sun had reflected off something in a thicket diagonally
across the road from the spot where Jefferson and Bob
had set up their camp.

His brow creasing in a frown, Daniel watched the
thicket. The orange glow of the reflected sun disappeared, as if whatever the light had been shining on had
just moved.

Somebody was definitely lurking in the woods. But
what he had seen was not necessarily sinister, Daniel
told himself. The sun could have reflected off a belt
buckle or something as innocuous as that. Or, the rays
could have been shining on the barrel of a gun.

Daniel wheeled his horse and dug his heels into its
flanks, sending it back down the road in a gallop. It was
certainly possible that the thieves had gotten ahead of
both Jefferson and the Gypsy caravan and were now
hiding in the trees, waiting until nightfall to ambush the
statesman. Daniel intended to find out, but he wasn't
going to investigate alone. There was still a little time
before darkness fell, enough time to fetch Quincy and
Murdoch.

They must have known that something was wrong

when they saw him riding hard down the road. Both men moved out ahead of the wagons on their horses to meet him. Before they could even ask any questions, Daniel called out, "There may be trouble up ahead. Jefferson's camped for the night, and I thought I spotted someone watching him."

"How far ahead?" Murdoch asked quickly.

"Maybe a quarter of a mile."

The wagons had come to a halt, and Anton and Gregor approached to see what was going on. Daniel hurriedly explained about the sun's reflection he had seen in the thick woods near Jefferson's camp, and the two Gypsies looked as worried as Quincy and Murdoch.

"We'd better get back there and take a look around," Quincy suggested.

"That's just what I had in mind." Daniel turned to Anton. "It would be better if you could keep the wagons here; I don't want to risk any of your people."

"The wagons will stay," Anton said without hesitation, "but Gregor and I will go with you."

"That's not necessary—"

Gregor broke in by rumbling, "There could be many of these thieves. You may need help, Daniel."

"We have not forgotten how you helped us," Anton added. "I will tell the people to park the wagons here beside the road."

Without giving Daniel a chance to argue further, the Gypsy leader returned to the wagons and spoke to the band in their own language. Then he quickly brought two saddle horses for himself and his brother and rejoined the others.

"Let us go," Anton said briskly. "The sun is down, and night will soon be here."

Daniel knew he was right. He turned his horse

around and heeled it into a gallop again. The four men followed him.

There were some small hills between the caravan and the spot where Jefferson had camped, elevations just high enough to hide the place from view as Daniel and the others approached. Before they topped the second hill, Daniel motioned to the right and veered his horse in that direction, leaving the road and cutting through the woods and fields. He wanted to approach the thicket from the rear, so that they wouldn't be noticed as easily or as soon. If there were thieves hiding in those woods, he wanted to take them by surprise.

After circling the hill the five riders reached a small creek, and Daniel noted the thicker trees and brush along the banks that would give them good cover as they neared the spot where he had noticed the suspicious glimmer of light. Still in the lead, he slowed his horse to a walk. Dusk was settling, bringing thick gray shadows, and the dimness made riding tricky. Also, he did not want to alert the highwaymen.

Daniel held up a hand to slow his companions and then lifted his flintlock, curling his thumb over the cock so that he would be ready to fire in an instant. Guiding the horse with his knees, he rode carefully through the trees, turning away from the creek and entering the grove that bordered the road.

Tension tugged at his nerves. There was no way of knowing for sure what waited for them up ahead, but they had to push on. So far they had heard no gunshots, no shouts, so he knew that if the robbers *were* waiting to ambush Thomas Jefferson, they had not yet launched their attack. But would Daniel and his friends be enough to stop them?

He brought his horse to a stop and slid off the saddle, motioning for the others to do the same. He caught the approving nod Murdoch gave him and was pleased that the big frontiersman agreed that they should proceed the rest of the way on foot. Daniel slipped ahead, squinting as he peered through the shadows.

Suddenly he saw movement about a dozen feet ahead of him. He stopped in his tracks, then realized what he had seen was the nervous prancing of several horses that were tied to some bushes. He counted quickly and got the number ten. One man for each horse meant that he and his companions were outnumbered two to one.

Well, those weren't such bad odds, Daniel supposed, when he had fighters like Murdoch and Gregor on his side.

He signaled for the others to move ahead. Murdoch came up beside him, then put a hand on his arm to stop him. The Scotsman gestured for Daniel and the others to wait, then glided ahead noiselessly, using all the skills his years in the wilderness had taught him. Few men were more gifted in the art of survival than Murdoch Buchanan.

A moment later Daniel heard a soft gasp and then a thump. He waited, tense with anticipation, until Murdoch reappeared.

"They left one man t' guard th' horses, just like I figured," whispered Murdoch. "He will no' bother us now. I spied th' rest o' th' scoundrels moving up t' th' road. I suppose they be about ready t' pay Mr. Jefferson a visit."

"Their visit's going to be delayed," Daniel said grimly. "Come on."

With their rear guard disposed of, the bandits could be taken by surprise, he hoped. At any rate, if Murdoch was right about what he had seen—and Daniel would never doubt the big frontiersman's eyes—there was no time to waste. He and his friends had to strike now, before the thieves had a chance to attack Jefferson.

Daniel hurried through the woods, lifting and cocking his rifle. His eyes searched for the highwaymen, and soon after passing the tethered horses, he spotted them crouched behind trees and bushes at the edge of the road. Across the way, some forty yards distant, Thomas Jefferson's campfire was clearly visible.

Even in the gloom, Daniel could see the lurking men raise their weapons and take a step forward. "Now!" he called softly.

Murdoch struck the first blow, leaping past Daniel and whipping his arm down as he threw the tomahawk he had carried ever since his first trip to the frontier. The tomahawk, making its deadly sound of revolving, uneven motion, sliced through the air, and its sharp blade sank into the back of one of the thieves. A scream tore from the man's mouth as he stumbled forward and fell.

Daniel and Quincy picked out their targets and fired at the same instant. One man spun off his feet under the impact of the ball that struck him; another staggered but managed to stay upright. A knife thrown by Anton flickered through the open spaces between the trees. With accuracy born of long years of practice, Anton found his target, and the weapon lodged in a highwayman's throat as he turned to face this unexpected threat. The man stumbled and pawed futilely at the handle of the blade buried in his flesh. As the knife came free it was followed by a fountain of blood, and the man pitched forward on his face and flopped around grotesquely in his death throes.

Murdoch pulled his brace of pistols from his belt and fired both weapons at the same time, the combined blast causing a thunderous roar. At the same time,

Gregor bounded forward, bellowing with rage, and scooped up one of the men as if he were a rag doll. The huge Gypsy flung the man against a tree, and there was a sharp crack as the man's spine snapped.

Once again, just as it had at Monticello, the nerve of the surviving gang members shattered like the breaking back. Most of them turned and ran. Daniel caught a glimpse of a tall, brawny figure trying to rally them, and as soon as he had reloaded his flintlock, he sent a round at the man. The shot missed, however, and the highwaymen's leader turned and darted into the growing darkness, fleeing like his comrades.

Murdoch and Quincy gave chase while Daniel, Anton, and Gregor checked on the fallen men. Three of them were dead, and two were badly injured.

Suddenly Daniel heard a familiar voice shouting. "What's going on over there?" Thomas Jefferson demanded. "I warn you, I'm armed!"

Daniel motioned for Anton and Gregor to fall back in the trees. He followed slowly, hoping that Jefferson would have enough sense not to venture far into the woods. A moment later he saw that the campfire had been doused, and he heard the rapid hoofbeats of a pair of horses. Jefferson and Bob had apparently chosen the prudent course and gotten out of there. They could make camp farther up the road, closer to Baltimore. Perhaps they might find a farmhouse where they could spend the night. Daniel certainly hoped so. Thomas Jefferson was a brave, proud man, but he was also an intelligent man, and after the gunfire and shouting, it must have been clear that this was not a good place to be.

Quincy and Murdoch trotted up and stopped when Daniel hissed at them.

"Those rapscallions have no' stopped running yet, Dan'l. What will we do about th' ones they left behind?"

"We'll leave them as well," Daniel replied, knowing that he was being cold-blooded. But these men had intended to steal money that was meant for the cause of freedom and liberty for the colonies, and he was not going to waste any sympathy on such scavengers.

"Come on," he said. "Let's get the horses and get back to the wagons."

"Do you think Mr. Jefferson will be safe tonight?" Quincy asked.

"That gang won't come back for a while, not after all the damage we inflicted on them. With any luck, they won't come back at all. We've made them pay a high price, and they still don't have anything for their trouble."

He hoped he was right this time. He hoped they had seen the last of the thieves.

Chapter Sixteen

After riding since early morning, Alistair Kane got off his horse in front of a broad, single-story log building and gratefully stretched his sore muscles. The journey into Virginia's Piedmont had proven days longer and far more tiring than he had expected, but the discomfort would be worthwhile once he had Roxanne in his power again.

An exhausted sigh came from Cyril Eldridge as the middle-aged spymaster dismounted as well. He and Kane knew from a conversation with a farmer the day before that the stream they now followed was the Rivanna River, but they were uncertain how far upriver the Reed plantation was located.

Perhaps they could find out something at this trading post, Kane thought as he ascended the four steps to the porch. A sign over the double doors read GRIFFIN'S MERCANTILE.

Just as Kane reached the doors, they opened, and a man ducked through and stepped out onto the porch. A young boy with light blond hair rode on his shoulders.

The lad was grinning happily as he said, "Ride horse now, Papa Geoffrey?"

"That's right, Dietrich," the man told the boy. "We'll ride the horse again."

Kane stopped in his tracks, and his eyes widened slightly as he looked at the man. Not only were his features familiar, but his voice was, too, and Kane realized that what he was seeing was a family resemblance. This man could only be a relative of Daniel Reed's.

Eldridge had come up the steps behind Kane, and he must have noticed the same thing. Moving smoothly, he stepped in front of the man and said with a smile, "Excuse me, sir, but would you happen to be Geoffrey Reed?" His accent was flawless; he and Kane had spent long hours practicing during their journey.

"That's right, sir," said Geoffrey Reed as he came to a stop, a puzzled expression on his face. "Do we know each other? I believe you have the advantage, sir."

"My name is Lester Wilkes," Eldridge said as he extended his hand, "from down Savannah way. I own a tobacco warehouse, and I was told to look you up because it's said you grow the finest tobacco in all Virginia."

"Well, I appreciate the compliment, whoever gave it to me," Geoffrey replied with a grin. He shook hands with Eldridge. "Up here on business, are you, Mr. Wilkes?"

"That's right." Eldridge gestured languidly at Kane. "This is my associate, Mr. Herman Lambert."

"Glad to meet you, too, Mr. Lambert," Geoffrey said as he shook hands with Kane.

Convinced that this man was the father of the traitors Daniel and Quincy Reed, Kane managed to put a friendly smile on his face. Eldridge had tumbled instantly to that fact and acted accordingly, and although Kane wished that Eldridge had chosen a more euphonious false name for him, he could not fault the spymaster's quick action.

Geoffrey lowered the blond boy to the porch and went on, "This young friend of mine is Master Dietrich Jarrott. He's staying with us for a bit. His sister is my daughter-in-law."

Kane didn't know what Reed was talking about, but it didn't really matter. What was important was finding out the location of the Reed plantation.

"Lester and I would like to discuss buying your tobacco crop from you, Mr. Reed," Kane said. "Would you be open to that?"

"I'm always open to a fair business deal, especially in uncertain times like these," Geoffrey replied. "Would the two of you like to come out to the house to talk about it?"

"Indeed we would," Eldridge answered without hesitation. "At the moment, though, we have to replenish our supplies. Perhaps you could give us directions how to get there?"

"Of course. In fact, why don't you gentlemen come out for supper tomorrow night?"

"We'd be honored, sir," Eldridge said. "And I think you'll like what we have to say. We'll pay you a good price for your crop."

"Excellent. We'll discuss it then." Geoffrey shook hands with each of them again, then said, "Right now, though, I have to get this lad home. I'm teaching him how to ride a horse, you know. He reminds me of my own two boys when they were little. We just came in to the settlement here to post a letter, and it gave Dietrich a chance to ride."

"The directions, Mr. Reed?" Kane reminded him, thinking that this isolated trading post and the few surrounding buildings hardly qualified as a settlement— except to primitive colonials like Reed.

"Oh, yes, of course. You follow this road—" Geoffrey pointed at the trail that wound along beside the river "—for about two miles. There's a bridge there, and you cross the river and continue northwest up the road on the other side. It veers away from the river a bit, but don't worry about that. A mile past the bridge, you'll come to a lane that turns off to the right. Follow it, and it will take you straight to my farm."

"We'll be there about dusk," Eldridge murmured.

"That'll be just fine. Good day, gentlemen. Come along, Dietrich."

Holding the youngster's hand, Geoffrey walked down the porch steps and led the boy over to a big bay gelding. Geoffrey swung up into the saddle and lifted Dietrich in front of him. He gave the reins to the boy and let him get the horse moving down the road.

"That was a stroke of luck," Kane commented quietly when Reed and the boy were out of earshot.

"And we won't squander our good fortune," Eldridge said, looking after Geoffrey and Dietrich with thinly veiled hatred on his face. Eldridge had never met the man before today, but Geoffrey's relationship with Daniel was enough to damn him in the eyes of the British spymaster.

"We're going out there tomorrow evening?" Kane asked.

"We're not going to wait that long," Eldridge said

with a sneer. "We'll pay the Reeds a visit tonight and find out if the Darragh woman and the child are really there." His already thin lips compressed even more. "I'm ready to conclude our business with them as soon as possible."

Night had fallen over the Piedmont as the two men approached the Reed plantation. The hour was late, after ten o'clock, and Eldridge was certain that most, if not all, of the inhabitants of the big house now visible through the trees had already gone to bed.

He hoped that was the case. He wanted to get inside, do what he had come to do, and slip out with none of the others in the house being any the wiser.

In the morning, they would find the Darragh woman and the child dead in their beds, and Cyril Eldridge would once again be the sole heir to the estate of Bramwell Stoddard, Lord Oakley, just as he was meant to be.

Eldridge had been careful to keep his plan from Kane. There had been a time when Kane had been ruthless and coldly logical in the service of his king, but ever since meeting the Darragh woman, he had been thinking with his heart instead of his head. It was plain to Eldridge that Kane still loved Roxanne and intended to win her back.

That would be an attempt doomed to failure, Eldridge knew, a complete waste of time. There was only one way to deal with this problem, and Eldridge intended to follow through with his plan. Once he had disposed of the patriot bitch and her whelp, he would tell Kane that they were not at the plantation after all. He would go through the motions of continuing their quest for a short time, then abandon it. Kane would be left unaware of the true fate of the woman he foolishly thought he loved.

Eldridge smiled in the darkness. Everything was falling together for him at last. Soon he would be on his way to England and the fortune that would be waiting for him.

"We've come close enough," Kane hissed in a whisper. He reined his horse to a stop, and Eldridge followed suit. They had halted in a thick stand of trees fifty yards from the house. They dismounted and started forward on foot.

Suddenly a man loomed out of the shadows.

"Who's that?" he challenged roughly. "What're you sneakin' around for?"

Eldridge froze, but the major stepped forward, saying forthrightly, "Is this the Reed plantation? Mr. Reed asked us to come out here—"

His quick stride and daring bluff worked well enough to bring Kane within reach of the sentry, who must have been roaming the grounds. Kane's arm whipped forward in a sudden thrust, and he rammed the dagger he had pulled from beneath his coat into the guard's chest. He let go of the knife and clapped one hand over the man's mouth, while with the other he wrenched the guard's musket out of his grasp. The man sagged toward Kane and then went to his knees. He tried to hit Kane, but the major ignored the feeble swings. Kane dropped the musket and reached down to grasp the handle of the dagger once more. He pushed hard on it, feeling the blade penetrate the last layers of muscle to reach the heart. He stepped back and let the dead guard fall forward on his face.

"Well, that was smoothly done, if I say so myself," Kane commented in a whisper as he hooked a booted toe under the dead man's shoulder and rolled the corpse onto its back. He stooped to retrieve his dagger and wiped the bloody blade on the man's coat before slipping it back in its sheath.

"Good work," agreed Eldridge. "Do you think that was the only guard?"

"Likely, but it's impossible to know for certain."

"I'll risk it," Eldridge declared. "I want you to stay here while I slip inside and have a look around."

"Stay here?" Kane repeated with a frown. "I thought we'd both go in—"

"Too risky," Eldridge cut in. "I want you to stay outside the house in case there's trouble and I need you to rescue me. We don't want them taking both of us prisoner."

Kane scowled. "All right, I suppose that makes sense. You go ahead. But at the first sign of trouble, I'll be in there."

"Right. If I locate the woman and the child, I'll fetch you, and we'll take them out of there."

"I'll be waiting." Kane sounded somewhat dubious, but he was an officer in His Majesty's army and would obey orders from a superior, at least for a time.

And all Eldridge needed was a few minutes and a little luck.

Mariel Jarrott Reed turned over restlessly in the bed. She was not particularly uncomfortable, but she was having a great deal of trouble falling asleep. She had slumbered earlier in the night, but something had awakened her, and now she could not drift off again.

If Quincy had been here, he would have put his arms around her and nuzzled her hair and whispered how much he loved her, and Mariel would have snuggled into the warmth of his embrace and dozed off easily. She was sure of it. But Quincy was far away, hundreds of miles to the northeast, making sure that Thomas Jefferson arrived safely in Philadelphia.

Reaching the decision to urge Quincy to accompany his brother and his friend Murdoch on that mission had been the hardest choice of Mariel's young life. Naturally she wanted her husband with her, but she knew how much the struggle for freedom meant to him, regardless of what he had told Daniel about having already done his part. She had listened to Roxanne talk so fervently about the fight for liberty that she too felt that as long as America was not free, none of them had done enough.

Besides, the idea of Daniel and Murdoch going off on an adventure and leaving him behind would have eaten at Quincy, and he might have resented her if he hadn't gone along. Mariel certainly did not want that.

She sighed as she stared up at the ceiling of the darkened bedroom. There was no point in worrying about the decision now. She had urged Quincy to go, and he had gone.

She sat up and swung her legs out of the bed. She knew she was not going back to sleep anytime soon, so she was not going to lie there and thrash back and forth futilely. She pushed back her long blond hair, put her slippers on, and stood up. She would go down the hall and visit the nursery that held the Reed plantation's unexpected influx of babies. She would check on Thomas and Elizabeth. Looking at them always made her feel better, as if Quincy were right there with her. And she could check on Joseph, too, while she was there. Since the ordeal of the twins' birth had left her so weak, Roxanne had done a great deal to help with the children, and Mariel felt a debt to her sister-in-law.

Still a bit shaky on her feet, Mariel picked up a robe and put it on over her nightgown, then opened the door of her room and stepped out into the hall. As she looked down the corridor toward the nursery, she was immediately struck by something strange. The door of the room was closed, but there was a thin line of light at the bottom of it. Someone inside the nursery had lit a candle.

Roxanne, Mariel thought. Of course, that was it. Roxanne was having trouble sleeping, too, and she had gone down to the nursery to look in on the babies. Mariel smiled. She would join Roxanne, and perhaps they could have some warm milk and a chat.

Still smiling, she tiptoed down the hall toward the nursery.

Eldridge's breath hissed between his teeth in a bitter, near-silent curse. He had never counted on this. He had slipped into the house without disturbing anyone. He had climbed through an open first-floor window and eased up the stairs to the second floor, his way illuminated by the stub of candle he had lit from the embers in the fireplace downstairs. Luck had stayed at his side as the first door he tried opened into the nursery.

But, bloody hell, he had never dreamed that there would be *three* babies there instead of one.

He stared down at the infants sleeping in their cribs, lit in the warm yellow glow of the candle he had placed on the dresser. All babies looked alike to him, and wrapped as they were in their blankets, he could not even tell if they were girls or boys. There was no way of knowing which of the brats belonged to the Darragh woman, and their hair color offered no clue, as each had the same tuft of brown hair.

Well, the answer was simple enough, he supposed, drawing a knife from under his coat. He would just have to kill them all.

Eldridge's features were a tense mask as he leaned over the first crib and carefully pulled back the blanket from the infant's face. He would have to strike quickly, slashing the chubby neck so that the child would not have a chance to cry out before it died. Eldridge moved the knife close to the soft, pale skin of the baby's throat.

Suddenly the door opened behind him, and a woman's voice said, "Roxanne? Is that—"

Eldridge whirled around, shock making his taut nerves jerk wildly. He saw a young woman with long blond braids standing just inside the door, a look of horror on her face as she stared at the intruder with the knife. Her mouth opened, and she emitted a high, keening scream as she threw herself at him.

"No!" she wailed as she reached for the knife.

Eldridge cursed again. Luck had deserted him, but only for the moment, he vowed. He could still accomplish what he had come to do. He would just have to kill this woman as well.

But the babies would die first. Savagely Eldridge backhanded the woman as she lunged at him. He put all the strength in his wiry body behind the blow, cracking her across the jaw and sending her spinning away.

The woman was pale and weak looking, but she seemed possessed of the strength of madness—or motherly love. She caught her balance and flung herself at Eldridge again as he tried to turn once more toward the cribs. This time he slashed at her with the knife, and the blade cut across one of her upflung arms and then ripped a gash across her chest and midsection. She screamed again, this time in pain, but she didn't fall back; she kept coming at him, striking at him.

Eldridge snapped a punch at her face with his free hand, and the blow connected solidly, jolting her head around. She fell to her knees in front of him, and he lifted the knife. Better to go ahead and kill her first, he decided. He was running out of time. He paused for an instant, ready to plunge the knife into the woman's body.

"Eldridge!"

The shout came from the doorway of the nursery, and Eldridge's gaze jerked up from his intended victim. His eyes widened at the sight of Roxanne Darragh standing there, looking not only beautiful in a long white nightgown but deadly as well. She held a cocked flintlock pistol in her hand, aimed unwaveringly at him.

Eldridge had just enough time to whisper the word "No!"

Then Roxanne calmly pressed the trigger. Smoke and flame spurted from the muzzle of the pistol, and Eldridge felt the heavy lead ball slam into his chest. The impact knocked him away from the blond woman, and the knife slipped from his fingers and fell harmlessly to the floor. Eldridge felt his life pouring from him like a river of molten lava. He fell to one knee and clutched at one of the cribs to keep himself upright. There was a crushing pain in his chest.

Damn it, this couldn't be happening! He was going to be Lord Oakley. He was going to be a rich man. He had played the deadly game of espionage for so many years. He just couldn't die here on the floor of a Virginia plantation bedroom. He was . . . he was . . . He was a dead man brought down by his own greed and ambition.

Kane heard the screams and then the shot, and he drew his pistol from his belt and ran toward the house. A grimace pulled at his face. Clearly Eldridge had run into trouble, bad trouble.

Kane didn't bother to sneak into the house. He kicked the front door open and bolted inside. There was shouting on the second floor, and he bounded up the stairs three at a time.

When he reached the landing, he saw light spilling through an open door down the corridor. The glow struck highlights in the lush red hair of the woman he remembered so well, the woman he loved. She was standing in the open doorway, and next to her were Geoffrey Reed and an older woman, probably his wife. Peering past Roxanne, Kane saw Cyril Eldridge's body sprawled on the floor in a pool of blood.

The spymaster's quest was over—but not Kane's. Roxanne was standing right there, within his reach at last. He leveled the pistol at the small group and bellowed, "Roxanne!"

They whirled around, horrified expressions on their faces. Kane saw the pistol in her hand, but smoke was still drifting from its barrel, and he knew it was empty. She must have fired the shot that killed Eldridge. Reed and the other woman were in their nightclothes and unarmed.

"Mr. Lambert!" Reed exclaimed. "What—"

"His name's not Lambert," Roxanne said coldly. "He's Major Alistair Kane, the British officer who held me hostage in Boston and sent me to England."

"That's right," Kane said with a smile. "Now stand away from those people, Roxanne. You and I are leaving."

"No," she said flatly. "I'll never go anywhere with you, Kane. You'll have to kill me."

She was no longer pregnant, and thin, wailing cries came from inside the room. A baby . . . more than one? That was a bit of a surprise, but nothing Kane couldn't deal with. He knew Roxanne, knew that she would not stand by and see harm come to any helpless infant, her own or someone else's.

"Come here to me," he threatened, "or I'll kill those children."

The older woman shrank against Reed's side, her hands flying to her mouth in horror. "You wouldn't!" she said in a choked voice.

"Yes, he would," Roxanne said. "I know him too well, Pamela. He'd do it, all right." She took a step toward him. "I'll have to do as he says. I'll have to go with him."

She walked slowly down the hall toward Kane, ignoring the cries from Reed and the woman. Bit by bit, she drew close to him, and Kane held out his free hand to her, keeping the pistol aimed at the Reeds. She was almost within reach.

"Come on, Roxanne," he uttered tensely. "Come on."

A stair creaked behind him.

Kane's head whipped around and he saw a stocky, sandy-haired man crouched at the top of the landing. The man had a fowling piece clutched in his hands.

"Get back, Roxanne!" the man shouted.

She had never intended to go with him, Kane realized. She had only been distracting him while this man slipped up behind him. She had betrayed him, and now there was no way out.

Kane's lips pulled back from his teeth. He might die here, but Roxanne Darragh would die, too. Daniel Reed would never have her. He looked at her again and pulled the barrel of the pistol in line with her face.

A shotgun boomed behind him.

Kane felt the blast rip into his back, the charge hitting him at point-blank range. It drove him forward, toward Roxanne. He tried to pull the trigger of the pistol, but his muscles no longer obeyed the commands of his dying brain. The pistol fell from his fingers, unfired.

He collided with Roxanne, and his arms enfolded her in a twisted mockery of an embrace. For an instant, they stood like that, their faces only inches apart, and Kane whispered her name one last time before his eyes turned glassy and rolled up in their sockets.

She stepped back and he fell, and then Hamish MacQuarrie rushed past the corpse to make sure she was all right. Geoffrey and Pamela hurried to her side as well, and Roxanne said with an urgent shake of her head, "I'm all right! But Mariel's been hurt. Come on, we have to see to her!" As she led them hurriedly into the nursery, she added, "Thank you, Hamish. You saved my life."

" 'Twas the least I could do," Hamish replied with a grin, "even if ye *are* related to the Buchanans. . . ."

They left Kane sprawled in the upstairs hallway as they hurried to tend to Mariel's injuries.

Unseen by the people in the nursery, one of the major's fingers twitched, then a second one. His hand pressed against the floor—then relaxed for the final time.

Alistair Kane and Cyril Eldridge were both as dead as the dreams that had brought them to America.

Chapter Seventeen

"**E**lliot? You've a visitor, dear."

Looking up from the chair where he sat reading, Elliot saw his mother standing in the doorway of his bedroom, a chamber barely large enough for his narrow bunk and chair, a far cry from his opulent sleeping quarters in the Beacon Hill mansion in Boston. Polly Markham looked and sounded a little excited, and Elliot was curious as to what visitor would provoke such a reaction.

He put his book aside, stood up, and followed Polly into the small sitting room at the front of the house. A man dressed in a fine suit and holding a tricorn adorned by a feathered cockade stood there talking to Benjamin. The visitor turned toward them as Elliot and Polly entered the room.

It was Mark Hutchins.

Elliot tried to conceal his surprise. What in blazes was Hutchins doing *here?* Had the Tory leader found out about Elliot's activities as a patriot secret agent?

That did not seem to be the case, however, because Hutchins was smiling and had been talking in a friendly manner to Benjamin. Now he extended a hand to Elliot.

"Ah, Elliot Markham!" he said heartily. "I've heard a great deal about you, sir, and it's a pleasure to finally meet you. I'm Mark Hutchins."

"Yes, I know," Elliot replied as he shook hands. "I mean, I've seen you around town, and people have pointed you out to me. You and Mayor Matthews have done a great deal to make us feel welcome in New York after we were forced to flee our homes."

Hutchins looked sympathetic. "The fall of Boston to the rebels was a great disaster. David Matthews and I and the other loyal citizens of New York felt it was our duty as subjects of the Crown to extend a helping hand. I know that the situation is perhaps not as comfortable as that to which you and your friends are accustomed, but that will change in time, Elliot, I assure you."

"Of course it will," Benjamin growled. "This damned rebellion will be put down, and when it is, things will get back to normal."

That was a futile hope, Elliot knew. No matter how the war ended, things would not "get back to normal," as his father put it. But he kept that thought to himself as he asked, "What brings you here, Mr. Hutchins?"

"I want to talk to you, Elliot. Would you care to take a walk with me?"

Elliot glanced at Benjamin and Polly. "Anything you have to say to me, you can say in front of my parents."

"Nonsense," Benjamin snapped. "There's no need

to be stubborn, Elliot. Your mother and I aren't offended, are we, Polly?"

"Of course not. You go ahead with Mr. Hutchins, Elliot."

"Well, all right," Elliot said with a shrug. "Let me get my hat."

A few minutes later Elliot and Hutchins were strolling down the street toward the docks. Hutchins opened the discussion by asking, "What do you know about me, Elliot?"

"I know you're a successful businessman and that the war hasn't hurt your interests too much . . . yet."

"Perceptive of you. You understand that if the rebels manage to win the victory in this contest, I'll be ruined."

"That much is obvious, Mr. Hutchins."

"Please, call me Mark. It will come as no surprise to you, then, that I am dedicated to the support of the Crown?"

"Of course not, Mark."

Hutchins looked at him slyly. "I've heard rumors that you yourself have done things to help our cause. Rumors dealing with a shipload of supplies brought down from Canada."

Elliot shrugged. "Such rumors are easy to start but difficult to pin down."

Hutchins laughed and said, "Don't worry, Elliot. You and I are on the same side. That's why I came to see you today. I have an invitation to extend to you."

At those words Elliot felt his pulse beat faster. He had an idea what Hutchins might be talking about, but it would be better to make the man come right out with it, he decided. "What sort of invitation?"

"You've heard of the King's Militia?"

"Well, I . . ."

"There's no need to deny it," Hutchins said in a quiet voice. "I know that you were at our meeting out on Long Island several nights ago. Your presence was noted and reported to me by some of our members."

Elliot stopped, forcing Hutchins to come to a halt, too. Looking directly in the man's eyes, Elliot said, "I hear rumors just as you do, Mark. The King's Militia sounded like an organization that wants the same thing I do—the utter destruction of these damned rebels."

"Exactly," Hutchins said. "That's why I've come to ask you to join our inner circle. We need men of your vision, Elliot."

Once again Elliot was forced to hide his reactions. He had been hoping to work his way into the upper echelons of the King's Militia over time, and now here was the head of the group asking him to become one of the ringleaders! It was an amazing stroke of luck.

Or was it? Elliot suddenly wondered. In the game of espionage, there was always the possibility of a trap.

"I'm flattered," he said after a moment. "But I'm not sure that I'm really the type you're looking for."

"Why not allow us to decide that? Anyone who could come up with a plan to supply the city's Tories by risking a trip to Canada is just the sort of man we must have to overcome the odds against us. You're clearly interested, Elliot, or you wouldn't have come to the meeting the other night."

"That's true." Elliot warned himself to take this slowly, not to jump at the opportunity too eagerly.

"So far, our leadership ranks have been composed of men from New York, but we've decided that it's time to invite a few of the Tories from Boston into our group. You're one of those few, Elliot. Please don't let us down."

He had drawn this out far enough, Elliot decided.

He thrust his hand out and smiled. "All right. I accept, Mark. It's time I started doing some real good."

Hutchins's hand closed around his in a firm clasp. "I'm sure you'll be glad you chose to join us. There will be a meeting of the inner circle tonight, and I'll introduce you to the rest of the men then. Is that all right with you?"

"It's an honor," Elliot said. "I'm ready to do whatever you require of me."

"Do you know a place called Corbie's Tavern?"

"I've been there," Elliot admitted. If the King's Militia had been keeping an eye on him, they would know he had visited the tavern in the past. He would have to be careful not to let himself be tripped up by a lie.

"Be there at eight o'clock. We'll be meeting in the back room."

"All right. Thank you, Mark."

"No," Hutchins said, "thank *you*, Elliot. I'm sure with your help we'll be successful."

With a jaunty wave Hutchins went on his way, and Elliot turned back toward home. Benjamin and Polly would want to know what Hutchins had discussed with him, but he did not intend to tell them the truth. He would say that Hutchins merely wanted to contribute some funds for the next trip to Canada to buy supplies.

As he walked he considered the possibility that this whole thing was an elaborate snare designed to entrap him. His instincts told him that wasn't the case; Hutchins had certainly seemed sincere in his invitation, and it made sense that the New York Tories would open their ranks to their brethren from Boston.

But even if it *was* a trap, Elliot knew he could not back out. He had a chance to find out what sort of scheme against the patriots was being planned by the

King's Militia, and he was not going to waste the opportunity.

After all, this wasn't the first time he had risked his life. He had been living on borrowed time since the day he had first agreed to become part of the patriot intelligence network. But then, Elliot mused, in a time of war, wasn't everyone living on borrowed time?

It stayed light fairly late on these June evenings, and there was still a faint reddish-gray reminder of the sunset in the western sky as Elliot made his way toward Corbie's Tavern. He had not told his parents where he was going, but they had not asked, either.

His mood was surprisingly buoyant considering that he might be walking blithely into danger. His main worry was that Casey might be in Corbie's and say something to give him away. The simple fact that she knew him would not be incriminating; a trollop like Casey knew many men. Elliot just hoped she was quick-witted enough not to reveal their status as patriot espionage operatives if she saw him with Hutchins and the other members of the King's Militia.

That was borrowing trouble unnecessarily, Elliot told himself. Casey was smart; she would know what to do.

The squalid tavern was smoky and filled with noisome odors, just as on his previous visit. Elliot walked inside and headed toward the bar, but before he could reach it, a pair of men fell in step beside him.

"Come with us, Mr. Markham," one of them said in a low voice that could not have been heard more than a foot away over the hubbub in the tavern.

So they had been waiting for him, Elliot thought. It did not surprise him that Hutchins had men watching for his arrival. He walked with them to a door at the back of the room. One of them opened it, then stepped aside so that Elliot could precede them. He did so, wondering just what he was stepping into.

He found himself in a good-sized room where nearly a dozen men waited, talking among themselves and sipping from mugs of ale. There was a long table in the center of the room, and seated at the far end of it was Mark Hutchins. The Tory ringleader glanced up at Elliot's entrance and smiled a friendly greeting.

"Come in, Elliot," he called. "We're waiting for one more man, and then we'll get started. Did you have any trouble getting here?"

"None at all," Elliot replied as he strolled to the head of the table and shook Hutchins's hand. He hadn't seen Casey anywhere in the tavern, and he was grateful for that. Now all he had to do was wait and see what information he could gather at this meeting.

As he looked around the room, he saw that some of the men in attendance looked familiar. Most of them were from New York, he supposed, although Hutchins had said that some of the Tories from Boston were being brought into the organization. Elliot did not know any of them well, but with luck he would get to know them better.

His worries about this being a trap had eased. One of the men handed him a mug of ale, and there was an air of conviviality in the room. This was a social gathering, Elliot mused.

The men who had brought him in had retreated to the main room of the tavern, and a few minutes later they reappeared with someone else, no doubt the last arrival Hutchins had spoken of.

The newcomer was slender and well attired, and Elliot was shocked when he saw the man's face. Avery Wallingford peered back at him, equally surprised.

"I believe the two of you know each other," Hutchins said to Elliot.

"Indeed we do. We've spent many interesting times together in Boston," replied Elliot, seeing Avery's gaze come to rest on Hutchins. Avery paled, and Elliot surmised he was about to say something about the situation between Hutchins and Sarah. Not wanting Avery to reveal what he knew about the affair, Elliot stepped forward quickly. Under the circumstances it wouldn't do to have Hutchins suspect Avery and Elliot of spying on him.

Elliot caught Avery's hand and pumped it, smiling broadly as he said, "It's good to see you again, Avery!" At the same time, his eyes sent an urgent message to him in hopes that Avery would understand the warning they held.

Slowly Avery's tightly clenched jaw relaxed.

"Hello, Elliot," he said, his voice trembling only a bit. "I see that you've been invited into this little group, too."

"You gentlemen are the first ones from Boston to be brought into our circle," Hutchins said as he stood up and strode toward them. He put a hand on Elliot's shoulder, then clapped the other hand on Avery's back. "We all know about your bravery and ingenuity in traveling to Canada to bring back supplies for our people. Everyone in this room—no, every Tory in New York—owes you a debt of gratitude, lads. You've served us well." He winked at them. "And you'll serve us even better in the future, I'll warrant. Well, come along and sit down. We've much to discuss."

The men took their places around the long table, and Elliot found himself sitting at Hutchins's right hand, with Avery beside him to the right. Avery's features were pale, but that wasn't unusual for him, and Elliot thought that no one would notice. Avery was controlling himself well, better than Elliot would have thought possible under the circumstances.

Hutchins began the meeting by raising his mug and intoning, "To the king!"

The other men echoed the toast and drank deeply, and then as the mugs were thumping back onto the table, Hutchins continued, "As you know, we have gathered here tonight to discuss the phase of our plan that directly involves us. Mr. Massey, how stands our armament situation?"

"We're well armed," growled one of the men. "Every member possesses at least a musket and a pistol, and enough powder and shot for our purposes are stored in the barn on Long Island."

Elliot, very interested in this information, was anxious to know what those purposes were, but he kept his mouth shut. It wouldn't do to appear too eager to learn the details of the plan.

"Very good," Hutchins said. He looked at the two newcomers and asked, "What about you men? Do you and Avery have any weapons, Elliot?"

"I have two pistols, and my father owns a musket I can use," Elliot replied. "I can't speak for Avery—"

"I have a pistol," Avery said tightly. "I can get a musket if need be."

"Well, we may not require any direct action from the two of you, so I think a pistol will be sufficient for now, just in case of trouble," Hutchins said. "You're probably wondering just what we're going to do with those guns and ammunition."

Elliot smiled slightly and inclined his head. "I *am* more than a little curious, I admit."

"That damned Washington is moving much of the artillery he used during the siege of Boston into this area, in preparation for the next phase of the conflict. He has set up a command post not far from here and is ready to tighten the rebels' grip on New York." Hutchins brought a fist down on the table with a resounding thump. "We are not going to allow that to happen, gentlemen! When the proper moment comes—when the rebels are already in a state of confusion—we will strike, attacking the Continental Army from the rear and seizing the artillery. We'll shell those damned rebels right into the Hudson River!"

There was a shout of agreement from the assembled plotters, and Elliot and Avery joined in. Elliot's head was spinning, even as he voiced his mock approval of Hutchins's plan. What he had just learned would be disastrous to the patriot cause. Although Hutchins had not mentioned what event was calculated to throw the American forces into a state of confusion, it was entirely possible that an unexpected attack from the rear would be successful.

Although the members of the King's Militia were not professional soldiers, neither were most of the men in the Continental Army. If Washington's artillery fell into the hands of the plotters, they could use it to shell the patriot forces to bloody ribbons.

Hutchins placed his palms on the table and looked around at the group, a solemn expression on his handsome face. "Well, gentlemen, what say you? Do we proceed?"

"Aye!" said the man called Massey. "We'll show those damned rebels what a big mistake they made by turning traitor!"

Other members of the group echoed that sentiment, and then Hutchins turned to the men from Boston and asked, "What do you think, Elliot? And you, Avery? Will our plan succeed?"

"It has to succeed," Avery answered before Elliot could say anything. "We must drive out those treasonous bastards."

Avery certainly sounded sincere, Elliot thought. That was good. Avery was apparently able to put aside his hatred of Hutchins for the moment and substitute a political hate for a personal one. It would certainly keep Hutchins from becoming suspicious.

"I agree," Elliot said firmly. "It's an excellent plan, Mark."

"Thank you," Hutchins murmured. From the pride in his voice Elliot surmised that the man had personally hatched the scheme. "Since we're all agreed, we will proceed with our preparations. You will all be notified when the time comes to act. Until then, God save the king!"

"God save the king!" sounded a chorus of agreement in response.

Elliot glanced at Avery, and for an instant he wished that he could tell him what was really going on. After all this time of working alone, treading the shadowy pathways by himself, it would have been nice to have an ally.

But Elliot knew it was out of the question. For all the hatred Avery bore Hutchins personally, he was still a Wallingford, still a zealous supporter of the Crown. He would swallow his loathing for the leader of the King's Militia and remain a loyal member. Elliot was sure of it, and as always, Elliot would continue to play the lonely hand he had been dealt. . . .

Chapter Eighteen

J ethro Tyler stalked back and forth across the clearing, fury pounding inside his skull like a hammer
striking an anvil. Even though it had been over a
week since half of his men and all his horses had been
lost in the ambush, his rage and frustration still burned
inside him. Twice now he had attempted to steal the
money from Thomas Jefferson, and twice he had failed.
Although it had been too dark to get a good look at the
men who had foiled the second attempt, Tyler was sure
they were the same ones who had interfered at Monticello.

But this time he knew that he was going to succeed.

Jefferson and the slave traveling with him would die, and Tyler and his men would finally reap their reward. And if anyone tried to get in their way . . . Tyler almost hoped that would happen. Maybe more killing would help ease his rage.

"You sure about this, Jethro?" asked one of the men seated by the fire. "We ain't goin' to get another chance if this goes wrong tonight. Jefferson'll be in Philadelphia tomorrow."

"Nothing's going to go wrong," Tyler snapped. "This time we'll get that money for sure."

"That's what you said last time," another man complained. "All that got us was a hell of a lot of trouble. There's only five of us left, in case you ain't noticed, Jethro."

Tyler stopped his pacing and turned sharply to address the man who had just spoken. He pulled the pistol from his belt and leveled it at the face of the startled and suddenly frightened highwayman, who swallowed hard and flinched as Tyler cocked the weapon.

"Four men can handle this plan as easy as five, you son of a bitch," growled Tyler as his finger quivered just over the trigger of the pistol. "The times when it went wrong before weren't my fault, damn it! Anybody can have some bad luck."

"S-Sure, Jethro, that's r-right," gulped the man. "It was just bad luck, like you said!"

Tyler spat on the ground near the man's feet, then visibly relaxed, as did the other men around the campfire. The one who'd had the gun pointed at him heaved a sigh of relief when Tyler put the weapon away.

"Tell us about the plan again, Jethro," another man said, anxious to change the subject.

"All right." Tyler started to pace again, glad for the

opportunity to talk through the scheme one more time before they put it into action.

"That little settlement down the road has only one inn, and Jefferson's staying there. We'll wait until later tonight, when everybody's asleep, then sneak in and set the place on fire. Jefferson will run out along with everybody else, and he'll bring the money with him. He's not about to leave it behind to burn. Then, in the confusion, while people are trying to put out the fire, we kill Jefferson and take the money." Tyler looked around at the surviving members of his gang. "Sounds simple enough, doesn't it?"

"It'll work, Jethro," one of the men replied. "It's got to."

That was the truth, Tyler knew. After being routed in the attack that had cost them half their men, the gang had taken several days to regroup, steal some horses, and get back on Jefferson's trail. They had done some hard riding to catch up with the politician before he reached Philadelphia, and the city was now less than twenty miles away. Jefferson would reach his destination the following day.

Unless Tyler and his men were successful tonight. And Tyler had every intention of being a rich man by this time tomorrow.

Murdoch Buchanan rolled over restlessly, half asleep but unable either to drift completely to sleep or come fully awake. He was vaguely aware of Natalia's warm form snuggled against him. The bunk in her wagon was too narrow for them, considering Murdoch's size and the fact that Natalia herself was well rounded in all the right places. But being crowded together under the covers had its advantages, such as the fact that Murdoch could feel every silky inch of the beautiful Gypsy woman pressed up against him.

Suddenly Natalia jerked violently in her sleep and sat bolt upright. A choked scream came from her throat.

Her reaction jolted Murdoch completely awake. In fact, as he tried to sit up, startled by Natalia's outcry, he slipped off the edge of the bunk and wound up on the floor of the wagon, his rear end thudding painfully against the planks.

"What is it?" he asked urgently as his big hand reached for the loaded flintlock that he always left beside the bunk. He was lucky he hadn't fallen on the rifle and made it discharge, he thought fleetingly as he tried to focus on Natalia in the darkness.

She was taking deep breaths and trying to calm herself. "I . . . I had a dream," she managed to say after a moment. "A frightening vision."

Murdoch felt a brief surge of irritation. The last time he had said anything about her visions, she had gotten angry and thrown things at him. He didn't want that to happen again, even though that argument had ended in passionate lovemaking. But he was still annoyed that she had disturbed them over something in which he placed little faith.

"I'm sure 'twas just a dream," he said soothingly, replacing the flintlock on the floor of the wagon. "If ye would like t' tell me about it, I'd be glad t' listen."

"You don't understand," she said, standing up and pacing back and forth as best she could in the narrow confines of the wagon. "This was more than a dream."

Murdoch pushed himself to his feet. "Another vine-covered cottage and a passel o' kids running about?"

"Don't you dare make fun of me, Murdoch Buchanan! This is important!"

He heard her voice shaking from the depth of emotion she felt and realized that he ought to be taking her seriously, even if all she had experienced was a simple nightmare. He put his hands on her shoulders and said quietly, " 'Tis sorry I be, Natalia. Now tell me what yer dream was about. Mayhap tha' will make ye feel better."

"All right. I . . . I saw fire . . . flames leaping high and smoke everywhere . . . and I heard gunshots. And there was a tall, red-haired man—"

"Tha' would be me," Murdoch said with a grin.

Natalia shook her head emphatically. "No! The man I saw wasn't you, Murdoch. He was someone I'd never seen before."

"What did he look like, then?" asked Murdoch. A tiny thread of worry was worming its way into his brain.

"He had red hair, like I said, and he was . . . well, not really handsome, I suppose, but distinguished looking, you might say. A learned man, I could tell that much, even though he did not speak in my vision."

The slight worry Murdoch had felt a moment earlier was growing dramatically. The man she was describing sounded just like Thomas Jefferson.

"Are ye sure about this?" he asked, his fingers tightening on her shoulders without his realizing it. "This was more than just a dream?"

"Oh, yes, I'm sure of it, Murdoch! That man I saw is either in danger now or will be soon. Remember the fire and the gunshots."

"I have no' forgotten," muttered Murdoch. He had already put on his pants, and he reached now for his buckskin shirt. As soon as he had pulled it over his head, he picked up his boots in one hand and his rifle in the other.

"I want ye t' stay here whilst I fetch Dan'l and Quincy. We'll make sure there be no trouble in th' village."

Natalia clutched his arm. "The man I saw in my vision—is he the one you call Jefferson?"

"Aye, could be," Murdoch rumbled. "I'm not saying tha' I believe in those visions o' yers, darling, but I intend t' find out if anything be amiss."

"Be careful, Murdoch. Just because I didn't see you in my dream doesn't mean there is no danger in store for you."

He bent and kissed her soundly.

"Dinna worry tha' pretty head about me. I'll be back before ye know it."

He fervently hoped there was nothing to Natalia's vision, but one thing was sure: This close to the end of their journey, he and Daniel and Quincy could not let anything happen to Thomas Jefferson and that money.

The Gypsies were camped in the woods at the edge of a little settlement south of Philadelphia. The village was small enough so that the inn was in plain sight as Daniel, Quincy, and Murdoch left the caravan and started toward the two-story building. The settlement was quiet, without even a dog barking. The only sound was the buzzing of insects in the warm summer night.

Daniel clutched his rifle in one hand and with the other rubbed his weary eyes. He had been awake when Murdoch came to alert him that there might be trouble. Daniel had taken the first watch, sitting with his back against one wheel of the wagon Quincy and he shared with Anton and Gregor, keeping his gaze fixed on the building where Thomas Jefferson slumbered peacefully.

"I tell you, I didn't see anyone moving around the place," Daniel said. He had been tempted to scoff when Murdoch spun the yarn about Natalia having some sort of vision of Jefferson in trouble. The big Scotsman had a fondness for whiskey at times, and Daniel wondered if he and Natalia had been drinking. Murdoch seemed completely sober and serious, though, and almost immediately Daniel regretted the thought. Murdoch was just about the most reliable person he had ever known, and if the frontiersman thought something was wrong, they had to investigate.

"Th' whole place looks mighty peaceful t' me," Murdoch said, "but th' rascals after tha' money have been known t' skulk around before now."

"Murdoch's right, Daniel," Quincy put in. "Maybe I'd better slip around behind the inn and take a look."

"That's a good idea—"

The three men halted abruptly when a voice called softly from behind them, "Daniel! Wait for us!"

They turned and saw Gregor and Anton trotting up to them. The big Gypsy said, "You did not think you could slip out without waking us, did you? A Gypsy sleeps with one eye and one ear open."

"If there is trouble, you may need our help," Anton added. He put his hand to his waist, and although Daniel could not see the motion in the shadows, he knew Anton was caressing the hilt of a favorite knife tucked into his sash.

"We're not sure anything is wrong," Daniel told the two Gypsies, his voice little more than a whisper. "We just want to take a look around the inn—"

Once again he was interrupted. Gregor leveled an arm that looked like the trunk of a small tree and pointed toward the inn.

"Look!" he shouted, no longer concerned about being quiet.

Daniel and the others whirled around, and he was shocked to see the red glare that suddenly spurted skyward from the rear of the inn. Flames licked around the corner of the building, and Daniel knew that the thick planks of the rear wall were ablaze.

The inn was on fire—just as in Natalia's dream.

"Come on!" Daniel shouted as he ran toward the inn. "We've got to get Jefferson out!"

"Fire!" bellowed Murdoch at the top of his lungs as he raced alongside Daniel. "Fire at the inn!"

Quincy, Gregor, and Anton added their voices to the uproar, and heads popped out of the windows of the houses they passed. The cry of "Fire!" was taken up by the villagers, who rushed from their dwellings. Many of the men were still in their nightshirts. Fire was a feared enemy to be fought by all, without delay.

Daniel saw movement at the side of the inn as a group of men, silhouetted by the flames, darted toward the front door. Something about one of them—a tall, brawny man—was familiar, and as Daniel drew nearer, the hellish red glow of the blaze illuminated the man's face. Daniel recognized him as the leader of the gang that had twice tried to rob Jefferson.

"Look!" Daniel cried to Murdoch, pointing at the man.

"I see th' scoundrel! Now we know who set th' fire! The thieves must have set th' inn ablaze t' drive out Jefferson and attack him when he runs out carrying th' money."

Already people were fleeing the building, stumbling and coughing in the clouds of smoke that poured from the open windows. Daniel recognized Jefferson and Bob; both men carried leather money pouches.

And at the bottom of the steps waited the thieves.

Murdoch pulled ahead of Daniel, his long legs carrying him with blinding speed toward the inn. Several yards before he reached the cluster of men about to attack Jefferson and Bob, Murdoch dove into the middle of the gang. One of them barely had time to shout, "Look out!" before Murdoch crashed into the tall, powerful leader. The two men went down in a heap.

In the meantime Daniel yelled to the other thieves, "Stand away from there!" They ignored the warning and swung around with guns raised to meet this unexpected resistance. Two men's pistols boomed.

Daniel went to one knee and brought his rifle smoothly to his shoulder. With the smoke billowing around them, it was difficult to aim, but he centered the barrel on one of the thieves and pressed the trigger. The flintlock snapped and ignited the charge of powder, and Daniel felt the reassuring pressure of the recoil against his shoulder as the rifle blasted. Smoke blossomed from the barrel to join the thick, eye-stinging clouds already in the air. The man at whom Daniel had aimed was jolted back against the railing around the porch by the impact of the heavy lead ball as it drove into his midsection.

Standing a few feet to the side of Daniel, Quincy fired, too, but his shot missed. There was no time to reload, because the highwayman who had been his target ran toward him, swinging an empty musket like a club. Quincy ducked and over the crackle of the flames heard the stock of the musket whistle through the air just above his head. Using his own empty rifle as a weapon, he smashed the butt of it into the thief's stomach. The man doubled over, gasped for air, and coughed as he gulped down a great draft of smoke instead. Quincy reversed his thrust and caught the thief on the side of the head with the rifle stock. Bone crunched under the blow, and the man went down limply, his skull shattered.

A few feet away, a pistol ball plucked at the leather vest Anton wore. Both his hands went to his waist and deftly withdrew a pair of knives from his sash. His arms rose in unison, then flashed forward. Firelight flickered on the twin blades as they flew across the gap of several yards between Anton and his target. The man was trying to reload his pistol, but gun and powder horn slipped from his hands, and he staggered backward when Anton's knives thudded into his chest, perfectly spaced and level, as if they had been aimed at either side of a bull's-eye. The thief crumpled to the ground, twitched a few times, and then lay still.

Another gunshot sounded as one of the remaining highwaymen fired at Gregor, who was charging forward like a maddened bull. The musket ball slammed into Gregor's body, high on the right side of his torso, just below the shoulder. The huge Gypsy's momentum carried him forward anyway, and he bellowed in pain and rage as he bowled into the man who had shot him. The robber tried desperately to slash at Gregor's head with the barrel of his musket, but Gregor swatted the weapon aside as if it were only a minor annoyance. He shrugged off the wound in the same fashion as his long arms swept around the terrified thief. Gregor locked his hands together behind the man and rocked back, tightening his grip and lifting the robber off his feet. The man's toes struggled futilely to find purchase on the ground six inches below. Gregor roared like a bear and squeezed, and there was a sharp crack as the man's spine snapped. The thief screamed and went limp in Gregor's grip, and the Gypsy flung him away like a child discarding a broken doll.

Meanwhile, Murdoch and the leader of the gang were rolling over and over in their struggle. Down on the ground the smoke was not quite so thick, and Murdoch was able to see the hate-contorted features of his burly opponent. Three times this man and his cohorts had tried to steal the money from Jefferson and kill the statesman in the process. Three times their plans had been thwarted. Now, this was to be the final confrontation, and both men knew it.

The man's punches grazed harmlessly off the side of Murdoch's head. The thief tried bringing his knee up in a savage blow to the Scotsman's groin, but Murdoch twisted aside and took the impact on his hip. Murdoch hooked a punch to his enemy's belly to bring the man's hands down, then rolled again and wound up on top as his hands locked around the man's throat.

The thief flung up a leg, hooked his calf in front of Murdoch's face, and threw him to the side. With a snarled curse the man pounced, landed on top of Murdoch, and drove his knee hard into Murdoch's stomach, forcing the air out of his lungs. Then his hands found a choke hold of their own around Murdoch's throat.

The big frontiersman's hands swept up, palms cupped to catch the air as he slammed them against his opponent's ears. Howling in pain from ruptured eardrums, the man loosened his grip on Murdoch's throat, and he was unable to fend off Murdoch's hands as they shot upward and locked around his neck again. The Scotsman's thumbs drove brutally into the soft flesh of the gang leader's throat. The man hit Murdoch in the face—once, twice, three times—but none of the blows dislodged Murdoch's grip. With his eyes bulging out of their sockets and his tongue protruding from his mouth, the man struggled for air that could not pass the death grip on his throat.

For long moments Murdoch held him there, watching the man's eyes turn glassy in the light of the fire, feeling the spasms that shook the man's body as his very life was squeezed out of him. Murdoch's shoulders bunched and he heaved upward, rolling over and putting his opponent on the ground. A horrible, grotesque gurgle sounded as the man went completely limp.

By this time, Daniel, Quincy, Anton, and Gregor were standing by, ready to help Murdoch. But the gang leader who had dogged Jefferson's trail all the way from Monticello was dead.

Daniel put a hand on his friend's shoulder and said, "You can let go of him, Murdoch. It's over."

Murdoch shook himself like a dog and pried his fingers loose from the dead man's neck. He stood up and glared down at the corpse. "Ye will no' be coming back t' plague us again, ye thieving bastard!" he growled.

"Who's there?" a voice called from the smoke. "What's going on?"

"Jefferson!" Daniel hissed. He jerked his head at his companions. "Come on!"

Led by Daniel, the five men faded away through the thick smoke, away from the inn where the fire was slowly being doused by the villagers. With Philadelphia so close at hand and this threat finally disposed of, there was no real need to conceal their presence from Jefferson, Daniel thought, but they had come this far protecting the statesman in secret. They might as well continue, he decided.

Besides, what they had done had been for the good of the colonies, not for glory or honor. The five men trotted into the night toward the Gypsy camp, where they could wash the soot from their faces and Gregor's wound could be tended.

The cause of freedom might not ever be secure, but for this night at least, it was a little safer.

Chapter Nineteen

Elliot paced back and forth nervously, although his room was so small that only a few steps carried him from one end to the other. He was in the grip of indecision, and it was not a feeling he liked.

Several days had passed since the meeting of the inner circle of the King's Militia at Corbie's Tavern. During that time Elliot had written a report for Tallmadge and Townsend, encoded it, and left it at the bakery to be delivered to them by whatever circuitous means the patriot spymasters had devised. He had heard nothing in return from them, however, and his nerves were stretched to the breaking point.

He knew that the powder and shot needed by the King's Militia for their secret attack was stored at the barn on Long Island where the meeting had taken place. It would be a simple matter to set fire to the barn, and the resulting explosion would destroy the munitions. But Elliot had received no such orders. He could always act on his own, of course, but to do so would certainly jeopardize his cover as a loyalist.

Ah, it was always so blasted complicated, Elliot thought as he punched one fist into the palm of the other hand. Life had been a great deal simpler a year or so earlier, when all he'd had to worry about was which doxy would share his bed for a night.

"Elliot," his mother said from the door of his room. Elliot swallowed a curse. He hadn't noticed Polly watching him. "You have a visitor."

"Mark Hutchins again?" Elliot asked in surprise.

"Hardly." There was a tone of disapproval in his mother's voice. "This is a young woman."

Elliot frowned. The only young woman he knew here in New York was Sarah Wallingford, and Polly knew her, too. And of course, there was always Casey—

Oh, no, Elliot thought. *She wouldn't come here, would she?*

"Thank you, Mother," he said, stepping past Polly and striding down the short corridor into the living room.

She stood there with a bonnet over her ginger hair and a shawl wrapped around her shoulders, but neither of those things could conceal the brazen cosmetics on her face or the neckline of her gown that revealed far too much of her large, creamy breasts.

"I'm sorry, Elliot," she said immediately as he came into the room. "I didn't want to come here, but I had to see you—"

Benjamin, frowning angrily, was sitting across the room, and he interrupted Casey's explanation.

"I thought you were more discreet than this, Elliot," he said. "It's bad enough that you still associate with women like this, but to bring them here to the home of your parents! Your mother is very upset."

"Well, I'm sorry if I offended your delicate sensibilities," Casey snapped. "I wouldn't have come if it wasn't important. I have to talk to you alone, Elliot."

Benjamin glowered at his son. "Don't expect your mother and me to leave," he said coldly.

"I don't," Elliot told him. He stepped across the room and took Casey's arm. "Come along. We'll walk outside."

"Try not to allow too many of the neighbors to see you," Benjamin called after them tersely.

"I'm sorry about that," Elliot said quietly as he and Casey walked along the lane in front of the house. "My parents have strict morals, and they've always been disappointed that I am such a heathen."

"You're no heathen," Casey said, slipping her arm through his. "Trust me, somebody like me knows the difference. You're a good man, Elliot Markham."

"You didn't come all this way to tell me that," he replied dryly.

"You're right, I didn't. I came to tell you that from what I've overheard at Corbie's, the King's Militia plans to strike tomorrow night."

Elliot stiffened. "So soon?" he exclaimed. "My God, someone has to do something!"

"Have you found out what they're planning?"

He hesitated. "I know part of the plan."

"Can you put a stop to it?"

Without gunpowder the plot could not proceed, Elliot thought again. "I *can* stop it," he said grimly.

"Then you've got to."

"I know." He swung around and walked quickly toward his parents' house. Casey had to hurry to keep up with him.

"I'll tell my parents I'm going out, then I'll saddle my horse."

"All right." She didn't ask what he planned to do, and he was glad of that.

He stepped inside, aware that Casey was behind him, and saw the hostility in Benjamin's glance. Ignoring it, he said, "I have to go out for a while, but I'll be back later tonight."

"Going to that trollop's crib with her, I'd wager," Benjamin growled.

"I'm sorry, Father," Elliot said, "but this is truly none of your business." He put his arms around Polly Markham. "I'll say good night now, Mother, since you'll no doubt be asleep when I return."

Polly brushed his cheek with a kiss and murmured, "Good night, dear."

He saw something in his mother's eyes, something that he recognized as fear for a loved one. She knew somehow, with a mother's instinct, that he was going into danger. Although there hadn't really been time to think about it, Elliot knew there was a chance he would not come back from this errand. As a secret agent it was a risk he always ran, but tonight, something about this leave-taking felt different, and a chill darted along his spine.

"I will be back," he said softly to his mother. "I promise."

"Please be careful," she whispered.

"Let the lad get to his slut, if she's that important to him," Benjamin said impatiently.

Elliot suppressed a surge of anger, and as he turned toward the door he smiled at his father and said, "Good night, sir."

Benjamin gave him a curt nod, and Polly moved

over beside her husband, put a hand on his shoulder, and squeezed hard as she watched Elliot.

Elliot took Casey's arm, reached for his tricorn, and left the room without looking back. He sensed that if he hesitated even slightly, he might not find the courage to go through with this.

"Take me with you," Casey said quietly once they were outside.

Elliot looked at her in surprise. "I can't do that," he said. "You have to go back to Corbie's—"

"To hell with Corbie's," Casey said vehemently, "and to hell with the life I led there! This is my chance to do something that really matters, Elliot. Don't leave me behind. Please."

For a long moment he made no reply as he walked to the small stable where he kept his horse.

"All right," he finally said. "My horse is sturdy and can carry two as well as one. But you have to do as I say."

She leaned against him, and he was conscious of the soft heaviness of her breasts pressing against him.

"Don't I always do as you say?" she murmured. "Like last time when you told me to turn over and—"

"That's not what I meant, damn it," he snapped. He reached for his saddle as they stepped into the stable. "Come on, help me get this on the horse. We've got a plot to smash."

Elliot got some knowing winks and Casey several lecherous stares from the ferrymen on the boat to Long Island. The men never would have guessed that this couple, bound for Farley's Neck and the Dawkins farm beyond, had anything other than pleasures of the flesh on their minds.

When they were riding up the road from the ferry

landing, Casey asked, "Now will you tell me where we're going?"

"A farm owned by a man called Dawkins," Elliot replied.

"Is he one of the King's Militia?"

"I suppose so. I never actually met him. But I know my way there. It's where the King's Militia had a meeting of the entire organization last week."

"Will they be there tonight?"

"Lord, I certainly hope not," Elliot said fervently. He knew Casey was not going to be satisfied until she had heard the whole story, and he couldn't blame her for wanting to know what danger she was riding into. Quickly he recounted what he had learned at the meeting and at the gathering of the ringleaders in the back room of Corbie's Tavern. He concluded by saying, "The munitions are hidden in that barn, and I intend to destroy them. The Militia probably has some men on guard there, but we'll have to deal with them."

"I can help you with that," Casey offered. "I've never yet met a man I couldn't handle."

"That's not quite what I meant," Elliot said.

She threw her head back and laughed. "I know. What I meant was that perhaps I could distract them. I can be quite distracting, you know."

Elliot certainly did know. Casey was riding in front of him, and he had an arm looped around her middle to steady her on the horse's back. From time to time he could feel the weight of her breasts on his arm, and his body told him he would rather be in a nice soft bed at this moment, with Casey distracting him as she did so well, rather than riding across Long Island to blow up a barn filled with gunpowder.

Although night had fallen, the hour was not too late, but the village of Farley's Neck was quiet as Elliot and Casey rode through. Elliot followed the route he remembered, and in a few minutes he spotted the silo that marked the Dawkins farm. The moon was small tonight, and clouds obscured it from time to time, but there was enough light to see the tall landmark that would be full of grain later in the summer.

Elliot turned the horse down the lane to the farm, pulling the animal back to a walk. He wanted to approach as quietly as possible, so as not to alert any guards posted about. He was sure Mark Hutchins was not careless enough to leave the vital powder and shot unprotected.

When they were close to the farm, Elliot reined in. He helped Casey to the ground and swung down to join her.

"We'll go ahead on foot," he whispered. He tied the reins to a sapling beside the lane.

In the faint light from the moon and stars, Casey looked nervous, and Elliot couldn't blame her. Her life was not without its dangers, of course, but they were different from the ones she faced tonight.

She squared her shoulders and whispered, "I'm ready. Let's go."

Elliot took her hand. His other hand went to his belt, where his pistol was tucked behind his coat. He loosened the weapon and held it by the curved wooden butt.

They walked quickly but silently down the lane to the farm. The house where Dawkins and his family lived —if the man had a family; Elliot didn't know—was quiet and dark, just as the village had been. Farm people went to bed with the chickens, Elliot recalled, and got up with them, too. He studied the distance between the house and the barn. The farmyard was large, and he felt certain the fire would not spread to the house. At any rate, the inhabitants would have plenty of warning when the kegs of gunpowder exploded.

Without speaking, he gestured for Casey to follow him as he headed toward the barn. So far no one had challenged them, and he saw no sign of guards. That was impossible, though, Elliot thought. Hutchins was smarter than that.

At that moment one of the big double doors leading into the barn creaked open, and a man stepped out. Elliot and Casey froze in the shadows next to a farm wagon. The man was little more than a silhouette against the barn, but Elliot saw a faint red glow and smelled tobacco. The guard was smoking a pipe.

Elliot put his lips next to Casey's ear and breathed, "We've got to draw him away from the barn."

"Leave that to me," she whispered.

Before Elliot could stop her, she had whisked off her bonnet and shawl and dropped them on the ground. She sauntered out of the shadows and walked openly toward the barn. The guard saw her coming, and Elliot's blood turned to ice when he saw the man lift a musket that had been leaning against the wall beside him.

"Eh? Who's that?" the guard called.

"Oh, sir, I pray you can help me," Casey said, sounding frightened and seductive at the same time. "I have lost my way, and I fear I have also injured my ankle."

Elliot saw that she was limping slightly. She let out a pathetic little whimper and sank down on her knees.

"I don't think I can go any farther," she said miserably.

"Hold on, girl, I'll help you," the guard said. "Let me get a lantern—"

"Oh, sir, my ankle hurts! If you could take me in first and let me sit down . . ."

"Of course." The guard tucked his musket under his left arm and hurried forward. As he did so, Elliot circled around the farm wagon.

Casey lifted her arms appealingly, and as the guard came up to her she murmured, "Are you alone here?"

"Aye, tonight I am." The man's teeth shone in the moonlight as he grinned broadly. "Or rather, I was alone until you showed up, girl. Now I'll have some company, eh?"

His words had taken on a flirtatious tone, and Elliot knew the man had gotten close enough to see how low-cut Casey's gown was. The man clearly planned to put the piles of hay in the barn to good use before the night was over.

No matter, Elliot told himself as a surge of anger welled up in him. The only use to which that hay would be put tonight was as fodder for the fire he intended to set.

He was close enough now. He stepped up behind the guard and made just enough noise to alert the man, who exclaimed, "Eh!" and started to turn around. Elliot slammed his pistol into the side of the man's head, and he dropped like a puppet with its strings cut.

"He said he was alone!" Casey hissed to Elliot.

"I heard him." Elliot tucked the pistol into his belt and bent to grasp the unconscious man's legs. Grunting slightly with the effort, he dragged the guard under the wagon, where thick shadow concealed his senseless form.

"Quickly," urged Casey. "We don't know how long he'll be out."

"Long enough," Elliot grated as he took Casey's arm and hurried toward the entrance to the barn. There was lantern light coming from inside the cavernous building, and Elliot slipped through the narrow opening first, with Casey behind him. He drew his gun again, in case the guard had been lying about being alone. Although it was difficult to see into the shadowy corners of the place, it seemed to Elliot to be empty.

But in the next moment he found out just how wrong he was.

Suddenly more light washed over the interior of the barn as two men carrying torches stepped out of empty horse stalls. Another man appeared in the doorway behind them, torch in one hand, pistol in the other. Elliot tensed and started to lift his pistol as Casey's fingers dug into his arm, but he stopped when he saw that the other men carried guns as well. There was no way he could shoot his way out against three-to-one odds.

It was worse than that, he discovered a second later. Mark Hutchins, accompanied by several more armed men, strolled into the ring of light in the center of the barn. He smiled warmly at Elliot and Casey.

"I'm very surprised to see you here tonight, Elliot. And who might this young lady be?"

Elliot tried to bring his nerves under control. He forced himself to sound calm as he replied, "She's just a friend of mine, Mark. What are *you* doing here?"

"Waiting for you," Hutchins said flatly. "Hoping that you wouldn't show up. But I appear to have been wrong about you, Elliot, just as I feared. You're not to be trusted, are you?"

Elliot laughed. "You can trust me, Mark. I'm one of the King's Militia, remember?"

"A new member," Hutchins pointed out. "And you still have not explained what you're doing here tonight." He peered at Casey. "I know you now," he murmured. "You're one of the doxies from Corbie's place. I knew one of them must have been spying on us, and it's clear now that it was you, my dear."

"She has nothing to do with this," Elliot said quickly. "She just came here with me because I asked her to. Now, why don't you stop being so suspicious, Mark—"

"Shut up!" Hutchins's voice lashed out at them. "Do you honestly think I'd ever trust you again, Markham? We saw the way you attacked poor Horace out there in the farmyard, enticing him with the woman and then knocking him out. You're spies, both of you, rebel spies!"

"You're out of your mind," Elliot said quietly, but he knew he could not convince Hutchins of their innocence. This was a trap, and he wondered if the King's Militia had let the information about the next night's planned attack slip on purpose, just to draw him out.

"I've no time for your denials," Hutchins said crisply. "Suffice it to say that I never trusted you men from Boston. I only brought you and Wallingford in to mollify others who thought you should be included. I suspected then that one or both of you might be spies, but once I had met you, I knew you had to be the secret agent. Wallingford is much too ineffectual a fop to be a rebel spy."

"Well, I can't argue with that," Elliot said dryly. "But you're wrong about me."

"If that's true, then I'll apologize later." Hutchins laughed. "It doesn't really matter, though, because there's nothing you can do to stop us." He slipped a watch from his vest pocket. "In less than two hours, General George Washington will be abducted from his headquarters by agents of the Crown. Failing that, he will be assassinated. And while the rebels are in disarray from the loss of their precious commander, the King's Militia will strike. Before this night is over, we will have crushed the progress of this damned rebellion."

Elliot glanced at Casey as Hutchins made his boast. The blood in his veins seemed to have turned to ice.

"I thought the attack was supposed to take place tomorrow night," he said.

"That's what you were *meant* to think. Soon our men will arrive and arm themselves. There are boats waiting to take us across to Manhattan. If you really *are* a loyal Tory, Markham, you won't be disturbed by any of this."

Casey's hands clutched Elliot's arm tightly, and he shuddered as he realized he had failed. He could not stop Hutchins's plan, and his shoulders drooped in despair and defeat.

Then something Hutchins had said made Elliot look up at the man, who was smiling triumphantly.

"You claim you never trusted Avery and me," Elliot said. "What about Sarah Wallingford? Does she know about your plan?"

Hutchins's eyes widened slightly at the revelation that Elliot knew of his affair with Sarah. Elliot felt a surge of satisfaction that he had been able to take Hutchins by surprise. But then Hutchins chuckled and said, "I don't know how you found out about us, but I would never take Sarah into my confidence about this or anything else important. She pretends to be a lady, but she's really just a trollop like Gingerhair there." The Tory leader grinned arrogantly. "Sarah Wallingford is good for one thing and one thing only, and that is to warm my bed."

"Liar!"

The harsh scream came from the doorway of the barn, and as everyone's eyes jerked in that direction, a pistol boomed. Hutchins rocked back as the ball hit him in the shoulder. Elliot barely had time to see Avery Wallingford standing there, a smoking pistol in hand, before he went into action himself.

A hard shove sent Casey sprawling out of the way as Elliot spun toward the nearest guard. The man had a torch in one hand and a pistol in the other. He was as startled as everyone else by Avery's unexpected appearance and the gunshot that had followed, and before he could bring his pistol in line with Elliot, Elliot kicked him in the stomach, grabbed the weapon, and wrenched it aside as he crashed into him.

The man fell backward and dropped his torch. A pistol blasted elsewhere in the barn, and Elliot heard the ball whip past his head as he whirled around. One of the men had already fired and missed, but another was drawing a bead on Elliot.

He dove forward, sprawling on the earthen floor as the man fired. The ball passed harmlessly over his head. Elliot squeezed the trigger as he landed, and his shot did not miss. The man staggered when the shot hit him in the belly, and the torch in his hand fell and landed in the hay.

The dry hay ignited with a *whoosh,* and the flames spread quickly. Hutchins had pulled himself into a sitting position with one hand clamped to his injured shoulder.

"Forget about them!" he screamed. "Put out that fire!"

Elliot's plan had been accomplished by accident— there was a fire in the barn, and if the flames reached the place where the powder and the shot were kept . . .

He heard Casey shout and looked around to see her struggling with one of the men to keep him from drawing a bead on Elliot. Elliot leapt to his feet and raced to her side. He smashed his empty pistol across the man's face, and the attacker went down. Casey gave him a kick for good measure.

Elliot scooped up the man's pistol and turned toward the other side of the barn, where the rest of the men were frantically trying to put out the fire. There was too much hay, though, and it was burning too quickly. The blaze was spreading rapidly, and Elliot realized that Casey and he had to get out of there before they were caught in the inevitable explosion.

Then he saw Avery walking calmly across the barn toward Mark Hutchins, reloading his pistol as he went. His features were drawn tight against his skull. Hutchins was scrambling backward, trying to get to his feet, but he was too weak from loss of blood; his shoulder and the side of his coat were sodden.

"What are you doing, Avery?" Hutchins cried. "Have you gone mad?"

Avery finished reloading his pistol. As he leveled the weapon he said coldly, "I'm not mad, Hutchins. I think I'm saner than I've ever been."

"You can't do this!" Hutchins screamed. "I'm the leader of the King's Militia! My God, man, help me! You're a loyal Tory!"

"I was," he said. "Now I'm just a man whose wife has been stolen from him."

Fired from a distance of less than three feet, the heavy lead ball crashed into the middle of Mark Hutchins's face and snapped his head back as it killed him. Hutchins kicked convulsively as the nerve impulses raced out of his ruined brain; then he lay still, and Avery calmly lowered the pistol.

Holding tightly to Casey's arm, Elliot ran to Avery's side.

"Come on!" he urged. "We've got to get out of here!"

From the corner of his eye Elliot saw that the men were abandoning their battle against the blaze and were racing out into the night. He knew he and his companions had to get as far away as they could from the barn if they were to survive.

Avery stared disdainfully at Hutchins's corpse for a final second, then turned and nodded to Elliot. With Casey they fled as the flames leapt higher and higher behind them.

They hurried across the farmyard and down the lane to the spot where Elliot had left his horse. He handed Casey up onto the animal's back and then swung into the saddle behind her. Avery disappeared into the trees bordering the lane and returned on his own horse. Elliot glanced at the barn as he wheeled his mount around. The structure was engulfed in flames.

It blew with an explosion that shook the ground beneath the horses' hooves. Flame and smoke billowed into the night sky, and a pillar of fire grew and grew as more explosions rocked the farm. The stone silo toppled like a gigantic tree under the force of the continuing detonations.

"Ride!" Elliot shouted as he kicked his horse into a gallop. He held on to Casey for dear life as they raced into the night, Avery galloping alongside. Behind them the dreams of Mark Hutchins and the King's Militia were blasted into a flaming debris that pattered from the sky like drops of fiery rain.

"I followed Hutchins," Avery said calmly as they cantered along the road between Farley's Neck and the ferry landing a half hour later. Far behind them, a red glow was visible in the sky from the fire, and Elliot hoped no one who was innocent had been hurt in the blast. That might be part of war, but it was the part he despised.

"I've been keeping an eye on him for a few days," Avery went on, "despite what you said about not watching him too closely, Elliot. I never expected to find him with the two of you tonight. I was afraid he might be having another rendezvous with Sarah, although it seemed ridiculous that they would come all the way to Long Island."

"Well, I'm certainly glad you carried your suspicions to the point of ridiculousness, Avery," Elliot said with a chuckle. "We'd never have gotten out of that mess otherwise."

"How . . . how much did you hear of what Hutchins said?" Casey asked, putting into words the question that had been nagging at Elliot since their escape.

"Enough to know that the two of you are quite likely patriot secret agents," Avery replied bluntly.

"Avery, Hutchins was a madman—" Elliot began.

"Oh, Lord, you don't think I care about that anymore, do you?" Avery interrupted. "Despite everything I've done to you, you've been a loyal friend to me, Elliot, and I'm beginning to realize that's more important than politics. I think I've grown up at last. At least I hope so."

Elliot was silent. Avery wasn't completely correct—for most of the past year and a half, Elliot had hardly been his friend—but if Avery wanted to think that, it was all right with him. The important thing was that they were all safe and at least part of the plot against the patriots had been ruined.

But that still left the attempt to kidnap George Washington. Elliot knew he had to get back to New York and alert the Continental Army, even if it meant giving up his dual identity.

"I'm not going to say you're right or wrong about

me," he told Avery. "But you know I've always had the best interests of our friends and families at heart."

"I know that. I saw more than enough evidence of it during our trip to Canada."

"We may not get to make another one," Elliot said regretfully. "After tonight, I'm not sure I can go back to New York, and it may not be safe for my parents to stay there, either. For that matter, you'll probably be in danger from the local Tories, since you killed Hutchins."

"Well," Avery said, "I suppose *I* can always take the ship to Canada, send it back with the supplies, and stay up there. I could even take Sarah and her parents, as well as your mother and father, Elliot."

Elliot looked over at him and saw the newfound strength in his face.

"You'd do that?" he asked.

"I think it might be best for all concerned."

Elliot heartily agreed with him; his only worry was whether or not Avery could be trusted, but after tonight he knew it would serve Avery's best interests to get out of New York, too.

"Thank you, Avery," he said fervently. "I wish I could join you. Right now, though, Casey and I have to get to New York. There's the ferry landing up ahead."

They approached the boat, which had stopped running for the night, but a pair of pistols displayed for the ferryman prompted him to roust his boys for a special trip to Manhattan. Elliot, Casey, and Avery were the only passengers, and when they reached the landing on the other side of the river, the ferryman asked, "You folks wouldn't have had anything to do with that big explosion I heard a while back, would you?"

"Best not to ask questions," Elliot advised him, "and to forget about what you've seen tonight as well."

He handed over a pouch of coins to pay for the man's trouble.

"That memory o' mine seems to be gettin' worse all the time," the ferryman said, grinning. "Good night to you, gentlemen, and to you, lady."

Elliot and Avery led the horses off the boat. They mounted up, Casey in front of Elliot once again. Avery rode in the direction of the house he shared with Sarah and her parents, but Elliot, intent on warning General Washington, headed for the headquarters of the Continental Army—hoping he was not too late already.

"We've both lost any chance of spying for the patriots in the future," Casey commented as they rode. "Too many of those men with Hutchins got away. They'll spread the story of what we've done."

"I know. My parents aren't ever going to forgive me. At least my father won't." Elliot sighed deeply. "He could never accept a damned rebel for a son. I just hope they'll go with Avery to Canada."

The fires of the Continental Army's camp came into view before they could discuss the situation further. Everything appeared to be calm. He rode up to the guard post at the perimeter of the camp, and when the sentries hailed him and told him to halt, he called out, "I have to see General Washington right away. I have an urgent message for him."

"And who's that urgent message from?" demanded one of the guards as he squinted suspiciously at Elliot and Casey.

"The King's Militia," Elliot replied.

"What was that?" asked a man who had just emerged from a nearby tent, his tall, lean figure silhouetted by the lantern light within. "Who are you, sir?" he asked sharply.

Elliot recognized both his voice and his stance.

"Operative Five," Elliot called, knowing that Benjamin Tallmadge would recognize him. Tallmadge strode hurriedly over to the guard post and motioned to the sentries.

"Let this man in," the patriot spymaster said. "I'll vouch for him."

A moment later Elliot and Casey were inside the tent, facing an astounded Tallmadge and Robert Townsend.

"What are you doing here, Operative Five?" Townsend wanted to know. "You're risking your cover as a loyalist. And who is this young woman?"

"This is Casey," Elliot told them. "And as you can see, she is certainly not a man, as you led me to believe. I'm afraid my cover as a loyalist is gone. Several members of the King's Militia know I'm a patriot agent, and no doubt all of them soon will. But it doesn't matter. They planned to attack this camp tonight, but their powder seems to have, well, blown up."

"And you wouldn't have had anything to do with that, eh?" Tallmadge said.

Elliot grinned. "Perhaps a little. But we must warn General Washington about the other part of their plan. They're going to try to kidnap him."

"That was their scheme, all right," Townsend said. "But we discovered it days ago by other means. Most of the plotters were taken into custody earlier tonight, but a man called Hutchins slipped through our net."

"You don't have to worry about him," Casey said. "He was in the barn with the gunpowder."

"It's a clean sweep, then," Tallmadge said, sounding highly pleased with the outcome of the night's action. "Everything turned out well . . . except for the Tories discovering that you've been working against them, Elliot."

"All things come to an end, I suppose," Elliot said with a shrug. "If you're sure the general is safe, Casey and I will be leaving."

"Where are you going?" Tallmadge asked.

Elliot slipped an arm around Casey's shoulders. "I'm not sure yet, but wherever it is, I think we'll go together. What do you think, Casey?"

She grinned up at him. "I think these gents have lost two of their best spies."

Still smiling, they left the tent, and Townsend called softly after them, "Godspeed to both of you."

Chapter Twenty

Philadelphia was abuzz. The Continental Congress was in session again at Independence Hall, and Thomas Jefferson had arrived with the small fortune he'd collected to support the war against the British. Richard Henry Lee, a delegate from Virginia, had issued a stirring call for independence from England, saying "That these United Colonies are, and of right ought to be, free and independent States." The Congress supported Lee's motion almost unanimously, and everyone in the city sensed that great things were brewing.

Under the circumstances it was not surprising that the small Gypsy caravan camped on the outskirts of town attracted little attention. There was a far more entertaining show taking place in the meeting hall of the Congress.

That was all right with Daniel. At the insistence of Anton, Gregor, and Natalia, he and Quincy and Murdoch had stayed with the Gypsies for a few days after their arrival in Philadelphia, but Daniel and Quincy were getting restless. Their wives and newborn children were at home in Virginia, and the men were looking forward to a visit with them before they were summoned to the war.

So it was that the three men were making preparations to leave, and only Murdoch was somewhat regretful. His relationship with Natalia had been passionate, but he had never expected it to last. Deep down, despite her visions, he knew that Natalia hadn't expected it to continue, either. But that did not mean they wouldn't miss each other.

Daniel and Quincy were packing some of their gear when Murdoch appeared in the doorway of the Gypsy wagon.

"Ye'd better come see this, you two." The big frontiersman sounded excited, and with a quick glance between them, Daniel and Quincy hurried to join him.

Having abandoned their Gypsy disguises, they were wearing their usual clothes, and it was a good thing, Daniel thought, because striding toward them through the camp was none other than Thomas Jefferson.

The statesman shook hands with Daniel and said, "It's good to see you again, and you, too, Quincy. Imagine my surprise when I noticed the three of you on the street the other day near the Independence Hall."

"How did you find us?" Quincy asked as he shook hands with Jefferson.

"Oh, I asked around town and discovered that you were staying with these good people." Jefferson waved a hand to indicate the Gypsy camp. Several Gypsies were gathering, their attention drawn by Jefferson's visit.

Most of them knew who he was and what he meant to the patriot cause. He smiled and went on, "I suppose it wouldn't do any good to ask what brought you here, or why you've been traveling with a band of Gypsies."

"Well, sir, I mean no offense, but that's our business." Daniel felt a twinge of remorse for having to say that to Thomas Jefferson, but he didn't want to burden the statesman needlessly with the knowledge of what had happened during the perilous journey from Virginia.

"Yes, of course," Jefferson said with a grin. "I daresay it's better not to know too much about certain things. Suffice it to say that I'm very glad to see all three of you and very gratified that you chose to come to Philadelphia."

He knew, Daniel thought. Jefferson knew or at least suspected the service they had performed by protecting him and the money from the band of thieves. But the less said the better, Daniel decided, and he changed the subject.

"We're just about to start back to Virginia, sir. Are there any messages you'd like us to carry?"

"No, thank you, Daniel. But I do have a favor to request of you."

"Anything," Daniel said sincerely.

"Don't leave just yet. Stay awhile here in Philadelphia, as my guests." Jefferson's voice dropped to a conspiratorial level. "Momentous events are in the offing, lads. If you stay, you might witness history in the making."

Daniel swallowed hard. He was touched by Jefferson's request, but Roxanne and Mariel and the children were waiting back home.

"I'm sorry, sir, but we can't—"

"Oh, yes, there's one more thing." Jefferson gestured toward the closed carriage that had brought him to the Gypsy camp. "I brought someone else with me who's been looking for you."

Daniel swung around, eyes widening in shock at the sight of the woman climbing down from Jefferson's carriage. The summer sunlight shone brightly on her thick red hair, and she was so lovely it took his breath away.

"Roxanne!" he exclaimed in amazement.

Unable to stop himself, he rushed across the road and pulled his wife into his arms. "Is it really you?" he gasped and then kissed her long and hard.

"Of course it is. I couldn't stay away from you, Daniel."

"Where's Joseph?"

"He's at the inn with Pamela and Geoffrey . . . and Mariel and the twins."

"Mariel!" Quincy cried out.

Roxanne smiled, but her expression grew solemn. "There was some trouble at the plantation. Major Kane and Cyril Eldridge showed up."

"Kane and Eldridge!" Daniel's hands clenched into fists. "If they harmed you, I'll—"

"You don't have to do anything. They're both dead. Mariel was hurt, but she's all right now."

"I've got to go to her," Quincy said anxiously.

Thomas Jefferson gestured toward the carriage. "I'll take all of you back to the inn. Your wife has told me the entire story, Daniel, and it's an incredible one. I was pleased to help her find the three of you, so that you could be reunited."

"Thank you, sir," Daniel said fervently. "I can never repay you for your kindness."

"Let's have no talk of debts," Jefferson replied. "After all, we are all patriots together, aren't we?"

Daniel smiled gratefully, his eyes damp with unshed

tears as he walked toward the carriage with his wife, his brother, and his friends.

Dinner that evening was a joyous occasion, as the inn's dining room was taken over by the Reed family, Murdoch Buchanan, and their Gypsy friends. Some of the guests might have been scandalized by the singing, dancing, and celebrating, but Daniel didn't care. His family was together again and safe, at least for the moment.

At one point during the impromptu party, he found himself sitting next to Jefferson, and as they watched Natalia teach Murdoch a Gypsy dance, the statesman said in a quiet voice, "Tomorrow I'm going to be presenting the final version of the document I was asked to write by the drafting committee. I want you and the others to come to Independence Hall for the presentation, Daniel. I don't think you'll be too bored."

"It will be our honor, sir."

Taking a rolled piece of parchment from his pocket, Jefferson spread it out on his knee and mused, "This has been a difficult document to write. It's impossible to please everyone, of course, but I hope the Congress will accept it."

Daniel read the words *The unanimous Declaration of the thirteen united States of America* at the top of the parchment. He could not make out the rest, but that did not matter. He would hear it the next day, when it was presented to the Continental Congress.

"Ah, well," Jefferson said with a grin as he rolled up the paper and put it away, "that's a subject to be dealt with tomorrow." He stood up. "Good night, Daniel. I believe I'll turn in a bit early tonight."

"Good night, sir," Daniel replied, standing and tak-

ing Jefferson's outstretched hand. "Thank you again
. . . for everything."

"And thank you, my young friend," Jefferson said
quietly. With a smile, he turned and slipped out of the
dining room while the singing and dancing and laughing
continued. Daniel watched him go, sensing the weariness in the man but knowing the strength that was there
as well.

Then he put his arm around Roxanne's shoulders
and asked her to dance. For tonight, at least, the worries
of history could be forgotten.

The next morning dawned hot and muggy. It was
very warm in Independence Hall when Daniel, Quincy,
Murdoch, Roxanne, Mariel, Geoffrey, and Pamela filed
into the gallery and sat down. The children had been left
at the inn with the servants who had come along on the
journey from Virginia. The gallery was packed, as if everyone in the city sensed that today was to be a momentous day. Daniel, Quincy, and Murdoch were forced to
stand at the railing along the front of the gallery while
the others found seats nearby. Below, on the floor, the
delegates filed in. Daniel spotted Jefferson, who looked
up, caught his eye, and smiled.

Suddenly a hand fell on Daniel's shoulder, and he
jumped up to look into a face he had not seen for long
months.

"Elliot!" Daniel cried in surprise.

His cousin Elliot Markham threw his arms around
Daniel and clapped him on the back.

"I knew that if we were ever to see each other
again, it would be here," Elliot said happily as he embraced Daniel, then Quincy. "How are you?"

"A lot older than that day a few years ago when I
arrived in Boston to visit you," Daniel said solemnly.

"Well, a great deal has changed since then," Elliot agreed. "I want you to meet a friend of mine." He turned to the young woman by his side. "Casey, these are my cousins, Daniel and Quincy Reed, and their friend Murdoch Buchanan." He grinned broadly as he put his arm around her shoulders.

Casey shook hands with each of the men and said, "I'm pleased to meet you. Elliot has told me a great deal about you."

"And no' more than half of it true, I'd wager," Murdoch said with a laugh. " 'Tis glad we be t' meet ye, lass, but how did ye come t' be here with this scoundrel?"

"Oh, I'm a bit of a scoundrel, too," Casey replied with a mischievous smile. "Elliot can tell you all about it later."

"What *are* you doing here, Elliot?" Daniel lowered his voice to a whisper. "Aren't you pretending to be a loyalist anymore?"

"That's over, I'm afraid. I've come to enlist in the army. There wouldn't be any openings on General Washington's staff, would there?"

"I'll see what I can do," Daniel told him. "What about Uncle Benjamin and Aunt Polly?"

"They should be in Canada by now, and I pray they stay safe through the rest of this revolution. I'm afraid my father didn't take it very well when he found out I was really a patriot. But the old boy surprised me, too. He said I was his son first, no matter what my politics, and that I am to take care of myself and we'll all be together again when this war is over." Elliot smiled a bittersweet smile. "That's just what I intend to do."

"Ssshh," Quincy said. "They're starting."

Casey sat down beside Roxanne and Mariel after all the introductions had been made, and the men and women turned to watch what was happening on the floor of Independence Hall. Thomas Jefferson was on his feet, reading from the document in his hand.

"In Congress, July 4, 1776. The unanimous Declaration of the thirteen united States of America. When in the Course of human events . . ."

The declaration continued, sweeping over the hall and the witnesses assembled there: the delegates, the fighters for freedom, the common people, everyone who had come to hear the desire for liberty put into words and set down for all time. History in the making, Jefferson had called it, and indeed it was, Daniel Reed thought. History was being made this day—July 4, 1776 —and the world would be forever changed.

A new nation had just been born.

ABOUT THE AUTHOR

"ADAM RUTLEDGE" is one of the pseudonyms of veteran author James M. Reasoner, who has written over sixty books ranging from historical sagas and westerns to mysteries and adventure novels. Reasoner considers himself first and foremost a storyteller and enjoys spinning yarns based on the history of the United States, from colonial days to the passing of the era known as the Old West. He lives with his wife, Livia, and daughters Shayna and Joanna.

In the British colonies of North America there arose a band of brave men and women who forged a free and independent nation. Their names live on today, as does their legacy, and we proudly call them Patriots.

PATRIOTS

by Adam Rutledge

❏ CANON'S CALL 29203-X

Boston, 1776. Determined to prove to his weary army of farmers and frontiersmen that victory is within sight, General Washington sets into motion his most audacious plan yet: the siege of British-held Boston. Success depends on the transport of Fort Ticonderoga's captured artillery across the rugged Berkshires and into the field of battle, a mission undertaken by Virginia's own Daniel Reed. He faces not only the bitter winds of winter but also a traitorious saboteur under his own command.

$4.99/$5.99 in Canada

❏ **LIFE AND LIBERTY** 29202-1

It is a treacherous time for freedom fighter Daniel Reed, who has thrown in his lot with General Washington's Continental Army. Risking exposure and death threats, undercover patriot and daring double agent Elliot Markham will fight a deadly battle against a lawless legion of ruthless criminals who could extinguish the flame of independence forever.

$4.99/$5.99 in Canada
